Praise for Novels by Brandilyn Collins

Over the Edge

"Tense and dramatic . . . a dense and compact narrative that holds its tension while following the protagonist in a withering battle."
—*New York Journal of Books*

"A taut, heartbreaking thriller . . . Collins is a fine writer who knows how to both horrify readers and keep them turning pages."
—*Publishers Weekly*

"A frightening and all-too-real scenario . . . very timely and meaningful book."
—*RT Book Reviews*

Deceit

". . . good storytelling and notable mystery . . . an enticing read [that poses] tough questions about truth and lies, power and control, faith and forgiveness."
—*Publishers Weekly*

"Solidly constructed . . . a strong and immediately likable protagonist. One of the Top Ten Inspirational Novels of 2010."
—*Booklist*

"Filled with excitement and intrigue, Collins' latest will keep the reader quickly turning pages . . . This tightly plotted mystery, filled with quirky characters, will appeal to suspense lovers everywhere."

—*RT Book Reviews*

". . . pulse-accelerating, winding, twisting storyline [that will] keep your attention riveted to the action until the very end."

—*Christian Retailing*

Exposure

". . . a hefty dose of action and suspense with a superb conclusion."

—*RT Book Reviews*

"Brandilyn Collins, the queen of Seatbelt Suspense®, certainly lives up to her well-deserved reputation. *Exposure* has more twists and turns than a Coney Island roller coaster . . . Intertwining storylines collide in this action-packed drama of suspense and intrigue. Highly recommended."

—*CBA Retailers + Resources*

"Captivating . . . the alternating plot lines and compelling characters in *Exposure* will capture the reader's attention, but the twist of events at the end is most rewarding."

—*Christian Retailing*

"Mesmerizing mystery . . . a fast-paced, twisting tale of desperate choices."

—*TitleTrakk.com*

"[Collins is] a master of her craft . . . intensity, tension, high-caliber suspense, and engaging mystery."

—*The Christian Manifesto*

Dark Pursuit

"Lean style and absorbing plot . . . Brandilyn Collins is a master of suspense."

—*CBA Retailers + Resources*

"Intense . . . engaging . . . whiplash-inducing plot twists . . . the concepts of forgiveness, restoration, selflessness, and sacrifice made this book not only enjoyable, but a worthwhile read."

—*Thrill Writer*

"Moves from fast to fierce."

—*TitleTrakk.com*

"Thrilling . . . characters practically leap off the page with their quirks and inclinations."

—*Tennessee Christian Reader*

Amber Morn

". . . a harrowing hostage drama . . . essential reading."

—*Library Journal*

"The queen of seatbelt suspense delivers as promised. Her short sentences and strong word choices create a 'here and now' reading experience like no other."

—*TitleTrakk.com*

"Heart-pounding . . . the satisfying and meaningful ending comes as a relief after the breakneck pace of the story."

—*RT Book Reviews*

"High octane suspense . . . a powerful ensemble performance."

—*BookshelfReview.com*

Crimson Eve

"One of the Best Books of 2007 . . . Top Christian suspense of the year."

—Library Journal, starred review

"The excitement starts on page one and doesn't stop until the shocking end . . . [*Crimson Eve*] is fast-paced and thrilling."

—Romantic Times

"The action starts with a bang . . . and the pace doesn't let up until this fabulous racehorse of a story crosses the finish line.

—Christian Retailing

"An unparalleled cat and mouse game wrought with mystery and surprise."

—TitleTrakk.com

Coral Moon

"A chilling mystery. Not one to be read alone at night."

—RT BOOKclub

"Thrilling . . . one of those rare books you hurry through, almost breathlessly, to find out what happens."

—Spokane Living

". . . a fascinating tale laced with supernatural chills and gut-wrenching suspense.

—Christian Library Journal

Violet Dawn

". . . fast-paced . . . interesting details of police procedure and crime scene investigation . . . beautifully developed [characters] . . ."

—Publishers Weekly

"A sympathetic heroine . . . effective flashbacks . . . Collins knows how to weave faith into a rich tale."

—*Library Journal*

"Collins expertly melds flashbacks with present-day events to provide a smooth yet deliciously intense flow . . . quirky townsfolk will help drive the next books in the series."

—*RT BOOKclub*

"Skillfully written . . . Imaginative style and exquisite suspense."

—*1340mag.com*

Web of Lies

"A master storyteller . . . Collins deftly finesses the accelerator on this knuckle-chomping ride."

—*RT BOOKclub*

"fast-paced . . . mentally challenging and genuinely entertaining."

—*Christian Book Previews*

Dead of Night

"Collins' polished plotting sparkles . . . unique word twists on the psychotic serial killer mentality. Lock your doors, pull your shades—and read this book at noon."

—*RT BOOKclub*, Top Pick

". . . this one is up there in the stratosphere . . . Collins has it in her to give an author like Patricia Cornwell a run for her money."

—*Faithfulreader.com*

". . . spine-tingling, hair-raising, edge-of-the-seat suspense."

—*Wordsmith Review*

"A page-turner I couldn't put down, except to check the locks on my doors."

—*Authors Choice Reviews*

Stain of Guilt

"Collins keeps the reader gasping and guessing . . . artistic prose paints vivid pictures . . . High marks for original plotting and superb pacing."

—RT BOOKClub

". . . a sinister, tense story with twists and turns that will keep you on the edge of your seat."

—Wordsmith Shoppe

Brink of Death

". . . an abundance of real-life faith as well as real-life fear, betrayal and evil. This one kept me gripped from beginning to end."

—Contemporary Christian Music

"Collins' deft hand for suspense brings on the shivers."

—RT BOOKclub

"Gripping . . . thrills from page one."

—christianbookpreviews.com

Dread Champion

"Compelling . . . plenty of intrigue and false trails."

—Publisher's Weekly

"Finely-crafted . . . vivid . . . another masterpiece that keeps the reader utterly engrossed."

—RT BOOKclub

". . . riveting mystery and courtroom drama."

—Library Journal

"Chilling . . . a confusing, twisting trail that keeps pages turning."
—*Publisher's Weekly*

"A thriller that keeps the reader guessing until the end."
—*Library Journal*

"Unique and intriguing . . . filled with more turns than a winding mountain highway."
—*RT BOOKclub*

"One of the top ten Christian novels of 2001."
—*christianbook.com*

GONE TO GROUND

BRANDILYN
COLLINS

GONE TO GROUND

Nashville, Tennessee

Other Novels by Brandilyn Collins

Over the Edge
Deceit
Exposure
Dark Pursuit

Rayne Tour Series
(cowritten with Amberly Collins)
Always Watching
Last Breath
Final Touch

Kanner Lake Series
Violet Dawn
Coral Moon
Crimson Eve
Coral Moon

Hidden Faces Series
Brink of Death
Stain of Guilt
Dead of Night
Web of Lies

Chelsea Adams Series
Eyes of Elisha
Dread Champion

Bradleyville Series
Cast a Road Before Me
Color the Sidewalk for Me
Capture the Wind for Me

978-1-4336-7163-0

Published by B&H Publishing Group
Nashville, Tennessee

Dewey Decimal Classification: F
Subject Heading: MYSTERY FICTION \ HOMICIDE—FICTION
\ ROMANTIC SUSPENSE NOVELS

Author represented by the literary agency of Alive Communications,
Inc., 7680 Goddard Street, Suite 200, Colorado Springs, Colorado,
80920, www.alivecommunications.com.

Scripture quotations are taken from the New American Standard
Bible®, Copyright © 1960, 1962, 1963, 1968, 1971, 1972, 1973,
1975, 1977, 1995 by The Lockman Foundation. Used by permission.
(www.Lockman.org) Also used Holman Christian Standard Bible
(HCSB), Copyright © 1999, 2000, 2002, 2003, 2009 by
Holman Bible Publishers. Used by permission.

1 2 3 4 5 6 7 8 • 16 15 14 13 12

For my niece, Laura Sheppard.
What a joy to see you grow
and to anticipate what you will become.

"What anxious moments pass between the birth of plots and their last fatal periods."

CATO, BY JOSEPH ADDISON

2010 Pulitzer Prize

Feature Writing

The Jackson Bugle

Gone to Ground

What happens to a small, quiet Southern town when evil invades in the form of a serial killer?

By: Trent Williams
October 29, 2010

(Excerpt)

Amaryllis, Mississippi, is a scrappy little town of strong backbone and Southern hospitality. A brick-paved Main Street, a park, and the legendary ghost in its old cemetery are all part of its heritage. Everybody knows everybody in Amaryllis, and gossip wafts on the breeze. Its denizens are friendly, its families tight. On the surface Amaryllis seems much like the flower for which it's named—bright and fragrant.

But the amaryllis flower is poisonous.

In the past three years five unsolved murders have occurred within this tiny burg. All the victims were easy targets—women who lived alone, ranging from age 48 to 64. Each was killed in similar fashion while asleep in bed—from a single knife stab to the neck. Inflicted with precision, each stabbing cut the victim's carotid artery, causing her to bleed out in a matter of one to two minutes. After being stabbed, the women were then stuffed into their bedroom closets. The reason for that remains one of the many mysteries surrounding the case. This strange M.O. has led to the dubbing of the murders as the "Closet Killings."

Three victims have been white, two black. The culprit, while unquestionably a monster and a coward, is no respecter of race.

Or anything else.

MONDAY
APRIL 25, 2011

Prologue

"GET ME A BIBLE AND SOME CIGARETTES—AND I'LL TALK."
Chief Cotter stared at the person facing him across the worn wooden table. Man, it was stuffy in the cramped interrogation room. And what kind of crazy stall tactic was this? He had no time for it, not in his present state of mind. He'd barely slept since Erika Hollinger's murder a week ago. And the pressure to nab the killer off the town's streets laid hard on him.

He fired back with a question.

The answer hit like a sucker punch.

MONDAY–THURSDAY
APRIL 18–21, 2011

Chapter 1

Cherrie Mae

YOU CAN TELL AN AWFUL LOT BOUT PEOPLE FROM CLEANIN their houses. Like the time I drug a hot pink thong out from under ol Ed McAllister's bed—a lacy little piece a cloth that wouldn't a fit round his wife's hiney in her best days. So what did Verna McAllister do to protect her husband's stellar reputation? Tried to hide her shock while swearin up and down she used that thong for a dust rag. Mm-hmm. Thing's no bigger than a piece a lint. Besides, who cleans that house, her or me?

I've had plenty other revelations. Like when I seen that hoard a sleepin pills stuck down in Alicia May Alkin's sweater drawer— enough to kill at least two and a half people. And her so happy and all after marryin the man a her dreams.

Words is just air. Faces tell you more, if you pay attention. (Most people don't.) But houses, they hold the darkest secrets.

Not that I go pokin round the places I clean. Well, maybe I do, but a woman's got to have somethin to keep her brain goin while she scrubs toilets. Like Sherlock Holmes said, "My mind rebels at stagnation." Besides anybody in this town'll tell you Cherrie Mae Devine's the best housecleaner around. I got my customer list—white and black folk alike—so full there ain't room for one more, and that's a fact. So I figure some rovin eyes now and then ain't gon hurt nobody. I always keep my discoveries to myself.

But mercy, what I seen today.

Austin Bradmeyer, mayor a Amaryllis, is a finicky man. Finicky enough he wants me cleanin his house twice a week—every Thursday and Monday—even though the missus don't work, so what she do all day? The mayor keeps his things just so, and that includes his fancy mahogany office. Big desk and leather chair, a straight-back settee, and huge shelves full a books. The top a the desk is always perfect, no cluttered papers, every pen in the wooden holder. Even his ash tray is always emptied into the trash can. (Which don't keep smokin from bein a nasty habit.) I happen to know that office is Mayor B's private little place. The missus ain't even allowed to go in there.

See, Mayor B ain't as nice and gentlemanly as folks think. I seen him more than once come home for lunch and yell at his wife over nothin. And I mean stompin round, red-faced mad. Fire in his eyes like the devil. So outta control he don't even care I seen him—as if anybody would believe my word over his anyway. Then he'll turn it off, just like that. Light a cigarette and go back to his plastics factory, no doubt smilin at everbody there.

I done lived long enough to know this: people can fool you. You think they one thing—they might be somethin else altogether.

Today, Thursday, Mayor B was at work as usual. His factory has a second shift that goes till 11:00 p.m., but the mayor keeps regular business hours in his office. Mrs. Eva B said she had to run out to Piggly Wiggly, and in case she didn't return before I was through, she left my check on the kitchen counter. The door slammed behind her on her way out. Mrs. B's always in a hurry.

I finished my dustin in the formal dinin room and headed to Mayor B's office, totin my fold-up, two-step stool. Have to drag that thing to ever room to dust up high. House cleanin would be a whole lot easier if I was six foot tall.

In the office I set down my stool and walked to the desk I done dusted a thousand times. And found myself eyein the shiny gold drawer handles.

Like iron filins to a magnet my hand reached for the top drawer. I glanced over my shoulder out to the front hallway, even though I knew nobody was there. My fingers pulled the drawer. It rolled open so easy.

Green hangin files is what I seen. Inside em, folder after beige folder with labels like "City Council" and "Downtown." But the one that caught my eye was "Closet Killings."

That sent a chill rollin down my back.

Three years and five victims. Then, just two nights ago—Lord, have mercy on us—a sixth. I could recite each name and date, knew each woman myself. The whole town did. The population a Amaryllis barely reaches 1,700, so who's not gon know everbody else?

I pulled out the manila folder. Laid it on the desk.

My heart took to trippin.

For a minute I almost put the file back. Didn't want to see, didn't want to know. Instead I opened the folder.

On top sat a full-page color picture a Martha Edgars, from the waist up. Blood all over her, a knife buried in her neck. She'd been shoved in a closet, clothes hangin round her. Her eyes was wide open like she died in utter terror.

I let out a little scream and tipped my face to the ceilin. *Jesus, Jesus, Jesus.* Couldn't pray no more than the precious Savior's name. My breaths got all staggery, and sweat popped down my back. I leaned against the desk and pulled in air.

Not that I hadn't known how Martha died. But to *see* it for myself . . .

I flipped over the picture. Couldn't bear to see it again. I lowered my eyes—and seen photo #2. Sara Fulgerson. Just as bloody. Knife just as deep in her neck, but the handle was different. Sara's eyes was closed. Like Martha, she was propped up against a closet wall.

My heart liked to beat right outta me. I pressed a hand to my chest.

Martha was my age—sixty-two. Sara, fifty-seven. Both white women.

What crazy voice in my head was it tol me to look at the third picture, I'll never know.

It was Sonya Stelligman, sixty-one. Another knife in the neck, blood everwhere. She sat in her closet. Sonya was a black lady, went to my church. I loved that woman.

Next I saw Alma Withers, only forty-eight when she was killed. Similar stab wound. Then Carla Brewster, sixty-four. Butchered the same way. Alma was white, Carla, black.

There they was—pictures a the first five murders, in order. That Mayor B, he was meticulous, all right.

My knees went weak. I huffed down into Mayor B's chair and leaned back, steadyin myself. Alma's photo still glared up at me, should I turn my face back to it. Last thing I wanted to do.

But there was one more killin—the most recent. Erika Hollinger, white girl jus twenty years old. Husband sent off to the Afghanistan war, then blown to pieces by a bomb six months ago. Erika had been a town wild child, raised by a single mother who drank too much. As for Erika's husband, Brent Hollinger, I'd cleaned his parents' house for years. Watched Brent grow. He was a good boy. I went to his and Erika's weddin—just about the only black face there. Later I went to Brent's funeral. Who'd a guessed within half a year Erika would be dead too. Now, two days after her murder I still didn't know when her funeral would be. The *police* had yet to release her body.

Somethin beyond me made my hand flip over Alma's picture. And there sat Erika. Knifed in the neck and bloodied, the ends a her thick brown hair clotted in red. Once pretty face all blotched and purple.

My body went to shakin. Good thing Mrs. B didn't choose that time to come home. Don't think I coulda moved.

The whole town knew the victims was all found in their closets. And that one person killed em all. The police said no doubt bout that, because ever crime scene was the same. Now I seen the proof. Each knife handle looked different, but from the size they all looked to be parin knives. Somethin ever woman would have in her kitchen.

I slapped the file shut. *Why* did the mayor have these pictures?

They had to come from the *police*. But those men were a tight bunch, two of em father and son. And Chief Adam Cotter ruled the roost. Cotter and Mayor B was tight, too. But the chief had kept a zipped lip on details a the Closet Killings. So to make an extra set a pictures a ever murder for Austin Bradmeyer—and let the man take em home? I couldn't see Mr. I'm-the-Boss-Here Cotter doin that, even for the mayor. Besides, why would Mayor B want those horrible things?

The grandfather clock in the front hallway bonged, bringin me back to my senses. I still had an office to clean. If Mrs. B come back she'd wonder what I been doin with my time.

I picked up the folder—with two fingers like I didn't want to touch it—and spread apart the green hangin file to drop it back in. That's when I seen the ring restin on the bottom a the file.

My heart knew what it was almost before my brain kicked in—and my muscles just plain froze.

Erika Hollinger, born Erika Lokin, got the ring from her mother on her sixteenth birthday, handed down from her great-grandmother. Far as I know she never took it off. Two days ago I seen Erika at the drugstore late that afternoon. She seemed upset. "How you doin?" I touched her arm. She shook her head in that determined way a hers—"I'm fine"—but wiped her eyes. Sad, her bein so young and losin a husband and all. So I took myself home and baked a batch a brownies and carted em over to Erika's house to cheer her up. We ended up sittin on her couch like two good friends—which we really ain't—eatin those brownies and watchin a movie. Around 10:00 I went home, and Erika said she was headed for bed. I tol her to wrap up the brownies so they wouldn't get hard. Erika rolled her big brown eyes but did what I said. She made a big deal a rippin off the plastic wrap while I watched.

And that ring was on her finger.

Sometime that night Erika was killed while sleepin in her bed. Just like the other five. When I heard the awful news yesterday I couldn't believe it. I called the police and tol em I been to Erika's house that very night. Chief Cotter said to come in and give a statement. He took me in that little interrogation room at the station and questioned me up and down. At the end he said, "You by any chance notice Erika's diamond ring on her little finger?"

Later that day I talked to Erika's mama. She also wondered if I seen the ring. Because when the police found Erika's body, she said, that ring was the only thing missin from the house.

Mayor B said nothin bout bein in Erika's house that night she was killed. Why should he be? In fact just this mornin the county paper ran a quote from Mayor B, sayin how sad he was that while he and the wife were safe at home, across town another woman was gettin herself killed.

Now here sat Erika's ring in Mayor B's desk drawer.

Somethin in my belly started to tremble. I set down the folder and picked up that ring. Looked inside the gold band. There they was— Erika's great-grandmother's initials: A.K.L.

I dropped the ring back in the folder like it was on fire.

Cherrie Mae, you know you crazy for what you thinkin. You know theys an explanation.

I looked from those awful pictures to the ring.

Trophies? I seen crime shows on TV. I know crazed killers keep such things. And we sure did have ourselves a crazy killer in Amaryllis.

But it ain't Austin Bradmeyer, Cherrie Mae, come on, girl.

Maybe Mayor B kept those pictures to remind hisself how much he wanted to catch the Closet Killer. Least that's what he says all the time.

Fine then. What about the ring? The *police* might a given him a set a those pictures, but *they* didn't even know he had that ring.

I heard the Bradmeyers' front doh open. My body jerked. I threw the picture file back in the hangin folder and slid the drawer shut. Snatched up my dust rag, heart rattlin in my chest.

"I'm back, Cherrie Mae!" Mrs. B called.

"Yes, ma'am. I'm in the office." Somehow my voice came out normal. I heard Mrs. B's footsteps comin and started dustin like my life depended on it.

Fact was, it did.

By the time I got outta that house, my mouth run dry and my knees wobbled. I loaded my car with all my supplies and the stool, and slid inside to rest my head against the steerin wheel. Surely I was as good as dead. Me, a woman livin alone in Amaryllis, and knowin what I did. What was I gon do? I couldn't keep quiet bout somethin this big. And I couldn't tell nobody neither.

Because who in town's gonna believe the likes a five-foot-high Cherrie Mae Devine when she says the mayor's the one who killed them six women?

Chapter 2

Tully

JUST AFTER LUNCH I FELL ASLEEP ON THE COUCH AND dreamed I was back in high school. Erika Lokin, a year older than me, was going all crazy over some new boyfriend. I kept saying, "Be careful." Didn't even know the guy, but that's all that came out of my mouth. I woke up on my side, eyes fixed on that Coke stain on the carpet I've been meaning to clean up. Day was warm as toast, but chill bumps ran all over me. My belly felt mountain-heavy, and my head hurt.

"Be careful."

I hated Erika Lokin—later Erika Hollinger—all through high school. She was way more sophisticated than me and so beautiful, with that thick brown hair and doe eyes, long lashes. My mouse-brown hair and too-round face couldn't hold a candle to hers. And she was fierce in her love for my Michael. She made no bones about the fact she wanted him back after he broke up with her and started dating me. In her mind she never let Mike go. Not till her dying day.

Will I burn in hell for being glad she's dead?

When I woke up from my dream the little square clock on the wall read 1:20. Mike would need to be at work at the factory by 3:00. I could hear him under the outside carport, country music cranking out his radio. Tinkering on his old fishing boat, I imagine. I could picture him with his shirt off, his powerful hand holding some tool, steel blue eyes squinting, and a cigarette hanging from his mouth. If things didn't go just right, that quick temper of his would crackle, curses spilling from his lips. My bad boy Michael. My heart since I was in eighth grade.

He'd had that swagger that so got to me. At thirteen, I knew he'd never look my way. I wasn't thin enough, pretty enough. And I was too quiet to *make* him notice. I watched him date Erika all my freshman year of high school. Then came that night at the school baseball game when he happened to sit next to me—without Erika.

Two days ago I was singing. Sewing clothes for my baby boy, due in two months. Nineteen years old and happy to be a mother. Now my mind had near shut down. I could hardly breathe.

You think you know where you're going in life. You think you got it all figured out. I sure did. My parents always expected me to go to college. Ole Miss, where they met. Instead their perfect daughter fell for the town rebel-without-a-cause, four years older. A man who got a job right out of high school, working the late shift at Mayor Bradmeyer's plastics factory, and waited for that daughter to graduate and marry him. My mother still mourns my wedding day. Thinks I threw away my life. "You're too smart not to go to college!" she cried when Mike and I got engaged. "Valedictorian of your class!"

Couldn't she see how he made me feel? How he'd acted like there was no other girl in the world? I refused to listen when she said he was no good. That he couldn't be trusted. I told my mother if I couldn't have Michael Phillips, I wouldn't *have* a life.

Now look at me.

Erika Hollinger thought she had it all figured out too. Married right out of high school, although college was never in her future. Then three days ago she up and tells me her latest news.

Yesterday, when I heard Erika had been murdered, I threw up. Victim number six, said the police. Stabbed, then stashed in the closet like the rest of them. Lots of blood. What other details they saw at the scene, they wouldn't say. But clearly it was the work of the same killer. And once again—no witnesses and no evidence.

Well, as far as *they* know.

People in town declare this and that about the murders. Everybody is a suspect, and nobody at all. They lock their doors and whisper their suspicions over the phone. I lock my doors too, when Mike is at work. He doesn't get off until 11:00 p.m.—long after dark, even in the summer.

My mom thinks the killer is somebody in the next town or beyond. Some psycho who creeps in, murders our women, then steals away. Couldn't be one of us, she says. Not in Amaryllis. I used to think that too. I *wanted* to believe it.

Now I know she's wrong. He lives right here among us, all right. But if I tell, I'm dead.

The killer is my husband.

Chapter 3

Tully

THREE DAYS AGO—ON MONDAY—ERIKA CALLED ME. AFTER years of stalking to a different aisle when she saw me in the grocery store. After spreading rumors about me in high school. From the day Mike and I got engaged when I was a junior, she hadn't spoken to me. Instead she threw herself at tall, muscular Bruce Hollinger, who'd always had a crush on her. Flaunted him around town like she didn't care a whit about Michael Phillips anymore. She married Bruce and made sure Mike and I weren't invited to the wedding, even though Mike and Bruce were friends. When Bruce went off to war and was later killed, I took Erika a casserole. She wouldn't even let me in the house. Standing right there on her front porch, she shoved the glass pan back at me.

"No *thank you,* not from the likes of you."

So why was she calling me now, while Mike was at work?

I stood in my kitchen with the phone to my ear, feeling like I had a basketball between my legs. At seven months the baby had dropped.

Just a week ago I'd had to stop my job as checker at the Amaryllis Piggly Wiggly because the doctor told me to get off my feet.

"Tully." Erika's voice vibrated right through me. "You need to come over and hear what I have to say."

"You have something to say, Erika, you can tell me right now."

"Oh, no." She gave a little chuckle. "I want to see your face."

My fingers tightened on the receiver. I didn't want to play her games. But I'd never been a match against Erika. She knew how to ride all over me. "I couldn't come if I wanted to. Doctor said to keep my feet up."

"Oh, right, you're pregnant." She singsonged the words. "You want Daddy around when the baby's born?"

"What's *that* supposed to mean?"

"Come over here now, Tully, if you know what's good for you."

"No."

"Fine. I'll tell your mother first." Erika hung up.

She knew she had me with that. My mother and I had enough strain between us, and I didn't need any more reason for the woman to remind me of my "mistakes." Besides, that comment about Mike being around for the birth—as if he wouldn't be—scared me to death.

In ten minutes I was lumbering up to Erika's front door, sweat rolling down my back, cursing myself for allowing her to rope me in. She waved me inside with a Karo smile—syrupy sweet and colorless. Sat me on the couch. Even told me to put my feet up. I said no, thank you. Swollen ankles or not, no way could I relax within a hundred yards of Erika Hollinger.

She perched prettily on the edge of her blue-flowered chair and leaned toward me, fingers laced. Her makeup was perfect, with pink blush and shiny lipstick. Like she wanted to rub it in how good she looked next to me. "I'm three months pregnant"—Erika looked me straight in the eye—"and Mike's the father."

The world spun down my spine.

Erika stood and with a flourish pulled up her T-shirt. "See?"

Her belly did stick out some, although less than mine had after the first trimester. But Erika had always been taller and thinner than me. I stared at that bump, my tongue numb.

Erika lowered her shirt and sat back down. Crossed a prim leg. "Don't believe me?"

With both hands I started to push off the couch. "I'm leaving."

"You might want to hear me out."

I jerked toward her. "Erika, you've been a conniving liar since I've known you."

"Oh, a big word from the smart one." Her head tilted. "But who can blame you for not believin me? Michael's good at keepin his secrets."

"He doesn't love you, Erika! He never has." Why couldn't I get to my feet? My legs were like water.

"Want proof?" Her voice hardened. "I've got it." She rose again, graceful as a swan, and glided to a knickknack case against the wall. Grabbed something off the middle shelf. "Here." She walked over to me and held out a picture. "See for yourself."

I glared up at Erika, refusing to take it from her hand. She positioned the photo upright, holding the top with two fingers.

My gaze pulled to the picture—and glued there. I frowned. Leaned forward to see better, despite myself. Erika lay on a bed in some clinic I didn't recognize, her shirt pulled up to expose her belly. A nurse stood over her performing an ultrasound, one hand pointing to the monitor. I could barely make out the grainy form of a fetus.

Holding Erika's hand, standing in half profile to the camera, was Mike.

My muscles gave out. I sagged back against the couch cushions, stunned betrayal whirling in me. Erika said not a word. Just pulled back the picture with a smirk on her face.

"Take your time." She resettled in her chair. "I know it's a shock."

I don't know how many minutes passed before I could speak. "Who took the picture?" Crazy question to ask first, but that's what popped out of my mouth.

"Another nurse." Erika sat straight-backed and chin up, so poised. Looking at her, you'd never know her soul played in mud. "I slipped her the camera when we went in, told her my boyfriend was camera-shy. He still doesn't know the picture exists."

My boyfriend.

Sudden rage shot through my limbs, propelling me to my feet. I headed for the door like a freight train, thinking wild thoughts . . .

That Erika had won. After all the years of high school and even my wedding, she'd actually taken Mike from me.

That wait a few months and elegant Miss Erika would look as fat as me—and wouldn't she deserve it.

And that no one on earth should die a horrible death more than Erika Hollinger.

"He's fixin to leave you, Tully," Erika called after me. "I've got some big money comin to me real soon. And then we're goin away together."

I couldn't respond around the brick in my throat. I fled through the front door and banged it closed so hard her front shutters rattled.

Her laughter chased me as I stumbled down the porch steps.

The rest of that day was a blur. When Mike came home from work that night I was already in bed, lying on my side away from him. Pretending sleep with my eyes wide open. Before my pregnancy I'd slept so sound Mike could walk around the bedroom and I'd never know it. But not lately. Every night I was hot and restless. As for *that* night, I didn't sleep at all. While Mike soft-snored through those dark hours, I alternately cried, pled with him, and attacked him like a lion-ess—without moving or making a sound.

By the next morning my veins simmered. Not till Mike was about to leave for work could I even speak to him. Then it all boiled out of me.

"I know about Erika."

We stood in the kitchen, me leaning against the counter for support. Mike was in his blue factory uniform, his head freshly buzzed.

"I know she's pregnant with your baby—and don't you deny it, Michael Phillips. She showed me a picture of you with her at the ultrasound."

Mike's face paled, then reddened. I saw the telltale vein throb at his temple, the hardening of his square jaw. He thrust back his shoulders and glared down at me. "*What* are you talkin about?"

"You denying it when she showed me proof?"

"There is no picture!"

"Then what did I see?"

"Danged if I know, Tully! You've gone plain crazy."

"Michael. I *saw* the picture. You were there. Holding her hand." My voice caught on the last word. Tears filled my eyes.

He turned away, breathing like a mad bull. Wiped the back of his hand across his mouth.

"She says you're going away with her."

He snorted, shaking his head.

"Is it true?"

"Erika's a liar, and you know it."

"Is it *true*?" I smacked him on the shoulder.

He spun around, fist raised. I barely flinched. He'd hit me plenty times since we got married—a shock I'd never in my wildest nightmares expected. Every time I'd just wither, but at that moment I didn't care. He couldn't hurt me more than he already had. "What're you going to do with us both pregnant, huh, Mike?" My mouth pulled as I fought bitter tears. "Guess you'll have to pick which baby you want most!"

His steel blue gaze could have cut glass. His fist hung in the air, his lips open and drawn back. We faced off, shaken and toxic.

Just like that my anger drained away. I slumped over the counter, face nearly touching the Formica. I could smell old sponge from where I'd wiped up a spill. My body shuddered with a sob. I wanted Mike gone, and I wanted him in my arms. I couldn't believe this was happening. Not now, two months from the birth of our son.

A stream of curses flowed from my husband's mouth. He stomped away and punched the wall. "I'm not leavin you." Michael growled the words. "No way would I ever want to be with Erika Hollinger."

"You *were* with her."

He smacked the wall again. "I'll kill her for tellin you that."

Fine by me.

I raised my face from the counter and fixed him with a dull stare. "I don't even know if I want you anymore."

He opened his mouth, then shut it. The door slammed on his way out.

I stumbled to the couch, fell on it, and sobbed. Life as I knew it was gone. No way could it get any worse.

No way.

Chapter 4

Deena

"THE POLICE IN THIS TOWN ARE IDIOTS. THAT INCLUDES TED Arnoldson, even if I was madly in love with him for two years in high school. And it *for sure* includes my ex, Mr. John Cotter himself. None of those five men would know a piece of evidence if they stepped on it—which is probably exactly what they do. You'd think with six murders in three years they'd ask for outside help. Hel*lo*, how about the State Police? Supposedly those guys know what to *do* with a crime scene. But nooo, the Amaryllis Police Department figures they've got to do this themselves. Egotists, every one of them. Worst of all Chief Cotter. And I'm not sayin that just because he used to be my father-in-law."

I positioned the last strip of five-inch-wide professional foil into place on Mary Harell's plain brown hair. I'd finally convinced her to go for a partial color—auburn lowlights. Dull Mary was about to become a new woman. She didn't want "that stripey look" I wore in my own hair. So I'd been careful to blend in the color.

Perfection, that's what I wanted for every client. That's why people kept comin back.

"Well, they'd just better find the killer soon." Mary had come in lookin pale, and her expression hadn't changed. Frankly it wasn't much different from the fear on everyone's face in Amaryllis. This was just too much. Nobody was sleepin at night, and pressure on the police was at an all-time high. A few days ago I'd have said that was good. Maybe Chief Cotter would finally allow some outside help in solvin these horrible crimes. Now the thought scared me to death.

But I had to keep up appearances.

"They *will* find him soon, if I have anything to say about it." I brushed auburn onto the last bit of foiled hair.

"What can *you* do?"

"Make noise, like I'm good at. Keep demandin the chief bring in the State Police. Make sure Trent Williams keeps coverin the case for *The Jackson Bugle*. Chief Cotter don't like lookin like a fool to the entire country."

Could I do all that now—really? Pursue the truth in this case and let the cards fall where I feared they would?

Mary fingered the smock I'd draped around her. "Trent's already in town. I saw him yesterday. Had an article in today's *Jackson Bugle*."

"I read it. Not much to it. As usual, police weren't talkin to him, and Erika's neighbors never heard a thing."

But for sure I planned to pump Trent for any new information. Amaryllis's most famous citizen always had time for Deena Ruckland. Fact was, Trent still had a thing for me. He and I had grown up on the same street, both without fathers.

We fell silent as I finished Mary's color. "If only just one of the murders had been outside of town in the county. That would have least brought in the sheriff's department for that crime. I swear I think the Closet Killer stayed in town on purpose."

I shut my mouth and put down my brush. "All right, Miss Beautiful."

Mary peered at her shiny head in the mirror. I looked away. Didn't want her to catch my eyes. Somehow, on this never-ending day, I'd managed to keep my voice even. Talkin's one thing I know how to do. That and hair. Everybody expects me to rattle on. But I didn't trust anybody lookin into my eyes that day. Sure as shootin the truth lay there.

"What now?" Mary shifted in her seat.

"You get to sit and let the chemicals process. I'll check on you in about twenty-five minutes." I handed her a stack of magazines.

Chin held high, I pushed my rollin cart to the back room and sank into a chair. Alone, thank heaven. Patsy, the gal who rented a station from me in Deena's Cut 'n' Style, was off sick. I should clean up the materials on my tray. Stick the comb in Barbicide disinfectant. Wash out the color bowl. But I didn't have the energy. I could only slump and stare at myself in the small mirror on the wall.

Thirty-two, nothin. I looked a dried up and blown away forty-five, at least. My straight brown hair was too long against my shoulders and needed a cut. Maybe Mary was right about the "stripey" highlights. Suddenly mine just looked overdone. My skin surely needed a tan. Even my hazel eyes—usually my best feature—looked dull.

I couldn't keep this up. My nerves were about to unravel. Spool right out across the floor.

All my life I'd watched out for my little brother. Stevie was slow-minded and easy to push around. Which too many people in this town got their kicks doin, ever since he was little. God has a special place in hell for those people. Think they can make fun of the weak. Truth is, if they knew what I knew, they might not tease so much. Stevie was a simmerin volcano. You could only push a person so far. But over the years I'd been the only one who'd seen him explode—in the safety of home. It was like he bottled up all his emotion until he could let it out in front of me.

Or so I'd thought.

For the past three years, since he turned twenty-three, Stevie had been livin on his own, with a steady job as janitor at the factory. He worked cleanin up durin the late shift, 3:00 to 11:00. He'd seemed to stabilize. Grow some confidence. When he came over to my place I saw no more of his temper. I thought he was growin up, learnin how to deal with his anger.

Until my brother showed up at my house two nights ago—the night Erika Hollinger was killed—covered in blood.

2010 Pulitzer Prize

Feature Writing

The Jackson Bugle

Gone to Ground

What happens to a small, quiet Southern town when evil invades
in the form of a serial killer?

By: Trent Williams
October 29, 2010

(Excerpt)

The population of present-day Amaryllis barely breaks 1,700.
Even so, it is the second largest city in Jasper County, surpassed by
Bay Springs seven miles to the west, with citizens numbering about
2,100. The entire county is home to a mere 18,000 people.

Before the Closet Killings the last murder on record for Amaryllis
dates back to 1905, when a lumberman by the name of Jack Brown
got drunk and shot his nemesis, Alton Wilkerson, during a fight over a
woman. The woman's name has been lost to history.

While Bay Springs is small, it benefits from the confluence of four highways within its city limits. By contrast Amaryllis has a much more sheltered feel, nestled along bucolic Highway 528, which meanders 22 miles between Bay Springs and Heidelberg. County Road 27, an even smaller and less traveled route, forms the town's eastern border. A driver along the pine tree lined Highway 528 comes upon Amaryllis almost as if by accident. A curve in the road—and the town appears. Driving east from Bay Springs, after a few outlying houses, one sees a left turn onto Main Street—a blend of brick-paved road and old storefronts. The drugstore—complete with soda fountain—the bank and grocery store, the hardware store, two hair salons, and one family diner all front Main. There isn't an unknown face on that street, unless, of course, it belongs to an out-of-town visitor. Amaryllis has enjoyed, even thrived, in its anonymity.

Now its separateness has taken on an eerie, bone-chilling aura.

"Where you headed?" Shirley Ludden asks a stranger as she sets a glass of water before him in her Flower Café. "Glad you stopped in. We love to meet new friends." Shirley is a rotund woman in her fifties, quick with a smile and known for her patience and listening ear. Not to mention the best peach pie in town.

But in the past three years Shirley's smile has slipped. "It's hard lookin' at a stranger now," she admits. "Hard even seein' folks I've known all my life come into my place. With every man I serve I think, 'Is he the one?'" She lowers her eyes, giving her head a little shake. "Come to think of it, how do you even know it's a man?"

Chapter 5

Tully

 THE SAME DAY MIKE SAID HE'D KILL ERIKA HOLLINGER HE was almost an hour late coming home from work.

I was already in bed, not wanting to see his face. I lay on my side facing away from the door, my belly heavy and my feet swollen. I had to put a pillow lengthwise between my knees for any comfort at all. When 11:10 rolled around with no truck pulling in the driveway, my body tensed up, like it already suspected the worst. By the time the digital clock read 11:30 I knew where Mike was.

With Erika.

I started to shake. I knew my Michael. He may have been sleeping with her, but he'd hardly gone over there on this night feeling amorous. He'd gone to beat the tar out of the woman who'd outted him to his wife. Mike does not like being told what to do. And he *sure* doesn't like being found out if he's done wrong.

Why had I married him? Why hadn't I listened to my parents?

For a crazy minute I thought about calling the police. But that would only make things worse between Mike and me. At the time all anger over his infidelity was gone, and I just wanted my husband back. Safe. I did not want him going to jail for assault and battery of some woman who wasn't even worth the trouble.

Finally at 11:50 I heard the truck. The engine cut underneath the carport. Mike soon walked into the bedroom, breath puffing, steps agitated. I didn't need to see him to *feel* the adrenaline rolling off him.

My insides went cold.

He disappeared into the bathroom. I heard the door shut hard, the shower go on. His usual routine. When he came out five minutes later I heard the plop of his uniform onto the floor.

He crawled into bed, breathing still erratic. He had to know I was awake, but he didn't try to talk. He just tossed and turned. It was a long time before he fell into the even breath of sleep.

What had he done?

I lay rigid as stone, expecting the phone to ring any minute, cops to beat on our front door. But . . . nothing. Just hot, smothering silence.

The next morning when I managed to pull myself out of bed, Mike was already up. I could hear him in the kitchen. Like a robot I picked Mike's uniform off the floor to throw in the hamper. It was a one-piece jumper-like thing, and as usual he'd peeled it off half wrong side out. My eyes fell on the inside tag at the top—and my hands stopped. I stared at the tag. Pulled it closer.

It didn't look right.

This was an older uniform, with different words on the tag, in different letters. Michael had been issued three uniforms, all the same. Two to wash and one to wear. This uniform was the right size—but it wasn't the one he'd put on that morning. I'd swear to it. I'd washed those clothes so many times I knew every square inch of them.

Like the hand of fate, Mike chose that moment to walk into the bedroom. He halted just this side of the threshold, eyes moving from my face to the clothes in my hands. His fingers twitched. He tried to cover up the nervous gesture by scratching his elbow.

I held up the uniform. "This isn't yours."

"'Course it is."

"It's not the one you put on yesterday morning."

"Yes it is."

"No, it's not."

"Tully. Shut *up*."

I glared at him, the fabric hot in my hands. Where was his uniform? Why did he need to change it?

"Mike. What did you do?"

"Nothin."

"What did you *do*?"

"Tully, we ain't talkin about this. Now or ever."

"I want to *know*!"

In a split-second he covered the ground between us. Wrapped his fingers around my throat and squeezed. I dropped the uniform. Started to choke.

"You hear me good, Tully." Rage contorted his face. "I came home at the regular time last night. Just like always. You got that?"

I couldn't *breathe*. Panic staggered through me.

"Tully!" Mike dug his fingers deeper.

My throat was caving in. Black dots swarmed over my vision. I tried to beg for my life but could only gurgle.

"Do you *hear* me?"

My head managed a nod.

Michael eased off. I pried my mouth wide and dragged in air. It skidded down my throat like fire.

"What time did I get home?"

I couldn't talk.

"*What* time?"

I panted hard. "Nor. Mal. Time."

"You see anything unusual?"

"N-no."

"You sure?"

"Huhhhhh."

"Tully!" He shook me.

"Yes!"

"Don't you forget it." Mike pushed me backward. I stumbled into the wall. "I'm goin fishin till work." He spat the words.

The world spun. I fell on the bed, chest heaving, tears hot in my eyes.

Ten minutes later I'd moved to the couch, not daring to speak. Mike stalked outside, carrying his fishing gear, but then returned. He snatched a cleaning rag from under the kitchen sink, wet it, and took it back outside.

What was he doing?

After a few minutes I heard him drive off.

My mind still shook. I touched my neck. If it bruised, how would I hide it?

The phone rang. I jumped. It had to be the police, asking about last night. I hesitated, then lifted the receiver and squeaked out a *hello.*

"Tully! Thank God you're all right." My mother's voice, all thick.

A dust whirl blew in my stomach. How did she know Mike had nearly choked me to death?

"Did you hear about Erika Hollinger?" Mom started to cry. "She was murdered last night, Tully, just like the others. They found her this morning in her closet . . ."

The phone slipped from my hand.

The next couple hours glazed by. My phone rang off the hook, rumors flying about the latest murder. It had been nine months since Carla Brewster. She'd been sixty-four. Erika was so much younger than all the other victims. Who would be next—a little girl?

Later that morning I lumbered outside to get the mail. The spring sun was warm on my face, and my veins ran cold as Turtle Creek. Mail in hand I reached for the door to go back inside—and saw dark red smears on the knob. I froze.

My finger lifted to graze the smear. It was dry.

I stared at it.

They say there are moments in your life you'll remember on your deathbed. I'd thought it would be times like Michael Phillips first kissing me. Our wedding day. The birth of our son, Michael Brent II, soon to come. But not anymore. The thing I'll most remember is the horrible sight of that smeared blood.

It hit me then. This was why Mike came back for the rag.

If he'd left blood on the doorknob, he surely left it first in the truck. He'd climbed into it that morning and seen the telltale evidence. Must have been in too much of a rush to notice the front door.

My life drained out my toes as I stared at that blood. Such a little bit of red to mean so very much. Shock stole through my body till I thought I'd pass out. Somehow I made it inside the house and collapsed on the couch. The mail scattered on the floor.

This couldn't be. Everything could be explained away. Somehow. The changed uniform. Coming home late, all agitated. Making me lie for him.

The blood.

He'd told me he'd kill Erika. But who'd ever believe he *meant* it?

And now he'd almost killed me.

I leaned back against the sofa cushions, giving my crowded lungs room to breathe. What was I going to do?

I'd fallen in love with Michael so *hard*. I couldn't help it. The flowers, the way he'd listened to me. The way he'd made this nobody feel like the most special girl in the world.

Where did that man go?

Now my whole life was different. I didn't even go to church anymore. I'd gone all my childhood. Had clung to Jesus and made Him part of my life. Jesus faded when Mike came along.

"You hear me good, Tully. I came home at the regular time."

The facts stared me in the face: Mike had killed Erika. And her death was just like all the others. The sixth Closet Killing. When the last murder happened nine months ago, that night, too, he'd come home late from work. Said something held him up at the factory.

The blood on the door.

My head snapped up.

I had to get rid of it.

On someone else's legs, I pushed to my feet and tottered to the kitchen. Bent down to pull a rag from underneath the sink. My gaze fell on a pair of yellow plastic gloves beside the rags. I stared at those gloves a long time.

After an eternity I made up my mind.

Heart still on hold, I reached for the items I needed.

A few minutes later on the porch, I cleaned the blood off the doorknob. I threw the soiled cloth in the washing machine, then hurried to get Mike's dirty uniform. I checked it all over—and found a few dark smears.

Blood? Or just dirt?

I threw the uniform into the washing machine and turned the water to hot.

There. I'd done my wifely duty.

In a fog I returned to the couch to lie down.

I pictured Erika's pulled-up shirt, the bump of her belly, and squinched my eyes shut. When I opened them I'd found myself staring at the Coke stain on the carpet. Same stain I was now staring at a day later while Mike was under the carport, tinkering on his boat. We'd hardly talked since yesterday morning. What was there to say?

The best I could hope for Erika was that she died quickly. My own death was playing out every minute, painful and slow.

Chapter 6

Deena

 IT HAD HAPPENED TWO DAYS AGO ON TUESDAY.

Bang, bang, bang.

The hard knocks on my front door at midnight near made me jump out of my shoes. I'd just watched the first half hour of Letterman, and was nearly asleep.

Bang, bang.

I yanked the drawer of my end table open. Snatched up my loaded Chief's Special—one of my two weapons. I kept a second gun just like it in the nightstand beside my bed.

"Deena!" Stevie's voice muffled from my tiny front porch. He sounded scared, like a little boy. "Open up!"

My heart lurched. I threw my gun back in the drawer—didn't want Stevie to know I had weapons around. Then ran to undo my various locks.

The minute the door cracked open Stevie heaved through it, pushin me backwards. I did an awkward two-step and caught myself before I fell. Stevie shoved the door closed and relocked it. He turned to face me, chest all aheave and cheeks pink. His green eyes looked wild, his hair was askew, and his hands waved in the air, nowhere to land. From waist up his blue work uniform looked wet. Worse, blood smeared the fabric. The whole front was red. And on the sleeves, especially the right one—more blood.

I reared back, a hand at my mouth. "What *happened* to you?"

Stevie paced, fingers in his hair. "I can't tell."

"What do you mean you can't tell?"

"I can't *tell.*"

"Stevie!" I caught him by the wrist. "Are you hurt?"

He looked down the front of himself, face twistin. "No."

"Where'd this blood come from?"

"I don't know."

I forced calmness into my voice. "It's on your uniform. You have to know."

"I can't tell you nothin. I didn't do nothin!"

"Where did this happen? When did you first see the blood?"

"I didn't see it. It was never there." His voice rose. I knew the tone of his lies, had heard it often when Stevie was in a desperate state. He strode away two steps, palms pressed to his temples.

I turned him around. "But it is there. We're both lookin at it."

"It's *not* there."

I surveyed him. "You're wet. Did you try to wash it off?"

"No. I didn't go in Turtle Creek."

Turtle Creek. That would be some chilly water in the spring. The biggest part of the creek ran through the back of the cemetery—just a block from my house—and down the hill near the large stone steps.

What had Stevie been doin in the cemetery? And whose blood was this?

My brother's teeth started to chatter.

"Stevie, come on in the den and sit down. You can tell me what happened." I pulled him by the arm, laughter rollin out from the TV. The sound grated my nerves.

"Nothin happened. I didn't do it." Stevie allowed himself to be led.

"Didn't do what?"

No answer.

I nudged him onto the couch and turned off the television. Took a seat in our mom's old rockin chair. "Listen now." I leaned forward. "It's Deena, your sister. You know you can tell me."

"No I can't!" Stevie flipped his hands up and down.

"Were you with someone who got hurt?"

"No."

"You didn't see anybody get hurt."

"No!"

"And it's not your blood?"

"I'm not bleeding." He squeezed his eyes shut. "Just my brain."

"Then whose blood is it?"

"I was so *mad*."

Oh, no. "Who were you mad at?"

"I don't want to talk about it."

"You *have* to talk about it."

"No, I don't!" Spittle shot from his mouth. "No, no, no!"

"Okay, okay." I held up my hands, palms out.

Stevie looked down at himself. "Get this *off* me!"

"You want to take off your uniform? Go ahead. I'll give you a robe to put on." And I'd throw those clothes in the washing machine fast, before anyone else saw them. Whatever Steve had gotten himself into, it couldn't be good.

Just like that, Stevie's expression switched to angry. His chin came down and his mouth tightened. His eyes lined into that mad-as-a-bull look I'd seen far too many times, and his voice thickened. "She made me do it."

Cold crept over my arms. "Who made you do what?"

He glared at me. "It's *her* fault."

"Sure. Sure it is."

"She's so mean to me."

Who? Lots of people had been mean to my brother.

"But she won't do it again."

"Why won't she do it again, Stevie?"

He leveled an evil grin at me, and my stomach dropped out. "Because I fixed her."

I licked my lips. Tried to keep my voice quiet, even as my heart hammered. "How did you fix her?"

He passed his tongue between his lips—and smiled.

My body went numb. Unbidden, those awful questions rose to the surface—about my brother's whereabouts at the time of the Amaryllis murders. He always claimed he'd been home alone. But who could prove it? My brother had been agitated the day after every one of those murders—and he'd never told me why. And every victim had hired him at some point to do work around their property. The police questioned Stevie after the second murder. He'd been rakin leaves in Sara Fulgerson's yard the day she was killed. But they couldn't pin anything on him, much as they wanted to. At the time I'd convinced myself the cops just wanted the murders "solved" to save their own shaky reputations. And what a way for my ex to get back at me for divorcin him and takin back my maiden name—lock up my brother. I'd fought John Cotter's suspicions—and the Chief's—at every turn. No way would I ever admit I had a few of my own, based on a gut feelin I'd carried around for years—that my unpredictable brother would grow up one day and do somethin really bad.

"Stevie. How did you fix her?"

He stood abruptly. "I got to go home."

I rose and caught his arm. "No, wait—"

"Leave me alone!" He threw my hand off him.

"But—"

"No!" He backed away, wrapped his arms around his chest and self-hugged—like he used to do when he was little. "I don't know nothin, Deena. Don't you say nothin to nobody. Don't you dare."

My head nodded. "I won't."

His face darkened. "You tell anybody, I'll hurt you."

I stared at him.

"Real bad."

He'd never threatened me before.

"You hear me, Deena?"

"Yeah. Yeah, Stevie, I hear you."

He headed for the door. I gathered my wits. "Stevie, let me wash your uniform. I can get it a lot cleaner than you will."

"I know how to wash my own clothes."

"Come on, Stevie."

"No!" He whirled around, hand raised. "Leave me alone!"

I cringed back. He glared at me, then turned again for the door.

Without another word he left. I stood on my porch and watched him run down the street to his little trailer, two doors away. Back inside my house I relocked and bolted the door.

Sleep would not come that night.

I sat up in bed, gun next to me on the covers. Somethin terrible had happened out there. In my heart I knew what it was. But I pushed the knowledge deep down, hopin against hope.

The next day brought news of Erika's death.

By the time the wildfire news leapt across town yesterday mornin, I was in the shop, cuttin Ruthann Becker's frizzy hair. When I heard the sirens peel out from the police station, down one block on Main, my veins iced. I dropped the shears and near stabbed my own ankle. Not five minutes later Theodore Stets ran over from the drugstore next door, sayin he heard the squad cars were parked at Erika Hollinger's house.

Erika, so young. Dead, just like the rest of them.

"She was mean to me." Stevie's words vibrated in my head. Erika had always been mean to him. Made fun of him unmercifully. I'd caught her at it once a couple years ago and near slapped her. She hadn't set foot in my salon since.

Now it was Thursday. In the back room of my shop, I felt like my insides had been hollowed out. Stevie hadn't talked to me since Tuesday night. I went down to his trailer this mornin to ask about the uniform. Had it come clean? He wouldn't answer.

Had anybody heard him bangin on my door? Or seen him runnin down the street in bloody clothes? Surely not, or the police would be all over him by now.

I glanced at my watch. Twenty-five minutes had passed since I left Mary Harell's color to process. Time to check on her.

Somehow I dragged myself to my feet and put on my perky face. Took a deep breath. The day wasn't even half over, and already it seemed like a lifetime. A choice weighed on me that I wouldn't wish on my worst enemy. I couldn't bear to give up my brother to the police. But if I didn't tell them what I'd seen—

How many more women would die?

Chapter 7

Cherrie Mae

AFTER MAYOR B'S HOUSE I HAD TWO SMALLER ONES TO clean before I was done for the day. I dusted and swept and scrubbed on automatic, my mind goin all directions.

What was I gon do bout what I seen?

I slumped into my own house a little after 4:00, wishin more than ever my Ben was still with me. He'd passed from a heart attack two years ago, just one year shy a retiring from his job at the bank. But I still talked to him and felt his presence in the house. And I still read the fine literature he'd introduced me to early in our marriage. Benjamin Bane Devine may only have been a high school graduate—like me—but I'm tellin you, that man was a reader. Chekov and Tennyson, Milton and Dante filled his head and stretched his dreams. Them dreams played out in his children. Both our son and daughter graduated college, Lester in business and Donelle in communications. Now they both had good jobs and families.

If only they hadn't moved out a state to find em.

I kicked off my shoes and headed to the refrigerator for a glass a sweet tea. Then to my favorite chair in the livin room, worn brown with a pop-up footrest. On the nearby table sat my Kindle e-reader, the fancy present my children gave me last Christmas. I couldn't understand why I'd want such a thing until Donelle tol me I could get lots a classic books for free. Wouldn't need to run to the Bay Springs library so much. Right now in my Kindle I was re-readin Alfred Lord Tennyson's *Idylls of the King*. I kept a little black notebook and a pen next to the Kindle so I could write down quotes I wanted to remember.

I set down my glass and collapsed in my chair. At sixty-two, I didn't know how many more years I could clean houses. Trouble was, I needed the money, and that wasn't likely to change anytime soon. But my ankles swelled ever day. At the end a work I always put em up fast as I could.

Gazin out my front window I could see my neighbor's house across Third Street. Esther Goins, in her seventies, used to live there by herself, another widow. Now a granddaughter and her husband had moved in. Esther was too scared to live by herself. Couldn't blame her. Our pretty little Amaryllis had turned into a war zone between regular folk and some crazy person.

"'Behold where Ares, breathin forth the breath of strife and car-nage, paces—paces on.'" I said the words aloud—words Sophocles coulda wrote bout our town today. Chill bumps popped down my arms. We didn't exactly have the Greek god a war in Amaryllis. We had a round-faced, half-baldin mayor. Wore what was left a his gray hair in what white folk call a comb-over. Not the likeliest a killers. But I seen what I seen.

Why on earth would Mayor B kill those women?

Did Mrs. B sleep so sound she wouldn't know if her husband slipped out at night? Or was she just not talkin?

The phone rang, and I jumped. I lifted the receiver off the table beside me, thinkin night would fall in a few hours and fear would leak into my bones like acid. Never failed when the sun went down. Now the fear would have a face attached—Mayor B's.

How would I ever step foot in that man's house again?

The ID said Thomas Howzer. I hit the *talk* button. "Hi, Lucelia."

"Cherrie Mae, just checkin on you. Tom and I still say you should sleep in our extra bedroom tonight. We'd feel better if you did."

"Thanks, but I'll be all right. You know I keep that billy stick right beside me."

"You can bring your billy stick with you."

"Lucelia, I cain't be sleepin at your house ever night. Besides, I'm safer now than I'll be in six months or so. That's his pattern."

"Patterns can be broken."

She was right, so I just grunted.

"Why're you so stubborn, Cherrie Mae?"

"I been stubborn since we was in first grade together. You just now figurin that out?"

"Now it really matters."

I arched my feet. They were beginnin to feel a little better.

Lucelia heaved a sigh. "You see the article in *The Jackson Bugle* today?"

A jolt went through me. "Didn't have time to read it this mornin." The paper still sat on my kitchen table. "Trent got an article in there?"

"Yup."

I was already pushin down my footrest.

"He got down here yesterday afternoon," Lucelia said. "I seen him carry his suitcase in next door, then he was right back out. Gatherin information, no doubt."

One thing bout Lucelia, she did know what her neighbors were doin. Ever time Trent came into town to cover the latest murder, he'd stay next door to her, with his sister and brother-in-law. "I'm gon read the article now. Call you later. Thanks again for checkin on me."

In the kitchen I sat down hard at the table and pulled the newspaper close. Shuffled to Section C—Local News. There sat the article.

Killer Strikes Again in Amaryllis

On Tuesday night, Erika Hollinger, 20, became the sixth murder victim in three years in Amaryllis, one and a half hours southeast of Jackson. Police are attributing the crime to the so-called "Closet Killer," who has stabbed all six victims in their own homes and left their bodies in a closet . . .

I read the rest a the article, lookin for some piece a news I didn't already know. Trent had talked to Erika's neighbors, none of em hearin a thing. The *police* didn't give him any more information than was rumored round town. No mention a the missin ring. Apparently Trent didn't even know I'd been at Erika's house that night. Thank goodness. I didn't want my name in the paper.

I heaved back in the chair, fear tumblin in my head. I should tell the *police* what I seen.

"No way, Ben, cain't do it." I looked toward the chair where my husband used to sit. "The chief won't believe me. He's too close to Mayor B. He'll tell the mayor lickety-split—and there goes my biggest housecleanin customer. And everbody else, too, when word gets round town I done snooped in the Mayor's desk. Meanwhile Mayor B will get rid a the evidence. Then guess who'll be his next victim."

But could I really just do nothin?

Maybe I should get Pastor Ray's advice. But once I tol him, that would put him in the same position as me.

If only I'd never looked in that drawer. This responsibility was too big.

"Shame on you, Cherrie Mae Devine," said a voice in my head. *"You been prayin for this killer to be caught. Now the Lord done sent you help— and you don't want nothin to do with it."*

I crossed my arms. My conscience could just hush.

Trouble was, it spoke the truth. Like Lord Byron said, "Man's conscience is the oracle a God." Sittin on this information would be like tellin the Lord *no thank You* for answerin my prayers.

Out a nowhere a stunnin realization hit. I done left my fingerprints all over Erika's ring.

Air whooshed out my mouth.

What if I tol the *police* I seen that ring—and Mayor B claimed I planted it in his file? And me bein the last known person to see Erika Hollinger alive. They could say *I* killed her.

"Oh, Ben. What am I gon do?"

Long minutes passed. My stomach growled but I paid it no mind. I pictured ever one a those murdered women. Martha. Sara. Sonya. Alma. Carla. And now Erika. I could see each a their smiles, hear their voices. None a them deserved what happened. Their blood cried out from the Amaryllis cemetery. And the remainin women in this town deserved to sleep in peace.

Did I *really* think I could turn my back on this? Imagine if another woman lost her life in such a terrible way cause I said nothin.

But which *police* officer could I tell? Any one of em would just go straight to the chief, who was too close to the mayor.

I shook my head. Nope. I couldn't talk to anyone a them.

Which left only one person to look into this mess—at least for now, till I got some proof.

Me.

The sun was settin by the time I pulled to my feet. As I searched my refrigerator for somethin quick to eat, I knew what I had to do.

If I got caught . . .

Well. I didn't want to think bout that.

Chapter 8

Tully

 AS I LAY ON THE COUCH MIKE CAME INTO THE HOUSE TO CHANGE FOR work. I tensed when he walked by, the air thick between us.

I hadn't been outside all day. My neck was bruised.

Without a word Mike headed for the bedroom.

I closed my eyes. Not even married a year and look at me. How was I going to live like this? And after my baby was born, what then? Would Michael one day threaten his life too?

I didn't even want to name my baby after his father anymore.

Mike's footsteps approached. I pretended to sleep.

"Tully." His voice cut down from the end of the sofa.

I lay still.

Mike slapped my foot. I jerked.

"I know you ain't sleepin'."

I raised my head. "What?"

Emotions rippled across his face. Anger . . . remorse . . . defiance. He stared at me, his mouth hard. "I want you to make sure all the doors are locked till I get home."

"They're always locked."

"You check em twice. Windows too."

Was he trying to convince me he didn't kill Erika?

"You hear?"

"Yes."

"And I don't want you goin to bed till I get home."

"But I get so sleepy, you know that."

"You don't have to get up in the mornin now and go to work. You can sleep late as you want. So sit up on the couch. And once it gets dark, take my gun from the nightstand and keep it beside you."

Mike had taught me to shoot soon after we were married. He had some kind of pistol—I didn't even know what it was. But I knew how to load it and pull the trigger. These days there likely wasn't a home in Amaryllis that didn't have a gun.

"Tully, I'm *talkin* to you."

"I hear you. Okay."

He put his hands on his hips. I could smell his last cigarette still lingering on his body. Who was I kidding—cigarette smell was everywhere in our house. I hated the smell of it. Why had I ever stood for that? Why hadn't I insisted he quit if he wanted to marry me?

He fixed me with a steely gaze. "You think I killed her, Tully?" It was more of a challenge than a question.

"Did you?"

"No."

We eyed each other.

"Then why'd you come home late?"

He shrugged. "Just extra work at the factory."

Something at the factory—same excuse as when Carla Brewster was murdered. If he'd really worked overtime, it would show up on his paycheck. Not that he ever let me see it.

"And your uniform?" *Give me something, Michael. Something I can stake the rest of my life on.*

"I spilled stuff on it and had to change."

If he'd just spilled something, where was the uniform? It would be his responsibility to wash it. And *why* did he nearly choke me to death?

Mike ran his tongue below his upper lip. "As for that picture of me with Erika—ever hear of Photoshop? I wasn't with her. If she was pregnant—which I wouldn't doubt, knowin her—I didn't know anything about it. Sure wasn't *my* baby."

Could that be true? I hadn't seen the picture for that long. Maybe it *had* been changed.

Surely Michael saw the wild hope in my eyes. He nodded. "See. Told you."

But the blood, Tully. The blood.

"Okay."

"That's it?" He scowled. "Just 'okay'? How bout 'I'm sorry I doubted you, Mike.'"

I swallowed. "I'm sorry I doubted you."

"Say it like you mean it."

"I'm *sorry* I doubted you."

Mike nodded, his lips twisting. "That's better." He turned to go. "See you tonight."

I lay like a stone until the front door closed behind him.

Not till the truck backed out of the driveway did I struggle to my feet. I headed into our kitchen and picked up a pair of plastic gloves from underneath the sink. Put them on. Then into our bedroom and to my dresser. I leaned over to slide out the bottom drawer, full of regular-sized clothing. One day I'd be able to fit into them again. I lifted the pile on the right, feeling to the bottom. My plastic-coated fingers brushed the small paper bag I'd hidden yesterday. I pulled it out, sat on the bed, and dumped out its contents.

Out rolled a swath of toilet paper.

Biting the inside of my lip, I unwrapped the paper, layer after layer, my fingers clumsy in the gloves. Finally the objects I'd so carefully protected lay before me.

Two cotton swabs, both stained red. The blood on the doorknob had been long dried by the time I found it. The only way I could swab it was to dampen the cotton.

Would a tiny bit of water make a difference in DNA testing?

Crazy, saving this evidence, then cleaning the rest of it off the doorknob.

I stared at the blood. Was it Erika's?

My nerves tingled. What was I going to do with this? If I took it to the police and DNA matched, they'd arrest my husband.

I closed my eyes, picturing the cops at our door, Mike's hands cuffed behind his back. Neighbors watching, word spreading across town. The look Mike would give me, his betrayer, as they pushed him into the squad car.

If they let him go, he'd kill me.

I stared at the swabs. I could take them down to the police right now. Show them the bruises on my neck. Mike wouldn't know—until they came to arrest him. Would they do that right away? If not I'd have to tiptoe around the house. Do nothing to set him off.

But what if he found out?

When I made these swabs, I wore plastic gloves, careful not to leave my own prints on the package. Just in case I sent it anonymously to police.

Now I couldn't even bring myself to do that.

The red cotton cried out to me, demanding justice. I couldn't stand to look at it anymore.

Carefully I rewound the two swabs in the toilet paper, then placed them in the bag. Returned the package to the bottom of my drawer.

I closed the drawer with a firm push, then turned around to face my empty bedroom.

And the rest of my life.

2010 Pulitzer Prize

Feature Writing

The Jackson Bugle

Gone to Ground

What happens to a small, quiet Southern town when evil invades in the form of a serial killer?

By: Trent Williams
October 29, 2010

(Excerpt)

Legend of the Amaryllis cemetery ghost dates back to the early years of the town. In 1871 Winifred Prathers, wife of the town's first banker, was mourning their young son's death from diphtheria. As she knelt at the grave in the gloaming, she felt a rush of cold air at her back. Turning, she beheld a figure in dark clothing, whose face she could not discern. Man or woman? The figure clenched both hands to its chest and bowed its head, as if grieving for her loss. "Who are you?" Mrs. Prathers managed—and the form fizzled into pieces that melted into the gathering darkness.

Sightings continued after that, the reports handed down from one generation to the next. Always the figure remained androgynous yet graceful, chilling yet empathetic, as if it mourned its own unrelinquishing form tethered between worlds, belonging to neither.

As Amaryllis grew, its cemetery spread to include land on the other side of Turtle Creek, which once formed its rear boundary. While the front of the burial place sits at street level, the back drops down a hill and into a small field that borders some of the finest homes in town. In the 1930s grand stone steps were built into that hill, affording easy access for the elite to pay respects to their deceased. Apparently the ghost applauded the stone steps as well. The specter was seen ascending and descending, as well as dipping its feet into Turtle Creek, known for its unusually frigid water. Perhaps the ghost found comfort in the creek, the one entity colder than itself. That is, until the Closet Killer appeared.

Chapter 9

Cherrie Mae

THE PHONE RANG A DOZEN TIMES BEFORE I COULD EAT my supper. Married friends checkin up to see how I was. Pastor Ray makin sure I was all right. I knew he'd be callin ever widow and single woman in his church. My son and daughter both called. "Mama, I just can't stand this worryin about you every night." Donelle's voice was tight-throated. "It's time you moved here to live with us. Memphis isn't that far away from Amaryllis. You could still visit your friends."

Sometimes the thought a movin in with Donelle sounded good. Specially when I drug home from cleanin houses, feelin so beat. But what would I do in my daughter's house all day while she at work, her husband too? And they kids in school? I didn't know nobody in Memphis. All my friends is in Amaryllis. I was raised here, my parents was raised here. I don't want to go nowhere. Besides it's not fair I should change my whole life cause a some blood-thirsty murderer. *He* deserves to pay for his crimes, not me.

That thought made me all the more determined to follow through on my plan. If Cherrie Mae Devine could help catch this killer and save Amaryllis, so be it. I had to walk in the shoes God done stitched for me.

I just managed to hang up from talkin to Donelle when the phone rang again. I answered on automatic.

"Good evening, Mrs. Devine. This is Trent Williams."

Oh, mercy, the reporter. Why hadn't I checked the ID before I picked up the phone? "Hello, Trent. I heard you was in town."

"Yes, ma'am." He spoke friendly enough but fast, like he was pressed for time. "Unfortunately I'm looking into this latest murder. I heard you visited Erika Hollinger the evening before her death. What did you two talk about?"

"Who tol you that?" Couldn't be the *po*lice. They didn't talk to Trent Williams. His prize-winning article on the Closet Killings last year hadn't made them look so good.

Maybe Erika's mama told him.

"It *is* true, isn't it?"

"Maybe. Maybe not."

"Can you at least verify that you were with Erika?"

"Nope."

He sighed. "Come on, Mrs. Devine, can you give me something? You're bound to have some important insights, as the last known person to see her alive."

My heart went a little softer. Trent was callin in favors as the local boy, and why shouldn't he? He'd made Amaryllis proud. "Trent, it's not that I don't want to help you. It's just that I done tol everthing I need to the *po*lice. And I don't want my name in the paper."

I sure didn't need any eyes on me if I was gon carry out my plan.

"Well, did Erika say anything to you that would indicate why someone would want to kill her?"

Did serial killers need a motive—other than they just plain crazy? "No. Was there a reason to kill the rest a those women?"

"I don't know, it's just . . . I've asked that question about every victim, hoping it'll trigger a thought in someone's mind. Some *reason* for all this." Frustration filled Trent's tone. "The worst thing about these murders is the randomness. If we could just make some sense of it all."

The *why* question. Trent's article had talked bout that. The whole town wondered why.

I shook my head. "Crime is common; logic is rare."

"What?"

"Sherlock Holmes."

Silence. Trent must be thinkin that one over.

"So, Mrs. Devine, do you have anything for me?" It was almost a plea.

What I had was my own question: did Trent know where Mayor B was during all six murders?

"Sorry, Trent. I need to go now."

"If you change your mind, please call me on this number. It's my cell phone."

"All right, young man. And I thank you for what you doin. Maybe one day you *will* find somethin to help crack this case." Goodness know the *po*lice weren't havin much luck.

"Oh, Mrs. Devine, one last thing. When you were with Erika, did she eat any brownies?"

My head drew back. "Why you want to know that?"

"I imagine if she did, that's something you told the police?"

"They tell you that?"

He sighed. "No. They're not talking to me."

I licked my lips. Smart as I knew Trent was, I done underestimated him. If he hadn't talked to the *po*lice, where'd he learn bout the brownies? Just went to show I couldn't possibly think through everything regardin these murders.

"Please, Mrs. Devine."

I was in over my head. Who was I to try to fix this case?

"Just say yes or no."

"Tell you what. I answer this one question, you got to answer mine."

"Deal."

"Okay then. Yes."

A pause. "What time?"

"What *time?*"

"When did she eat her last brownie?"

"That's two questions."

"Come on, Mrs. Devine, it's important."

My mind spun back. Hadn't Chief Cotter wondered the same thing? As I remembered, Erika stuffed a brownie in her mouth bout the time I got up to go. "I guess around 10:00."

"Great. Thank you very much."

"Uh-huh." I blinked myself back to the present. "Trent, don't you go puttin my name in your article, you hear?"

"I'll let you remain anonymous, I promise."

"All right. Now my question." How to say it without givin anything away? "In all your talkin to people, you notice anybody not able to account for where they was durin the murders?"

"I wish. Maybe that'd get us somewhere. You thinking about someone in particular?"

I knew I shouldn't a said anything. Now I had to lie. *Lord, forgive me.* "No."

"You sure?"

"Can't a body just wonder somethin?"

"Sure. Okay." Trent didn't sound convinced.

"I really got to go now."

"Please call me if you think of anything else? If you have some thought, maybe I can help run it down for you."

If he only knew. "Okay, Trent. Bye now." I hung up the phone before he could say another word.

For a long time I sat at the kitchen table lookin out the back window. Why did Trent want to know bout them brownies?

Wish I hadn't answered his question. Somehow—didn't quite know how yet—that was gon get me in trouble.

One thing I did know. Next time I took to wantin to bake for somebody I was gon think twice. Never know what kind a mess it could get you in.

Chapter 10

Deena

AT 5:30 I FINISHED WITH THE DAY'S LAST CUSTOMER. BETSY Luvall's gray hair was perfectly coifed for another week. My head ached, my feet hurt, and my mind turned like a whirlwind. I waited with Betsy while her husband came to get her—he wouldn't let his wife go anywhere by herself, even in the daytime. Then I locked the door while I counted the day's money.

I wished I could go home and be alone. After a day's work I was always talked out. People thought I could chatter forever. That it came naturally. They were wrong. Unless I was nervous, talkin was simply a part of my business. Folks expect it from their hair stylist.

But Trent Williams had called an hour ago, wantin to see me. For him it was part work, part date. Let him dream on. I saw it as an opportunity to gather information. Had anyone seen my brother, or an unknown figure, runnin through the cemetery or down our street? Or worse yet, comin to my door. Chances were good no one had seen a thing. The streets of Amaryllis always did roll up tight after dark, even before the murders started.

Still, what would I do if someone *had* seen Stevie? If he hadn't given *me* an innocent reason for bein covered in blood, he sure wouldn't come up with one for anyone else. Chief Cotter would throw my brother in the slammer and grin while doin it. So would John. Amaryllis folks wanted these murders solved. How easy it would be— finally—to pin em on the town "half-wit."

But what if my brother *was* to blame?

I let myself out of the salon, makin double sure the door was locked. I slipped into my car, parked out front on Main, and drove the five blocks to my house. Supper wouldn't be anything fancy. I told Trent I had some leftover spaghetti sauce—take it or leave it.

Since Trent had come down from Jackson to cover our first murder in Amaryllis, we'd sort of teamed up. He knew I cut about all the white folks' hair in town. (The blacks went to my friend Rochelle's salon. Nothin racial about it. I just didn't have the trainin or equipment to do black hair.) And the white folks who weren't my clients likely came into my salon for Patsy, so either way I heard their talk. The only white people who never darkened my door were the three Caucasian members of the Incompetent Five—the Amaryllis police force. Not that I wanted em in my salon anyway. My ex-husband, Officer John Cotter, and his father the chief would have to be crazy to let me stand over them with a pair of shears. And with the Chief tellin all his men what to think, say, and do, it was no puzzle why Ted Arnoldson wouldn't set foot in my place either.

A block before my house I drove by the Amaryllis cemetery, rememberin the game Stevie and I used to play as kids. "Hold your breath till it's passed—or you're dead!" I'd elbow Stevie in the back of Mom's car. He never was any good at not breathin. He died a thousand deaths passin that cemetery by the time he was ten.

Once, when I was eleven and we drove by the cemetery at night,

I could have sworn I saw the Amaryllis ghost. It was floatin between headstones in the middle of the grounds. I screamed and pointed, but at that moment the ghost melted away. I've never seen it since.

At home I locked the front door and checked to see my two guns were in their places and loaded. Call me obsessive, but I checked them every day. I put the spaghetti sauce in a pan to warm and started heatin water to boil some fresh pasta. I hadn't been home ten minutes when my bell rang.

"Hello?" I called through the closed door.

"It's me."

Trent's voice, deep and kinda sulky. Frankly the man's voice was the sexiest thing about him. On looks I'd give him a five. His brown hair was good—better when he was in town and I could cut it. But his face was thin and long, and his jaw line weak. Total opposite of my hunky ex. But then, John Cotter had plenty other issues.

Click, click went my multiple locks. I opened the door and stood back. Trent was dressed in khaki pants and a short sleeve blue shirt. The fabric set off his blue eyes. Stickin out his front pocket was the ever-present small spiral notebook and pen. Always the reporter.

"Hi there, Deena." He leaned down his lanky frame and gave me a hug. His half-day growth of beard scratched my face.

"Hi, Trent. Been a long time since I've seen you." Christmas, to be exact. He'd come home to Amaryllis to spend the holiday with this sister and brother-in-law.

"Too long." He looked meaningfully into my eyes.

Uh, yeah.

"Come on into the kitchen. Water's about ready to cook the pasta."

I led him back, my brain churnin. This had to go right. Trent had always been open with me, especially two years ago when Chief Cotter had tried to pin Sara Fulgerson's murder on Stevie just because my brother had raked leaves in her yard the day she died. Of course he'd left fingerprints on her back door—she gave him lunch that day.

Trent had told me everything the cops had on Stevie—nothin more than the print and a boatload of speculation. Trent didn't believe Stevie could've killed Sara, or Martha a year earlier. But now after four more killings, if someone had whispered to Trent about Stevie runnin around all bloodied on the night Erika died, would Trent tell me?

I had to find out what time Erika was killed.

In the kitchen Trent leaned against a counter, one foot crossed over the other. Without askin, I fetched him a Dr. Pepper with plenty of ice. That's all Trent drank, mornin, noon, and night. Probably took showers in it.

I dumped spaghetti in the boilin water and stirred the sauce in the other pot.

He sniffed. "Smells good."

"Yeah. Always better the second day." I set the red-stained wooden utensil on the spoon rest. "So. You got here yesterday, I hear."

"Not till mid afternoon. I was way on the other side of Jackson when I heard the news. I'd been there with Zeke, covering another case since Tuesday morning."

Zeke was his supervisor. "Yeah, I know." Trent's sister, Sally, and I had both left messages on his cell phone Wednesday mornin. "Sally told me she finally got through to Zeke, askin him where you were. He said you and he had been up all night Tuesday followin leads on your story, and then you had to run to a court session for all day Wednesday."

"Yeah, that's a crazy case. But the minute I heard about Erika I begged off to come here. Just had to stop by home first for some extra clothes."

He'd probably broken every speed limit gettin to Amaryllis. "You write another article for tomorrow?"

"Yup. Barely made my deadline after the autopsy."

"The chief'll love it." If anybody in this town hated Trent, it was Chief Cotter. "What's it gonna say?"

Trent slid a forefinger up and down his glass. "I talked to my contact at the facility in Jackson after Erika's autopsy. Of course toxicology will take awhile, but like the other murders, I doubt they'll matter. Erika's pending cause of death is from the same kind of wound—a stab to the neck that cut the carotid artery. In fact he said the single stab was done exactly like the other victims—same precision, same placement. Which means it had to be the same perpetrator."

Which also meant, like the others, she bled out in just a minute or two. Must have been an awful lot of blood.

I stirred the sauce, keeping my eyes averted. "Did he tell you what time she died?"

Trent set down his glass. "How much do you want to know? It gets kind of technical. And . . . gory."

I shivered. We were talkin about a person I knew. As much as I'd disliked Erika, I wouldn't have wished this on her. I steeled myself. "Tell me."

A shadow dropped down Trent's face. "They can never tell time of death exactly. But I did learn the condition of the body when the coroner got to the scene around 10:00 a.m. She was nearly in full rigor mortis, which normally takes about twelve hours—but there are all kinds of variances to that."

Hope lifted its head. Could Erika have been killed as early as 10:00 p.m.? Stevie was still at work.

"But the pathologist said Erika had one kind of partially digested food in her stomach—brownies. Food normally goes through the stomach in four to six hours. I'd gotten a tip that a woman had been eating brownies with Erika, maybe as late as 10:00—"

"Who?"

Trent shook his head. "Anonymous source."

"Oh, come on, Trent."

"I can't. Maybe later."

My heart kicked around. "So she was killed sometime between 10:00 and 4:00 in the morning?"

"Well, based just on stomach contents. But when they put it together with everything else like rigor mortis and body temperature, they narrowed it to between 11:00 and 2:00."

No.

The sauce started to bubble. So red. Why hadn't I cooked somethin else? I turned off the burner, fightin to look calm. "You sure she ate a brownie at 10:00?"

"That's what I heard. But that doesn't mean she didn't eat one after that. The visitor left at 10:00, so who's to say what happened later. Still, when you look at all the factors, the timeline looks pretty good."

No it didn't. It looked *horrible*.

I threw a glance at Trent and nodded. The expression on his face snapped my eyes back to him.

He surveyed me. "Why are you so curious? You never asked me this about any of the other murders."

"No reason."

"You sure?" He tilted his head.

I couldn't relax around Trent, not tonight. He was too keen on gettin his story. "Of course."

The noodles looked nearly done. I busied myself with pluckin one out to sample. Al dente. I turned off the burner and lifted the pan to the sink to drain. I could feel Trent's eyes borin through my back.

"If you know something, Deena"—Trent's voice had gone quiet— "I need to hear it."

"What could I possibly know?"

"You tell me."

I set down the drained pan of noodles none too lightly and turned around. "Is this the only reason you're here, to find out what I know? I thought we were friends."

He flicked a look at the ceilin. "We *are* friends. And there's no need to be dramatic."

"Fine then. Let's eat."

"Fine then."

If I hadn't perfected my motor mouth I don't know how I'd have made it through the rest of that evenin. Trent and I talked about all the murders, goin over everything we knew, which wasn't much. All the while my mind chanted, *Stevie could have killed her. Stevie could have killed her.*

If Trent noticed I was on edge, he didn't let on.

With supper done and dishes in the sink, I was talked out. We moved into the livin room. I took the rockin chair, leavin the couch for Trent. No use sittin close to him and gettin his hopes up.

"I need to tell you something." He stretched his left arm across the back of the couch.

"Shoot."

"I'm moving to New York."

I gaped at him. "New *York*?"

A smile crept across his face.

"Why? How?"

"The *New York Times* wants me to come write for them."

The *New York Times*? "Trent, that's amazing! That's the big time."

His gaze dropped to the floor. Slowly he nodded. "Yup."

What was he holdin back? "Why aren't you more excited?"

"I am excited. Guess I'm just trying to soak it all in."

"Is it because of your feature on Amaryllis?"

"Gone to Ground" was wonderfully written, capturing the heartache, the questions, and the sense of fate in Amaryllis after the murders started. It painted the picture of a small town turned upside down—and still lookin to turn itself aright. Trent started work on the article after the murder of Carla Brewster. After the piece ran in

The Jackson Bugle, Zeke submitted it for a Pulitzer Prize in the feature writing category. And lo and behold, it won.

Trent rubbed his long fingers against the couch. "That's what they said. I was blown away when I got the call. But now I'm just wondering what a Southern boy like me's gonna do in New York."

"Show em what you've got, that's what."

Trent took a deep breath and licked his lips. Sat up straighter. Clearly he was about to say whatever was eatin at him. My heart did a two-step. Was it Stevie?

The air around us changed.

"What is it, Trent?"

He hesitated. "You want to come with me?"

Relief hit me, followed by shock. I stared at him. "*Me?*"

He nodded, color tingeing his cheeks. He picked at his shirt, one foot in a nervous pump.

I let out a tinny laugh. "What would a Southern girl like me do in New York?"

Trent raised a shoulder. "Explore the city. Think of it, Deena." He leaned forward. "All the sights of New York. The Empire State Building, the Statue of Liberty. Central Park. The neighborhoods and stores and crazy places you can't even dream of in Amaryllis. We could get married. You'd get away from the killing here. Be safe."

Married. *Married.* "Like New York is safe?"

"A lot more than here. I could stop worrying about you."

My pulse went fuzzy. What to say? "This is . . . amazing. I still can't believe what's happened to you. Remember that time in the school cafeteria during seventh grade? You told me when you grew up you wanted to own a successful business. And I remember thinkin, wow, wish I had a dream like that—"

"Deena."

"Instead of just wishin people would quit teasin Stevie—"

"Deena."

"When I couldn't seem to stop it—"

Trent half stood and caught my wrist. "Be quiet." My mouth hung open. He was close enough for me to see the flecks of darker blue in his eyes. "Just . . . listen to me."

"Okay."

He let my arm go slowly, as if makin sure I wouldn't flit away. He eased back to the edge of the couch.

Outside my neighbor's dog barked. A car drove by. Trent and I looked at each other.

"Thing is . . ." Trent swallowed. "That day in seventh grade? I only told you half my dream—and of course it never came true. But the other half was that you were in it. You were with me."

Not a single word would come to my tongue.

"I've loved you since fifth grade, Deena. All the way through high school, when you had a crush on Ted Arnoldson. And later when you married John Cotter. When it leaked out about all his girlfriends, I wanted to strangle him 'cause he'd hurt you. I was happy when you divorced him. I knew I'd finally get a chance . . ."

How had I not seen he cared this much? "I—"

"*Don't.*" His hand jerked up, palm out. I could see his shirt move from his heartbeat. "Don't answer now. I'll be here for a few more days. Just think about it."

My head nodded.

"And don't worry about money, I have enough to start out. That $10,000 award for the Pulitzer—I saved it for us."

For us. So many thoughts went through my mind I couldn't begin to sort them out.

Trent's gaze dropped. Awkwardness crept between us and hung there. I played with the collar on my blouse. I didn't want to deal with this, not now. How did Trent think he could take me away from Stevie, anyhow? Who'd look after my brother if I was in New York?

Unless he was in jail.

Trent pushed to his feet. "I need to go." He wouldn't meet my eyes. "Thanks for supper."

Numbly, I rose. "No problem. Thanks for comin. Tell Sally and Ray hi for me."

"Sure."

We reached the door. I placed my hand on the deadbolt. "Do they know you're goin to New York?"

"I just told them. They're excited for me."

The last sentence sounded almost defensive. "I'm excited for you, too, Trent."

He firmed his lips. "See you soon, Deena."

"Yeah. See you soon."

I watched while he walked down my porch steps. As he climbed into his old Ford he gave me a small wave. I waved back.

The door relocked and bolted, I leaned against it and closed my eyes. The smell of spaghetti lingered. Suddenly it was sickening.

With draggin steps I entered the kitchen. I eyed the dishes in the sink and shivered. The sauce looked like blood.

As I rinsed plates and scrubbed pans, two thoughts pulsed in my head. One—no way I could go with Trent, and he had to know that. And two—if he cared so much about me, would he do *anything* for me?

Like help me with my brother, no matter what Stevie had done.

FRIDAY
APRIL 22, 2011

Chapter 11

Tully

THURSDAY NIGHT I SAT UP LIKE MIKE TOLD ME TO, HIS gun on the coffee table. Who were we fooling? My muscles turned to rocks while I waited, and the baby wouldn't stop kicking.

I couldn't keep doing this. I was already about to fall apart.

Finally in bed next to Mike, I couldn't sleep. Again. How could I relax, beside a killer? When I did doze off, I had nightmares. Twice I jerked awake, sure I felt a knife at my neck.

Friday morning I dragged around, hot and fat and weepy. In the shower I couldn't stop crying. I dressed in shorts and a T-shirt. Put makeup on my neck, trying to hide the bruises. I hoped my OB-GYN wouldn't notice. He'd be busy at the other end.

"Wait." Mike spoke up as I was fixing to leave. "I'm goin with you."

"To the doctor?" Mike never went along. He couldn't stand to see a man checking me.

His face darkened. "Got a problem with that?"

"I was going to meet Mercy at the soda fountain afterwards." Mercy was a friend from high school. Worked afternoons at the Bay Springs Dollar General Store.

"I don't want you seein Mercy."

"Why?"

"You need to stay home, off your feet, remember? You got no business runnin around with friends."

"I stay home *all day* with my feet up on the couch."

"Good. That's the way Doc wants it."

My eyes burned. Mike was going to cut me off from everybody. As much as I'd hated Erika, I wished I had her courage. She'd have stood up to him.

Maybe she did. Now she was dead.

I picked up the phone.

"What're you doin?"

"Calling Mercy to tell her I can't see her today."

Or tomorrow. Or ever.

As we headed out to the truck, something inside me gave way. This was it, and I'd better face the truth. Either I'd live the rest of my life like this—or I had to do something about it.

Chapter 12

Deena

NO SLEEP FOR ME THURSDAY NIGHT. HOW'S SOMEONE supposed to sleep when she thinks her brother's a killer? I watched my digital clock tick through the hours, its red numbers like demon eyes. At 1:00 I knew Stevie was guilty. By 2:00 I'd convinced myself he *couldn't* have pulled off the murders. He wasn't smart enough. Would have left bloody prints everywhere. Besides, why would he kill the first five women? They never did anything bad to him.

By 3:00 I was beatin myself up for ever thinkin such awful things about my brother.

Four o'clock and I was back to the bloody uniform. Stevie's obvious lies. Erika's time of death.

Who had been with her the night she died? I had to convince Trent to tell me.

Trent. How was I supposed to tell him I didn't want to go to New York? I'd break his heart.

On the other hand runnin away right now seemed mighty temptin. I could leave this mess behind. Start over. Work in a fancy New York salon.

By the time I stumbled from bed, I knew I had to make Stevie talk to me. What had he done with that bloody uniform? What if he washed it, and the blood didn't all come out? It was evidence just waitin for the cops to find.

But what if he was guilty? I couldn't protect a killer. Besides, if I messed with evidence, I could get in serious trouble.

I took a shower and got dressed. Drank a bunch of coffee to fry my already fried nerves. A half hour before I had to open the salon I strode to Stevie's trailer. His threat echoed in my head.

"I'll hurt you. Real bad."

This was crazy. I should just leave this alone.

At his door I hesitated, then knocked hard and long, the metal clangin beneath my fist.

No response.

Give it up, Deena.

I walked down the trailer to my brother's bedroom window and rapped on the glass. "Stevie, get outta bed! I need to see you."

Still nothin. I banged again. "Stevie!"

A growl drifted from inside. "Go away, Deena!"

"I'm not goin away. I want to make sure you're all right."

"I'm fine."

Sure he was. All bloody Tuesday night, with Erika killed as early as 11:00.

"Stevie, if you don't let me in, I swear I'll bust your door down!"

"You do and you'll be sorry."

I leaned against the trailer. "*Why* are you actin like this?"

"Go away, Deena." His voice hardened. "I mean it."

"I have to talk to you, and I don't want any neighbors to hear." I threw a glance to either side. On my right was the Fredericks' house.

Gary would be at work, but Betty stayed home with a two-year-old. Did she have a window open? On the left sat the Dragers' little place. They were a young couple, both workin. Probably gone by now.

"Stevie, open the door!"

"*No!*"

My head lowered. I rubbed between my eyes, starting to cry. *Dear Lord, how can this be happenin?*

I cupped my mouth against my brother's window. "Stevie, you *have* to tell me what happened Tuesday night."

No answer.

"Stevie!"

"Deena, I'm warnin you." His words seethed. "Go. A*way.*"

The hairs on my arms raised. I pulled back from the window. He was just actin like this because he was scared. Hadn't I seen him do that enough as a child?

I leaned in once more. "The cops'll come after you. Then what?"

"Why should they?"

"You *know* why."

"You gonna tell em?" The words spat like fire. "Huh, Deena?"

"No."

"Do I need to come out and make *sure* you won't?"

My heart dropped. I turned away. *What was that you said about New York, Trent?*

Gazin down the street, I fixed on the cemetery. I pictured my brother stumblin through it in the dark, tryin to wash off blood in Turtle Creek. He often cut through the graveyard and down the stone steps on the other side to go to work. Quickest way to the factory, which sat a third of a mile beyond. But he never walked through that unlit place at night.

What if he'd dropped some piece of evidence near the creek?

Hurryin back up the road, I jumped in my car and drove around the block to the rear of the cemetery. Parked near the stone steps and trotted up to the top of the knoll. The sun was already warm and not a breeze to be found. My body heated up, sweat at the back of my neck.

Straight ahead were all the graves. Turtle Creek splashed to my right. I swished through the grass toward it, eyes riveted on the water.

Along the bank weeds were pressed down, as if someone had stomped through. I stared at them. What Monday of the month was comin up?

The fourth.

Church volunteer ladies would be out here in a few days, pullin those weeds. If this was any kind of evidence at all, they'd take care of it.

Easin closer to the shallow water, I peered into it. A dragonfly hovered above a rock, the creek a-shimmer in the sun. Nothin glinted in the light. No knife blade.

Well, why should there be a knife here? The weapon was left in Erika's neck. Still, what if there'd been a second knife? Or . . . somethin else?

My heart fluttered as I made my way down the creek, searchin for anything out of place. Anything that screamed my brother had been there. My blouse grew damp and my head pounded. By the time I reached the point where the creek went beyond cemetery property, I felt sick in my stomach. Not because I'd found anything. Because I even had to *look*.

Eyes burnin, I slumped my way back up the creek and down the stone steps. The day had just begun, and I was exhausted. And I looked like the dickens. Checkin in my rearview mirror, I pushed bangs out of my eyes and wiped perspiration from my forehead.

One thing I knew, as I drove toward Main Street. After I closed up shop for the day, and while Stevie was at work, I had to find a way to get into his trailer. Once upon a time I'd had a key. Maybe it was stuck in some junk drawer.

I had to get that bloody uniform out of my brother's house.

2010 Pulitzer Prize

Feature Writing
The Jackson Bugle

Gone to Ground

What happens to a small, quiet Southern town when evil invades in the form of a serial killer?

By: Trent Williams
October 29, 2010

(Excerpt)

The apparition in Amaryllis's cemetery is not the only kind of ghost in Jasper County. Along Highway 528 and elsewhere in the area are the ghosts of numerous settlements, once bustling burgs and now little more than pine trees and a few scattered buildings.

Amaryllis's history is much like that of its once neighboring towns—except for how it got its name. Founded in 1877 by Roland Marks, Amaryllis cut its acreage out of the longleaf yellow pine forests surrounding Highway 528—at that time a mere dirt and gravel road. The lumber business was booming in Mississippi, aided by the building of railroads. Marks, hard-working and entrepreneurial since his teens, thumbed his nose at the area's successful "Big Four" logging companies and built his own saw mill. Marks's wife, Lucinda, was an avid gardener, her favorite flower, the amaryllis, gracing their front yard in early spring. The blooms were no small feat, given the county's ubiquitous red clay dirt. Legend has it that as a birthday present Marks eventually allowed Lucinda to name the town, sure that she would dub it Marksville, or perhaps even Roland. Lucinda had other ideas. When she decided to call the town after her favorite flower Marks was livid, considering the moniker far too feminine for the home of his hard-scrabble business. But Lucinda stood her ground, and Amaryllis it became.

Marks Mill continued until 1908 when, unable to compete with the Big Four, it stuttered to a halt. Still, Amaryllis managed to hang on while nearby settlements such as Acme, Waldrup, and Paulding faded away due to the lumber mills' eventual demise. Bradmeyer Plastics, the factory that today employs almost a fifth of the town's working citizens, wasn't built until the 1950s. In those lean in-between years, Amaryllis lost many people but clenched its teeth and hung on.

It is that same tenacity and will to survive that has fueled its citizens in the past three years since the Closet Killings began.

Chapter 13

Cherrie Mae

THANK HEAVEN FOR FRIDAYS—THE ONE WORK DAY I GIVE myself a two-hour lunch. After cleanin houses all week, my ol bones needed the rest. Especially after doin the big two-story McAllister house Friday mornin. It had been almost a year since I pulled the pink thong out from under the McAllisters' bed. Verna McAllister and I ain't spoke of it since. But tell you one thing—she give her husband a lot colder eye than she used to.

At my kitchen table before I left for work I'd read Trent's latest news story on Erika's murder. He kept his word and didn't use my name, givin "anonymous" information bout Erika eatin brownies, and how the autopsy report backed that up. Erika was killed with the same "precise stab wound to the neck" that the other victims suffered. Course, I already knew that. What hit me hardest was the estimated time a the murder—somewhere between 11:00 p.m. and 2:00 a.m. I had to stop readin for a minute when I saw that.

Erika mighta died just one hour after I left her? What if I'd stayed longer?

That guilty thought stuck to my insides like a big burr. I had to beg Jesus' help to pry it loose. Then it hit me. Maybe this is why the Lord put me in a position to solve this terrible crime. He was givin me a way to find justice for Erika.

"Oh, Lord, help me do that." I gazed toward heaven. "And Ben, you keep close to Jesus up there the next few days. I'm gon need all the help I can get."

Heart heavy, I left to start my work day.

As I cleaned the McAllister house my thoughts kept churnin. What if Mayor B got rid a that evidence in his drawer before I could get to it? And on the night Erika died, did he leave his house just before 11:00, tellin Mrs. B he needed to go to the factory and check on somethin as the second shift ended? She wouldn't think anything bout it. Then after Erika was killed and the mayor said he was home at the time, Mrs. B just kept her mouth shut, never dreamin her husband coulda done it.

If only I could talk to Mrs. B about Tuesday night. But I couldn't figure how to bring up the subject without puttin her on guard.

At 11:30 I drug myself home and ate some leftover turnip greens. The pot liquor from the greens tasted mighty good on a piece a corn bread. Then I turned on my little laptop computer, a Christmas present from my son and daughter two years ago. Hardly used the thing. Now it would be my savin grace, along with the camera they got me the year before. Crazy notion my kids have, that I need such things. Maybe God was behind that too.

Sittin at the kitchen table, I took a picture a my refrigerator, covered with photos a Donelle and Lester, and all the grandbabies. Then I pulled that cable connector thing out a the camera bag and stuck it in the computer. Now how in the world did I get the pictures from one place to the other? I stared at the camera and all its buttons.

Ah. That dial right there.

Up on the computer came a beautiful sight—the program to get the pictures. I fussed with it awhile, slowly goin through the steps. And lo and behold, I ended up with that lovely refrigerator photo on my computer. Saved and safe.

Cherrie Mae, you ain't such a dummy.

I leaned back in my padded kitchen chair and rubbed my top lip.

Monday I could wear a pair a loose pants and drop the small camera in my pocket. The trick would be to get Mrs. B out a the house. Five minutes is all I'd need. But five minutes could be hard with Mrs. B. That woman had a mind a her own.

Did she know her husband had left their house Tuesday night? Surely she did.

I pushed to my feet and made for the phone to dial Cory, Pastor Ray's wife. As much as I didn't want to say nothin to anybody, I had no choice. At least Cory knew how to keep her mouth shut.

She answered on the first ring.

"Cory, it's Cherrie Mae."

"You okay? It's the middle of a work day."

"I'm on a lunch break. Listen, I wonder if you'll do me a little favor. Ain't this comin Monday mornin when our church weeds at the cemetery?" Our Baptist church and the Methodist church took turns the fourth Monday each month. Saved the town some money, and besides, we all wanted the graveyard lookin right. Everbody had at least one loved one buried there.

"Yes, it's this Monday. I'll be there. With the warm weather now, there'll be lots of work to do."

Thank You, Lord. "You know if I didn't work I'd be right there beside you."

"I know that, Cherrie Mae."

"But I was thinkin, with it bein spring and all, you could use some extra hands. You need to call Eva Bradmeyer, see if she'll put in an extra day to help you."

"But her church's month isn't till May."

"I know. But Mrs. B'll be willin to help."

"How do you know that?"

"Well, I just figure."

Cory was silent for a minute. "Don't you work at the Bradmeyers' on Mondays?"

"Yes, ma'am, Thursdays too."

"You working there this coming Monday then." It was a statement, not a question. I could hear the tone buildin in Cory's voice.

"Mm-hmm."

Cory made that little sound she do, with her tongue hittin her top teeth. "Why do you want to get Mrs. B out of her house?"

I looked at my camera. "Cory, this is somethin you don't want to know."

"Do tell."

"Ain't lyin to ya."

I could practically hear the wheels turnin in her head. As a pastor's wife Cory had to know when to keep a confidence, but that don't mean she don't have curiosity like the rest a us.

"Will you do it for me, Cory?"

"I can't lie."

"You don't *have* to lie. You done tol me there'd be a lot a extra work."

"I know, but . . . I've never called Mrs. B with that kind of request before. She'll think it strange."

Not half as strange as her husband bein out the night Erika Hollinger got killed. "Do it, Cory. We been friends a long time. You know if I'm bringin this up, it's got to be important."

"What if she says no?"

"Who could say no to you? You one a the sweetest women in town."

"I don't . . ."

"Please."

She sighed. "Will I ever know what this is about?"

"Most likely. But in the meantime I got to remind you that you cain't say nothin. And I mean even to Pastor Ray."

Silence. I waited her out.

"Okay, Cherrie Mae." Defeat touched her words.

Yes! "Thank you so much. I'm mighty grateful. Call her now, all right? And lemme know what she say."

"You are full of mischief, you know that?"

Better that than full a somethin else. "Thanks again, Cory. I look forward to hearin back from you." I hung up before the woman could change her mind.

I sank back in the chair and lowered my chin. A long shudder took hold a my shoulders. I was really gon do this.

The clock on my wall ticked. The phone didn't ring. I got up and washed out my plate and fork. Ate a couple chocolate chip cookies. *Come on, Cory, where you at?* Maybe Mrs. B was out.

Five minutes before I had to leave, my phone went off. I liked to jump five feet. I snatched up the receiver and saw the pastor's ID. "Hi, Cory?"

"It's done." She didn't sound happy.

"She give you a hard time bout it?"

"No, not at all. Said she'd put in an hour or so late morning."

"Thank you!"

"I have no idea how I'm going to explain to the rest of the women why I called Eva Bradmeyer."

"Don't tell em. When she show up, jus say, 'Eva! So glad you could help us out on your month off.' She'll say, 'Glad to do it.' And that'll be that."

"Cherrie Mae, for a Christian woman you sure got a lot a cunning in you."

If she only knew. "'The games one plays are not the games one chooses always.'"

"You quoting somebody again?"

"Maxwell Anderson."

"Who?"

"Cory, thanks for your help."

As I drove off to clean the Trangells' house, I prayed Mayor B didn't touch that horrible file a his this weekend. And that, come Monday, I'd still find the courage to do what I had to do.

Chapter 14

Deena

I LUGGED MYSELF THROUGH THE DAY, ONE CUT AND STYLE blendin with the next. At my short lunch break I drove down to Stevie's and banged on his trailer again, beggin him to let me in.

A glutton for punishment, that's me.

"Get outta here, Deena!" he hissed through the door. "You knock one more time, I'm comin after you."

He meant it, too. I heard it in his tone.

If I got into his trailer, and he found out . . . I didn't want to think what he'd do to me.

Back at work and frustrated, somehow I had to wash and style Norma Dodderman's hair without diggin my fingernails into her scalp. She wanted two inches cut off—a radical thought for her. Fortunately, Norma's one person in town who can yak even more than me. She had all kinds of wild theories about the Closet Killer—everything from the cemetery ghost to some Mississippi Bureau of Investigation policeman who'd hated workin with Chief Cotter and now wanted to get back at him.

That last idea didn't seem so far-fetched.

Patsy, at her own station, was cuttin Tom Leringer's hair. He was one of the checkers at Piggly Wiggly. Patsy was tall, rail-skinny, and bleached blonde. She had a crazy laugh that would cut off in the middle, like she had the hiccups. Not that she was laughin much at this conversation. Tom was short and squat, and had hair about as black as you could get. Mutt and Jeff had nothin on the two of them. Both were also talkers and put in their own two cents. All I had to do was clench my jaw shut and mutter *uh-huh* once in awhile.

I liked Tom, even while I distinctly disliked his sister, Letty June. Now *that* was another person who never set foot in my shop. She treated Stevie about as badly as anyone in town. Had ever since she and Stevie went to school together. The ugly woman clearly had some mighty poor self-esteem goin on, and tried to raise herself by belittlin the weak. It didn't help that she worked Stevie's shift at the factory. My brother did his best to steer clear of Letty June. I felt sorry for the woman's husband. How he stood her, I didn't know.

I'd just got through with Norma around two o'clock when the phone rang.

"Go ahead and get it, Deena." Norma dug cash out of her purse. "I'll just put the money on the counter."

"Thanks." I grabbed the receiver. Betty Frederick, the neighbor between me and Stevie, was on the line.

"Deena, you better get over here. The cops are at your brother's house."

I froze. My own frightened eyes stared at me from the mirror.

"You hear me?"

"I hear. Thanks." I punched off the line and whirled toward the back room for my purse.

"What happened?" Patsy's voice filtered behind me.

I rushed back through the salon, nearly slippin on Norma's two inches of hair on the floor. My mind churned out questions. Why were the police there? Where was the uniform? Did they have a warrant?

Stevie, why wouldn't you listen to me?

In my car I flew up Main, barely slowin to turn right on Second Street. As soon as I hit Maxwell I could see two police cars parked in front of the trailer. I skidded up behind the last one and carved to a stop. Ran up Stevie's cracked sidewalk, leavin my purse and keys in the car. The trailer door stood open, Chief Cotter's broad backside straight ahead in the tiny front room. I jumped inside and spotted John on the left, hands on his hips as he faced Stevie. All three men snapped toward me. My brother looked scared to death, one hand thrust in his hair.

"What are you doin here?" I threw my demand at John.

"We're the police, Deena. We don't need your permission to be here."

Well, hello to you, too. At six-two, John stood a half-foot taller than me. I hated that I had to look up at him. His muscles and rock-jaw good looks didn't make me like him any better. It would've been one thing if he'd kept his fine physique for *me* when we were married, when I happened to be madly in love with him. But no, he'd had to go cattin around all of Jasper County.

"You got a warrant?" I turned to Chief Cotter. He was givin me his I'm-serious-as-a-heart-attack look, his bottom lip pushed upward. The expression made his big jowls look even heavier. He carried a clipboard with a piece of paper and pen attached.

"Now, Deena, let's not get all hot 'n' bothered here." The chief gave me the dismissive glance of an elephant to a gnat. "We came to talk to Stevie."

"He doesn't want to talk."

"He was doin just fine till you got here. In fact, he let us in."

"If he let you in, it's because you intimidated him! You know he has no idea of his rights." Any figure of authority made my brother nervous. *"Do* you have a warrant or not?"

"Deena." John's voice climbed sharp. "Get outta here and leave us to our work."

"I take it that's a *no.* So you can just leave."

"This ain't your house." My ex took a step toward me.

I stood my ground. "Stevie, tell em to get out. They need your permission to be here."

"But it's too late." He twisted his hands, his forehead a mass of wrinkles. "I already let em in."

"It's not too late—"

"Steven." Chief Cotter thrust the clipboard in my face to block my sight of my brother. I pushed it down. "We hear you ran home from work Tuesday night like your pants were on fire. That true?"

Oh, no.

My brother's shoulders hunched. His eyes bounced from the chief to John. "I don't remember."

"Well, the person who saw you sure remembers."

"I don't know."

"You come straight home after work last Tuesday?" Chief Cotter leaned back, arms crossed.

My brother looked at the floor and shrugged.

"This person said you didn't. Said the time you were runnin across town was about 12:30 in the mornin."

Twelve-thirty? No way! Stevie had shown up at my door at midnight.

"And this person who saw you? Said you had somethin all over the front of your clothes. Looked like blood."

No, no, no. "Stevie! Tell them to get *out.*"

"Was that blood on your uniform, Steven?"

"I don't know!"

"You have to know, Steven. Either it was or it wasn't."

My brother darted a panicked glance down the hallway toward his bedroom. He looked as obvious as a cookie thief wipin crumbs from his face.

Chief Cotter honed in. "I'm just goin to look around, with your permission, Steven." He held up the clipboard and snatched the pen from it. "Sign here."

Sign a paper? "No!" I grabbed my brother's arm and shook it. "Don't sign anything. Tell them to go! You can *do* that."

The chief's beady gray eyes shot lasers at me. He shoved his big self between me and Stevie and forced the pen into my brother's hand. "Sign it, Steven."

Stevie did as he was told.

Flexin his shoulders, Chief Cotter pushed past me and lumbered down the narrow hall. John stood back and let him pass.

My brother's mouth flopped open and closed like a fish on a riverbank.

I faced him, my back to John, my eyes bugged. Everything in my expression read, *"The uniform, Stevie! They can't find the uniform!"* His face paled even more, but he couldn't bring himself to speak.

I whirled on John. "What's the matter with you, why can't you leave him alone?"

John's face reddened. "You are pushin me way too far."

One of his favorite lines from our marital fights. I stomped around him and headed after the chief. John caught my wrist. "Deena, *don't.*"

"Don't you *don't* me." I shook off his grip and kept goin. He grabbed me again. "*Get* your hands off me!"

He sunk his fingers into my shoulders and jerked me around. My hand pulled back to slap him—then hung in the air.

"Go ahead, do it. I'll arrest you for assaultin an officer."

"I wouldn't *be* assaultin an officer, I'd be punchin my ex."

He seethed. "This isn't about you and me, Deena. It's about women dyin in this town."

"Stevie's got nothin to do with that!"

"We think he does." He gave me a shake. "Can't you see past your own blindness? You *can't* protect him from this."

"I can protect him from cops who need a fall guy. That's all this is about—so your father can announce he's got a suspect—"

From Stevie's room at the other end of the trailer came the sound of drawers bein opened and closed. I wrenched away from John and flung myself down the hall, sick in my stomach. John could be right, he could be *right*, and I'd never bear the thought of it. "Chief!" I rounded the corner into my brother's messy room.

Adam Cotter stood back from his rummage in the closet and cast me a bland look.

"You *can't* be in here." I couldn't keep the panic from my voice. "I'll testify against you in court, I swear it. You forced my brother to sign that paper!"

"Your brother got somethin to hide, Deena?" He tilted his head in that smirky "come on now" expression I'd always hated. I wanted to hit him. "Well?" He leaned toward me.

"No."

"Then what're you so worried about?"

"You know he's not competent enough to keep you out of here."

"He's competent enough to be employed. Live on his own. He signed the consent."

A squeak filtered down from the center of the trailer—the opening of the bi-fold door to the stacked compact washer and dryer. I leaned out of the bedroom to see John checkin inside.

My heart leapt to my throat.

He pulled a Bradmeyer Plastics uniform off the top of the washer and straightened. Held it up to examine it. I wanted to fly at him, scratch out his eyes. But I couldn't move.

Slowly John's head turned my direction. He eyed me for a moment, then looked back to the dark blue fabric. "Dad."

"Yeah." The chief pushed me out of the doorway. I floundered two steps into the hall and leaned against the wall.

"Take a look at this."

My tongue dried up. I cast a wild glance toward the front room but couldn't see Stevie. The chief hunched up the hall and took the uniform from John's hands. He held it close to his face, frownin. Then exchanged a meaningful glance with his son.

"What is it?" The words blurted out of me. *Shut up, Deena, shut up.*

The chief ignored me and headed for Stevie. I stumbled after him. As I passed John, I gave him a look that could have melted stone.

"What's this, Steven?" Chief Cotter pointed to the front of the uniform.

Even as I sidled into the room I could see huge splotches of reddish brown against the dark blue. *Great, Stevie.* A lot of good puttin the thing on top of the washin machine did.

A spasm flitted across my brother's cheeks. "I don't know."

"Looks like you got somethin on your clothes here."

Stevie shrugged.

"And it sure does look like bloodstains."

No response.

"You cain't tell me what it is?"

"No."

"Or how it got here?"

"No."

I jumped to my brother's side. "Stevie, shut up. Don't say anything."

The chief's eyes hardened. "Deena, I've been mighty patient with you. Now I'm askin you *real nice* to be quiet."

Chief Cotter's "real nice" was as trusty as a snake in the grass. "Stevie, *don't* say anything."

Adam Cotter's head pulled back. "John, get her out of here."

John took hold of my arm. I jerked away. "You can't throw me out of my own brother's house."

"Leave or I'll arrest you." John reached for his cuffs.

"Wouldn't you just love to arrest me." I turned narrowed eyes on my ex-father-in-law. "You go right ahead—and see what a judge says when I tell the court you questioned someone who can't even understand his rights. Anything you think you've found in here will be thrown out."

The chief surveyed me. I'd hit every policeman's sore spot. Last thing they wanted was for evidence to be thrown out. But he had his signed permission, and that was that. "You know about this, Deena?" He gestured toward the uniform with his double chin.

I glared at him. He mocked me with a half-smile. "I'll take that as a yes."

My veins ran cold. If they arrested me for hidin evidence—who'd help Stevie then?

"Steven." The chief focused on my brother. "I'm sayin again, this looks like blood to me."

Stevie threw me a panicked look. I shook my head hard: keep quiet.

"Is it blood, Steven?"

"I'm not tellin'."

"Where'd it come from?"

"I don't know."

"It's on your uniform. You should know."

Stevie's expression blackened—his response to being cornered in a lie.

"What day did you wear this uniform, Steven?"

"Tuesday."

My heart fell to my feet. *Why* had he answered *that* question?

"Tuesday? You sure?"

My brother nodded. Suddenly he thrust his face inches from the chief's. "I didn't do it!"

No, Stevie, *no.*

"Didn't do what?"

I wanted to run outside, cover my ears. I couldn't stand to hear what my brother denied. Because I knew from childhood that whatever he said he didn't do—he'd done it.

"I didn't kill that girl!"

Chapter 15

Tully

BY THE TIME MIKE LEFT FOR WORK, MY MIND WAS MADE UP. I pulled my laptop computer out from under the couch and plugged it in. The thing dated back to my sophomore year in high school. Mike didn't like seeing me on it. All I did was check Facebook pages of my friends, but to Mike, that was too much. "What're you sayin about me?" he'd demanded more than once. I'd learned to put my computer away while he was home.

Sitting on the couch with my feet on a footstool, I positioned the laptop on my huge belly. It took forever to boot up. Finally I pulled up the Internet and Google. I stared at the screen. How to begin? Then typed in a search: *Mississippi private lab.*

Over 200,000 hits came up. I did a double take. How was I supposed to wade through all that?

The fifth listing on the first page caught my eye: "Crime Fighters Critical of Mississippi Crime Lab." An article from March 2009. Great, just what I was afraid of—some lab botching tests of my swabs.

I clicked on the link.

According to the article, law enforcement agencies complained a lot about the state crime lab in Jackson. With a backlog of as much as ninety days, it took too long to get to cases. One district attorney said the lab "caused so many headaches" he didn't care that it cost more to send evidence to a private lab.

That cinched it. A private lab was the way I should go. I could see results before turning them over to police. And no way did I want to wait ninety days for a result.

The article mentioned Scales, a private lab in Brandon, about fifteen minutes from Jackson. I read on. This could be my answer. Then I saw the cost. From $500 to $700 for each DNA sample. No way I could get that kind of money.

Suddenly it hit me. How could I be so dense? I didn't *have* a sample of Erika's DNA, so how was a lab supposed to tell me if my swabs contained her blood?

My head fell back. *Stupid, stupid, stupid.* I had no idea what I was doing here. And even if I had something from Erika, I could never afford running *two* samples. If I wanted to go ahead with this, I was stuck with only one choice. I had to give the swabs to the Amaryllis police.

No way.

I set the computer on the coffee table and lay down on the couch. For a long time I stayed on my side, one hand under my cheek. Slowly a plan begin to form. In my mind I took apart the plan, looked at it up and down and sideways. I saw no alternative—other than doing nothing. And that was no longer a choice.

Pulling in a large breath, I heaved my big body to sit up. I put my computer away, then pushed to my feet. I lumbered into the kitchen for my purse and went outside. Got into my car and backed out of the driveway. Funny, my lack of emotions, now that I was really *doing* something. I shoved them way down inside me. I was just driving to the Bay Springs Piggly Wiggly, that's all. One action at a time.

Don't think, Tully. Just do.

At the store in Bay Springs I bought a yellow pad of paper and the smallest package of regular sized envelopes I could find. I mixed these in with other grocery items we needed anyway. A high school boy—was I really in his shoes only a year ago?—helped me out to my car.

Back home I put the food away, then set to work. Out came the plastic gloves from under the sink. I washed my hands with them on. Dried off the gloves with a paper towel.

From my dresser drawer I pulled the package containing the two swabs. I took one from the bag, rolled the other one back up and returned it to the drawer. The second swab would be backup in case something happened to the first.

At the kitchen table I addressed an envelope to Chief Cotter at the police station. Next I pulled a piece of yellow paper from the middle of the pad. Using a black pen I wrote in block letters:

THIS SWAB HAS BLOOD ON IT I FOUND AFTER ERIKA HOLLINGER'S MURDER. I THINK IT'S HERS. PLEASE TEST IT *FAST*. IF IT MATCHES HER DNA I KNOW WHO KILLED HER. WHEN YOU HAVE RESULTS, PUT A RED PIECE OF CONSTRUCTION PAPER IN THE STATION WINDOW IF IT'S NOT A MATCH, AND A GREEN PIECE IF IT IS.

I sat back and viewed the note, careful that no part of my arm touched the paper. Was that good enough? I wanted to pour out my fear, say hurry, hurry, I'm dying here! Would they even pay attention? What if they thought this was from some weirdo and ignored it?

Please, God. I know I haven't talked to You much lately, but . . .

With a tissue I wiped off the stick part of the swab, even though I'd never touched it without gloves. Then wrapped it up in another tissue and put it in the center of the paper. After folding the note twice I slid it in an envelope. At the sink I wet the finger of my plastic glove, ran it across the gummy surface of the envelope flap, and sealed it up. I fetched a stamp from a kitchen drawer, dampening it also with a wet-gloved finger, and pressed it on the envelope.

I stood, plastic fist pressed to my mouth, eyeing the package. The envelope showed a small bump from the wrapped swab.

Had I missed anything?

Mentally I went over every step I'd taken. When I was satisfied, I slipped the envelope into my purse along with a fresh paper towel, folded. Only then did I take off the gloves.

No way could I mail this in Amaryllis.

Once again I drove to Bay Springs. I parked outside their post office and used the paper towel to pick up the envelope by its corner. My heart skipped and splashed like a rock over water. For a long time I stared at the outside mailbox, unable to move. My throat grew thick, and my hands started to shake. Once I did this, there was no taking it back. If I'd forgotten anything, if somehow they traced it to me and Mike found out . . .

Stop thinking, Tully.

I glanced around. Saw no one nearby. Holding the envelope close to my stomach, I struggled out of the car and stepped to the mailbox. Its last pickup was posted at 5:00. I'd just make it.

The metal door opened with a squeak. I dropped the envelope inside, making sure to hold on to the paper towel. Banged the door shut.

Done.

My knees turned wobbly. No second thoughts now. No matter what happened, there was no turning back.

Quick as I could, I got in the car and drove away.

Going down Highway 528 I turned on the radio with trembling hands. I needed to find a song to hum along with. Something to keep my mind from churning. I pushed channel after channel, harder each time, until my finger got sore, and I couldn't hold the tears back any longer. I was still crying when I pulled into our driveway.

When I walked through the door the phone was ringing.

Mike. He was probably calling to check on me during a break. Make sure I wasn't out running around.

I hurried to the kitchen and snatched up the phone. "Hello?" I couldn't keep from panting.

"Tully, you hear what happened?" It was Mercy.

My insides stilled. In a flash I pictured a postman in Bay Springs pulling my envelope from the mailbox, the Amaryllis police magically aware of where it had come from—

"The police took Stevie Ruckland down to the station." Mercy's voice sounded tight, excited. "They think they have him this time, Tully. He's the Closet Killer."

Chapter 16

Deena

I PACED IN THE SMALL LOBBY OF THE AMARYLLIS POLICE Station, cell phone to my ear. Inside the interrogation room Chief Cotter and John were ganged up on Stevie. I'd shouted to my brother to refuse to come down to the station, but Chief Cotter had him too scared to listen. Even as they hustled him out to a squad car, I ran alongside. "You can keep quiet, Stevie! You can demand a lawyer!"

He just walked along like a lamb led to slaughter.

I'd jumped in my car to follow them to the station.

Now that the chief and John had Stevie alone in a room, who knew what he'd say. Despite my demands, they wouldn't let me stay with him. "He's a grown man, Deena." John jabbed the air with his forefinger. "I'm tellin you *one more time* to back off, or I'm puttin you in cuffs too."

I had one last look at my brother, slumped and forlorn at the room's small rectangular wood table, before John closed the door in my face.

Come on, Trent, pick up! Where was his nose for news when I needed it? Half the town had to know about Stevie by now.

The line clicked in my ear. "Hi, Deena."

"Trent! They've brought Stevie to the station for questioning."

"What?"

"They're talkin to him right now, and who knows what on earth he's sayin."

"Why'd they come after him in the first place?"

I hesitated. "Somebody said they saw him runnin home Tuesday night after work all agitated. And the police think they found somethin at his house."

"What'd they find?"

Twelve-thirty, the witness had said. They were off by a good half hour. Twelve-thirty gave Stevie all the more time to kill Erika. But how could I tell the cops I'd seen him at midnight?

"You got to do somethin, Trent. They practically barged into his house without a warrant. You know Stevie couldn't figure how to tell em no."

I reached the front of the station and pivoted, pacin away from the door. What was goin *on* in that room? I wanted to rush inside and punch out the police. Punch out my brother. *Why* hadn't he listened to me?

Stevie *had* killed Erika, hadn't he. And the others. He really was a murderer, and I didn't know what to *do*.

"Deena. What did they find?"

It came back to me then—the words Chief Cotter had thrown at Stevie the last time he was a suspect. "You *mad*, Steven?" the chief had pressed. "You carryin a boilin rage around inside you?" That was the chief's theory. The Closet Killer carried hidden rage—and murder was the way he let it out.

I slid to a halt and leaned against the wall. My brain would hardly think straight. Stevie *did* carry hidden rage. And how could I keep the bloody uniform secret now? Chief Cotter would splash the news all over town. "A dirty uniform. They claim it's got blood on it. And Stevie won't say what it is." I wasn't about to give away anything the police didn't know.

"Give me five minutes, and I'll be right there."

"Where are you?"

"At my sister's house, workin on today's story. See you in a minute."

I hung up and closed my eyes. My chin fell to my chest. This was a nightmare. If that uniform had Erika's blood on it, Stevie was doomed. So was I. They'd find out he'd come to my house. That I knew about it and covered it up.

The world started to swim. I staggered to a chair and sank into it. Somehow I managed to call the salon and tell Patsy to cancel my appointments for the afternoon.

"I heard they took Stevie in." Her tone sounded guarded, as if this time she just might believe he was guilty.

Was that how Amaryllis would respond? *Somebody* needed to pay for these murders—might as well as be Steven Ruckland?

"It's a mistake. *Again.* They'll clear it up."

"Yeah, I'm sure—"

I punched off the line. Set down the phone and dropped my head in my hands. A voice drifted from the interrogation room. Couldn't tell whose.

The station's door opened. I straightened up to see Officer Chris Dedmon walk in, his black face sheened with sweat. Chris was in his late thirties, a father of four, and a deacon at the Baptist church. I'd gone to school with his younger sister, Rowanda. "Deena." He nodded my direction. "You all right?"

I shook my head.

"I hear they got your brother in there."

"News travels fast."

"Well." He indicated the radio clipped to his uniform. "I have my connections."

"He didn't do this, Chris." I *had* to keep sayin that. For my own sanity.

"People aren't always what we think."

I shot him a look to kill. "That's it, then? Guilty until proven innocent?"

He rubbed the side of his short-cropped head. "Didn't say that at all. I just said people aren't always what we think."

Of course he was right. How many times had I seen a story on the news about a man no one would have expected bein some serial killer? A family man, a husband and father. That BTK killer in Wichita had even been active in his church, like Chris Dedmon. "Right. That would make *you* the perfect candidate."

He shook his head and sighed. For the first time I noticed the bags around his eyes. And his face looked worn. Come to think of it, John had looked awful tired too. If the Amaryllis police force was lackin in sleep, it could only be due to the pressure of findin the Closet Killer. And that pressure made it all the more likely they'd pin the murders on the easiest suspect.

The station phone rang. Chris answered it. Dully I listened to his end of the conversation. Apparently the caller had heard rumors about arrest and wanted confirmation. "Sorry, ma'am, I can't talk about that right now. Rest assured as soon as we have news to tell the town, we will."

Hope glimmered in his voice.

My stomach turned over.

As Chris hung up, Ted Arnoldson came in the door. Terrific. In my eyes Ted rated not much higher than my ex. The man was full of himself, walkin with a swagger and puttin on airs. Judgin by his off-duty designer clothes and the sports car he drove, Ted had to be up to his eyeballs in debt. Police officers don't make that much money. But Ted always had to appear better than everybody else. Why in the world did I ever have a crush on that man?

Ted gave me a curt nod. "Deena."

I stalked out of the station to wait for Trent outside.

After two excruciatin minutes he pulled up to the curb across the street. He ran over, wavin to somebody up the road. I turned to see Theodore Stets outside the drugstore, peerin at me. "They take Stevie in?" Theodore called.

Forget half the town. All of Amaryllis knew by now. I looked away, my throat locked tight.

Trent took my elbow and pulled me close to the police station, out of the sun. "Tell me what you know."

I regarded him, suddenly half-sorry I'd called. Was this Trent, the man in love with me, askin? Or Trent the reporter?

"I told you what I know."

Trent gave me a keen look. Fine, let him wonder.

He shook his head. "He'll need an attorney."

"He hasn't got any money for one, you know that. And neither do I."

"Then he'll be assigned a public defender. But sounds like a lot of damage is already done. The attorney will have to work backwards. I mean, you have to wonder—is Stevie even capable of understanding his Miranda rights? If a lawyer could get everything he says in there thrown out—that would be major."

Wait, this was all too fast. Trent was talkin how to mount a defense, and I was still hopin I could just take Stevie home.

"Maybe my brother won't say anything. You know how he is when he's cornered—he just shuts down. The more scared he is, the more he refuses to talk."

Or he'd lie. And if the police caught him tellin lies . . .

The door to the station opened. I jerked my head up to see Chief Cotter step out, holdin Stevie by the arm. John was close behind. My brother's wrists were cuffed, and his face looked like a steel mask.

"Where you goin? What'r you doin?" I jumped around Trent to stand in their path.

"Deena, move aside." Chief Cotter's crisp tone warned he was out of patience.

"But—"

The chief pulled to a halt and shot me a look like a laser beam. "We've arrested your brother for the murder of Erika Hollinger. He's on his way to the county jail." He pushed me aside and escorted Stevie to his police car. John opened the back door, Chief Cotter pressed Stevie's head down, and they forced him in.

As they drove away I stood rooted to a sidewalk that dipped and rolled, and threatened to swallow me whole.

2010 Pulitzer Prize

Feature Writing

The Jackson Bugle

Gone to Ground

What happens to a small, quiet Southern town when evil invades
in the form of a serial killer?

By: Trent Williams
October 29, 2010

(Excerpt)

Adam Cotter came to Amaryllis as chief of police a decade ago,
upon retiring from the Mississippi Bureau of Investigation after 25
years. The MBI is a branch of the state's Highway Patrol and a not
unusual gateway through which small-town Mississippi can acquire
experienced chiefs of police. Amaryllis was thrilled to welcome Adam
Cotter, who hailed from the area. Before Cotter's arrival, his son, John,
was already an established officer on the town's five-man force, and
thereby protected via the escape clause in the state's nepotism law.

Adam Cotter could not have hired his own son, but since that son preceded his arrival to the force, they can now work together hand-in-hand. Or fist-in-fist, as some in the town claim. The three other officers, Orin Wade, Ted Arnoldson, and Chris Dedmon, together total 29 years of serving as Amaryllis's finest. Wade and Dedmon are African-American, the two-to-three ratio a little under the town's demographics, which run almost an even fifty-fifty between whites and blacks.

Since the Closet Killings began, opinion on the effectiveness of the town's police has also split down the middle, although not along racial lines. Some Amaryllis citizens will tell you their law enforcement is doing all it can to solve a string of murders with little to no evidence. Others will point to the chief's ego as the main stumbling block to finding a suspect. Their view is based on one indisputable fact: the chief has refused to ask for outside help from the Mississippi State Police, who have more equipment, manpower, and training.

Here, too, the historical tenacity and separateness of Amaryllis plays a part. In the past the town's citizens wouldn't have wanted the rest of the world "barging in and telling us what to do," as one business owner put it. Chief Cotter, along with his close friend Austin Bradmeyer, owner of Bradmeyer Plastics and mayor for fifteen years, have enjoyed free rein to run the town as they see fit. But the desire for separation has begun to slip. Talk to people on Main Street today, and you're likely to hear folks question why national media hasn't paid more attention to the serial killings in their tiny town. "You can turn on a cable news channel and watch 'em run video of some fight on a school bus," said Curtis Paltrow, owner of the town's only gas station. "But they're not interested in *five people* dead?"

As for Chief Cotter's investigation, talk to anyone in law enforcement, and in their honest moments they'll admit egos abound in the field. Each jurisdiction has their own way of doing things. One doesn't want the other "butting in." Chief Cotter points to his own years of investigative experience and the paucity of evidence in the

Closet Killings, and says, "What do you expect the State Police to do that we haven't done? We've collected every piece of evidence there is—and that hasn't been much. We've canvassed every street numerous times. We have the files; we know the details. They don't. Plus, the State Police don't know our people, our town. They *aren't* equipped to handle this case as well as we are."

And some whisper, "They couldn't handle it any worse."

Chapter 17

Cherrie Mae

THE SCOTTS' PHONE RANG AS I STOOD ON MY STOOL TO dust the top a their bookcase in the front room. Two more minutes, and I'd be done with another work week, thank the good Lord. A tangy smell cut the air. Laverlle Scott did love her Lemon Pledge.

It would be another half hour before Laverlle got home from her job at the bank. And Tony Scott would be busy for hours at his work in Bay Springs. The Scotts was one a my three black families in town. Ever week I let myself into their house with my own key. My check always waited for me in the big bowl on the counter, on top a the bananas.

The phone rang a second and third time before the answer machine come on. I heard Tony's voice greet the caller, then a long beep.

"Oh, Laverlle, I forgot you ain't home yet." The wispy voice of Laverlle's mother, Trixie, come from the machine. "I wondered if you heard bout Stevie Ruckland bein arrested for Erika's murder."

I dropped my dust rag.

"This time I hear the *police* say they got some good evidence. They'll probly end up chargin him with all the murders."

My tired feet hopped me off the stool and into the kitchen.

"And tonight they's—"

I snatched up the phone. "Trixie? This is Cherrie Mae. What you sayin?"

"Cherrie Mae? Oh, you cleanin house there?"

I'd only cleaned the Scotts' house at this same time for ten years now. I pushed down my impatience. "Stevie's been *arrested*?"

"Yes."

"Why?"

"Don't know entirely. They took somethin from his house. Tonight they's a town meetin. Chief Cotter set it. Rumors are goin everwhere, and the station phone been ringin off the hook. He figured might as well tell everbody at once what happened. People so scared. They want somethin done."

This was awful. The *police* jumped the gun on me. "What time's the meetin?"

"Seven o'clock. At the elementary school."

Seven. My achy body would fuss me up and down for draggin it out on a Friday night. But that's just what I was gon do. "What else you know, Trixie?"

"Oh, I heard all kinda things. One person say they found his fingerprints inside Erika's house. Another tol me they had shoe prints. Somebody else say they had his hair, too, stuck in Erika's fingers. I don't know what's right from rumor."

Hair? The Jackson lab couldn't a run DNA tests for hair yet—that took time. Even I knew that much.

I rubbed my forehead. "I'll be at the meetin. You?"

"Wouldn't miss it for the world. I cain't wait to clap for the chief findin this awful killer."

"You don't know he's guilty yet."

"If they arrested him, I do. They wouldn't arrest him without good reason."

My mind flashed the picture a Erika's ring in Mayor B's file. "You don't know that either, Trixie. They's so much pressure on those men to make an arrest."

"That just got em workin harder. Now it done paid off."

"That just got em too anxious to 'solve' the case—right or wrong. Like Samuel Butler said, 'Justice, while she winks at crimes, stumbles on innocence sometimes.'"

She made a disgusted sound. "Whose side you on, Cherrie Mae?"

"I hope you right, Trixie. I really do. But let's wait and see what the *police* say. Worst thing we all could do is relax when that killer's still out there."

"Well, that's true." She sounded like a balloon with the air let out.

"I'll write Laverlle a note and tell her your message, since I cut it off."

"All right then. See you in a few hours."

I put the phone in its cradle and leaned against the counter. *Why* did this have to happen today? As if my shoulders didn't have enough to bear, savin the town. Now I had to save an innocent man from death row too. Because it would take a mighty lot a evidence to convince me Stevie Ruckland was the Closet Killer. Poor man hardly had enough sense to come in out the rain. Mayor B done gave him a janitorial job when no one else would hire him. Couldn't prove it, but I bet sister Deena had been behind that. I could picture her cuttin Eva B's hair and talkin how Stevie needed a job—

A new thought hit me. I sank into a kitchen chair. What if Mayor B made Stevie do some dirty work to throw the *police* off track?

Without that job at Bradmeyer Plastics Stevie couldn't keep his trailer. I knew that boy was proud a livin on his own. What if Mayor B said he'd fire Stevie unless he went to Erika's house? Once inside Stevie'd surely leave his fingerprints. Mayor B could a come along later, wearin gloves, and killed Erika.

But how could the mayor trust Stevie to keep quiet bout bein told to go over there, specially with the *police* leanin on him? And why would Erika open her door to Stevie Ruckland in the first place? As for the mayor sendin him over there *after* Erika was already dead—well, that was just too crazy to imagine. Stevie'd surely come unglued at a sight like that.

I sighed and tipped my face to heaven. "Ben, you see Jesus round up there, tell Him I could use His help."

My joints hurt. I pushed to my feet while I still could and went back to the front room to finish my work. Before packin up my step stool and supplies, I wrote Laverlle the note.

At home on a Friday night I usually eat while watchin the news, then settle in to read a few hours. Not tonight. From the minute I hit my door I fretted and stewed, barely able to choke down some leftover barbecue chicken and green beans. Puttin my throbbin feet up in my chair didn't help neither. I tried to close my eyes and rest while I could. But my mind kept cookin up pictures a Stevie in jail, scared to death. While I sat here, knowin a key piece a information that I couldn't tell nobody bout yet cause I had no proof.

How in the world would I sleep tonight in my own bed while that boy tossed on a hard, cold cot?

Half a me wanted to stand up in that town meetin and point my finger at the mayor. The other half reminded me how dumb that would be. Sure's you livin that evidence would disappear from

Mayor B's desk before the *police* ever got there. *If* they believed me enough to look in the first place.

Dear Lord, what am I gon do?

At ten minutes to seven I got my miserable self up and into my car to drive to the elementary school.

Chapter 18

Tully

I PARKED AT THE SCHOOL, MY STOMACH ALL SHAKY. I shouldn't even be here. After my running around in the afternoon, I should be putting my feet up. And what would Michael do when he heard I'd gone?

But I couldn't stay away.

My brain hadn't stopped whirling since Mercy's call. If only I'd waited to mail that swab. I'd taken a huge risk for nothing. This had to mean Mike wasn't guilty. Right?

If only I could believe that.

Truth was, Stevie Ruckland's arrest could only mean they got the wrong man. "Evidence" on him was nothing new. Last time that surfaced nothing came of it. Meanwhile, how could I explain how Mike had acted since Erika was killed? If the police knew what I knew, would *they* explain it away?

When Chief Cotter got the swab in the mail, what would he do with it?

Please let the evidence on Stevie be real this time.

The atmosphere in the elementary gym was nothing like the usual happy anticipation before a school play. The air smelled of dust and sweat and fearful hope. A strained, grim quiet hung over the crowd. Metal folding chairs had been set up in every available spot. Most were already taken. Townsfolk perched down the long rows, some exchanging nervous whispers. Others sat rock still, staring at the empty stage as if a treaty to end World War III was about to be signed. The looks on their faces punched me in the gut. They *wanted* this to be right. They wanted to feel safe. To have their town back after three nightmarish years.

Now that the Stevie Ruckland train was rolling down the track, it would take a mighty big switch to stop it.

My hands were hot. What if the make-up on my neck sweated off? I felt like a giant sign hung on me—*Ask Tully Phillips what she knows.* I looked around for Mercy but didn't see her. My parents had to be here, but the last thing I wanted was to sit next to my mother. She'd take one look at my face and know something was wrong.

I waddled up the side of the gym, looking for a place to sit. Up front stood Officers Orin Wade and Ted Arnoldson, pointing out empty seats to people. Orin Wade caught my eye. I cringed. On a normal day Officer Wade intimidated me. He was short but muscular, and his eyes could bore right through a person. He waved at me. My heart skidded. I looked away, pretending not to notice. From the corner of my eye I saw see him head toward me.

They knew, didn't they? Already. Somehow. They were going to pull me up on that stage, force me to talk—

"Tully."

I turned, my throat dry as burnt toast.

"Follow me. There's a seat up front."

No.

I didn't want to sit up front, under Chief Cotter's eye. I wanted to sit in the very middle seat of the very middle row, where I could blend in.

"Come on, Tully." Officer Wade gestured with his head. "You need to get off your feet."

Like a prisoner, I followed, feeling the eyes of every person in the gym on my back.

The policeman led me to the *first* row and pointed. There in the center was one empty chair. Next to it sat Deena Ruckland, arms folded, glaring at the stage.

My heart clutched. "I couldn't. She's probably saving it—"

"No, she's not. Just no one wants to sit by her." The last sentence was muttered half under his breath.

Poor Deena. What it must be like for her, caught between a family member and the town.

I could be in her shoes. The thought terrified me.

"Go on now, sit down." Officer Wade nudged my arm. "We need to get started."

Was God punishing me by saving me that seat? I cast one last desperate glance around—and saw too many people staring at me.

"Thank you." My voice croaked.

Head down, I shuffled to the chair. As I settled my heavy body I noticed the Jackson reporter, Trent Williams, on the other side of Deena. He focused on a notebook, scribbling.

Deena glanced at me. She blinked. "Hi, Tully."

"Hi." I wanted to say so much more, but my tongue froze.

Sudden silence fell like a shadow. Clothes rustled as hundreds of heads moved to watch Chief Cotter and his son, John, mount the side steps to the stage. Officers Wade, Arnoldson, and Dedmon fell in behind. The chief stepped to the podium, his big belly forcing him to stand back and lean into the mike. Adam Cotter wasn't a tall man. His age showed—thinning hair and lines down the sides of his mouth.

He intimidated me too. The way he walked—like he owned the town. Like he could do anything he wanted.

The four officers took seats lined up behind the chief. A show of unity.

Deena made a disgusted noise.

Chief Cotter tapped the microphone, sending thumps out over the upturned faces.

"All right." His gaze cruised the crowd. Surely he felt Deena's stabbing eyes, but he wouldn't look at her. "Thank y'all for comin. It's unusual for me to call this kind a meetin, but I reckon y'all have a strong need to know what's happened. And frankly our station phone was ringin off the hook. I figured this was the easiest way to stop the rumors and get the truth out. Now, I can't tell you everything, as this is an ongoin investigation. But I'll tell you what I can."

Just tell me enough, please. Enough evidence against Stevie Ruckland that I could believe my own husband.

"And before the details, let me give a public thanks to our fine officers." The chief half turned toward his men. "They've had many a sleepless night workin on this case. Since Erika Hollinger's death last Tuesday none of us has hardly slept. I know when a crime hasn't been solved it can look like nothin's bein done. That couldn't be further from the truth."

"*Truth.*" Deena spat the word under her breath.

"One other thing, on behalf of Erika's mother, Mrs. Lokin. Erika's body has now been released to the family. Mrs. Lokin asked me to inform y'all that her daughter's funeral will be at the Methodist Church this Sunday at two o'clock."

Erika's funeral. Would Mike drag me there to keep up appearances?

"Now for the information I have for you. This afternoon we arrested Steven Jay Ruckland for the murder of Erika Hollinger. We're well aware that's only one of the six murders committed in Amaryllis. We will continue to look at our evidence on each of the other five crimes and press charges accordingly. But for now our main suspect—a man we've been watchin for some time—is off the streets. And that gives us great relief."

"Amen to that," someone behind me whispered. Deena's chin lifted in defiance.

Chief Cotter wiped his forehead. "This mornin we received a tip from an Amaryllis citizen who saw Steven Ruckland runnin home after his shift at Bradmeyer Plastics like he was in a major panic. The time of his comin home was later than usual—twelve-thirty."

Deena's head shook.

"The next day the witness heard about Erika Hollinger's death. Even then this person wasn't sure what he or she may have seen on Stevie's clothes. But by this mornin the witness realized we needed to know. We're glad for that decision. You never know if somethin you've noticed may be crucial information. It's always best to tell the police and let us sort it out."

Trent's pencil scratched against his notebook.

"Based on this information Investigator John Cotter and I paid Steven Ruckland a visit at his trailer this afternoon. We asked if we could talk inside his house. He let us in and allowed us to look around. When we asked him questions about runnin home last Tuesday night he could not—or would not—explain his actions." Chief Cotter pushed out his upper lip. "In a subsequent search through his home we found a dark blue Bradmeyer Plastics uniform on the top of his clothes washer, not yet run through a cycle. There were large stains down the front and on the right sleeve. These stains appeared to be blood."

Air sucked out of my lungs. Gasps rose all around me. I glanced at Deena. She sat like granite, mouth in a hard line. Clearly not surprised.

She *knew* this? And she still didn't think her brother was guilty?

I pictured the blood on my own doorknob. On the swabs.

"When questioned about the stains, Steven Ruckland could not explain their presence. Investigator Cotter and I then confiscated the uniform as evidence. We took Steven Ruckland to the station for further questioning. At the station Investigator Cotter and I took the uniform into a closet where we could block out light. There we sprayed the uniform with a substance called Luminol. This substance causes blood to glow a bluish color under black light. The stains on Steven Ruckland's uniform *did* glow, indicatin they are indeed blood."

Murmurs radiated through the gym. My fingers squeezed into my palms.

Chief Cotter held up a hand. "Now let me make it clear, we don't yet know if that blood is human. And we certainly don't know if it belongs to Erika Hollinger. But the bloody uniform, along with the witness's statement regardin Steven Ruckland's behavior Tuesday night, *and* his apparent lack of veracity under questioning, both at his residence and at the station, gave us enough reason to arrest him for Erika Hollinger's murder.

"As you may know, an initial hearin before the judge must take place within a few days of arrest. Since taking Mr. Ruckland into custody, we've scrambled to do what must be done before Monday, when that hearin will occur. Of high importance is testin the Bradmeyer Plastics uniform to see if it provides a match with the DNA of Erika Hollinger. Our state lab would take weeks to do this. I have instead chosen to take the uniform to a private lab, which has agreed to run the tests immediately. Yes, this will cost us more money. But the safety of Amaryllis is involved. And if you ask me, y'all are worth it."

Mumblings of agreement fluttered around me.

What if the DNA matched? My brain tilted at the possibility. Stevie *would* be guilty—and Mike innocent.

But that wouldn't happen. Even now I could feel Mike's fingers around my neck. *"You hear me good. I came home at the regular time last night. Got that?"*

Chief Cotter placed his hands on his wide hips and looked over the crowd. He still wouldn't even glance at Deena. "Of course I will also be meetin with the district attorney to go over what we have."

What did he have, really? Blood—who knew from where? And suspicious behavior on the night Erika was killed. The same two things I had on Mike. Except Mike had *told* me he'd kill Erika. And he had good reason. Why would Stevie? Was he even capable of murdering someone?

The chief rubbed his jaw. "That's all I can tell you at this point. I'm not takin questions, and none of my men can answer your questions either. We'll continue to work on this case. Meanwhile if any of y'all have information you think is important, please contact the station. That's it, and I thank y'all for comin out."

Chief Cotter turned away from the podium. The gym buzzed to life, chairs scraping and voices humming. Those voices held hope for the first time in years.

Deena didn't move, her head hung. Trent patted her arm, but she didn't respond. He hesitated, then got up, mumbling something about getting quotes.

I stayed rooted to my chair. The noise level rose, but all I could hear was the grief moaning like wind around Deena's shoulders. Where were all her friends? No one came up to give her a hug, say they knew Stevie couldn't be guilty. But then, why should they think that? Listening to Chief Cotter, it sounded like he was.

Maybe Deena even thought Stevie had done it. And the idea was killing her.

My chest burned. I wanted to get up, walk away without looking at Deena. Go back to my life and my house, my marriage. Let Stevie take this rap. He didn't have a wife. He didn't have a son ready to be born.

Get up, Tully. Go.

The burning increased until I thought my veins would burst. The whole rest of my life swam before me—and still I couldn't move.

Seconds ticked . . .

Tocked . . .

Time stopped.

"Deena"—I heard myself blurt out the words—"Stevie didn't do it."

Chapter 19

Deena

AT FIRST TULLY PHILLIPS'S WORDS DIDN'T REGISTER. MY mind had gone to some other plane. I couldn't think. Couldn't feel. Even my rage at Chief Cotter had faded. I only knew one thing: I was utterly alone.

I should go to New York with Trent. If Stevie was convicted I'd have to leave this town.

"Deena." Tully's voice again.

Her words hit home. I jerked around and stared at her. "*What* did you say?"

Tully's face paled. No rosy cheeks from her pregnancy. And no life in her gaze. Tully was a pretty girl, with those milk chocolate eyes and generous mouth. She'd just never known it. I'd seen her glow in the past few months, but now her shoulders drooped and anxiety wrinkled her forehead.

Her mouth opened, but no words came out. Tears glistened in her eyes.

"Did you say Stevie didn't do it?"

She swallowed hard.

The way she'd said it. And the way she was lookin at me now, cringin like a kitten. As if she knew who *did*. I leaned in close. "You know who killed Erika?"

Tully glanced left and right, hands twistin in her lap. Her head shook.

She knew somethin. She did.

Energy rolled through me. I grasped her elbow. "Come on, let's get outta here."

Tully allowed herself to be led. I propelled her toward a side door, ignorin the snatches of conversation around us. Tully waddled more than walked and couldn't move very fast. *Come on, come on!* A woman behind us called my name, but I didn't slow. Somewhere along the way my anger at John and the chief came back, and it felt *good*. Got my heart beatin.

Outside I aimed Tully toward my car. If I let her go, she might change her mind and melt away. "We need to talk."

"No."

I'd take her to my house. Pin her down until she *told* me—

Tully pulled out of my grip. "I need to get home. My feet should be up, and my ankles are swelling—" She let out a sudden sob.

"But you said—"

"I didn't mean it."

"Yes, you did."

"Deena!" The woman called again.

"Tully." I leaned forward to look her in the eye. My heart kicked against my ribs. Whatever this was, I couldn't lose it. "You know somethin. You can't back down on me."

Her face crumpled. She buried her face in her hands.

Footsteps pattered toward us. I tried to move Tully aside, turn our backs to the person. *Not now!*

"Deena, wait." The woman behind us puffed for breath. "It's Cherrie Mae."

Cherrie Mae. I swung around to see one of the most beloved people in Amaryllis. A generous Christian woman. Cherrie Mae barely topped five feet, but she bristled with life. And you never quite knew when she'd come out with some crazy quote.

But right now I couldn't be interrupted, not even by Cherrie Mae. "Hi. I was just tryin to talk to Tully—"

Cherrie Mae waved a hand. "That can wait."

"No, it can't."

"Yes, it can."

Tully ogled us both.

Cherrie Mae's tone sharpened. "Deena, I *got* to talk to you. Trust me, you want to hear what I got to say."

Tully moved back. "I'll go."

I caught her arm. "No, wait!"

"Stop!" Tully jerked away.

I stepped in front of her.

Cherrie Mae peered at Tully. "Baby, you all right?"

"I'm fine. Deena, get out of my way."

Oh no you don't. "You're not goin till you tell me what you know."

"I don't know *anything*."

"Yes, you *do*."

"Who, you, Tully?" Cherrie Mae edged closer. "What do *you* know?"

"What?" Tully looked at Cherrie Mae in a daze.

"You know somethin?"

Tully shrank away.

"Cherrie Mae, please." My throat tightened. "We were tryin to have a conversation—"

"Look to me like she leavin."

"She's not leavin." My eyes pled with Tully. "Please don't go."

"Wait a minute." Cherrie Mae raised her tiny hands. "This bout Stevie?"

In the parkin lot car doors slammed. Somebody's engine started. Tully wiped her cheeks.

Cherrie Mae pulled her head back. "Let's all slow down a minute. Seem like something . . ." She looked from me to Tully, her eyebrows risin.

I frowned at Cherrie Mae. For the first time I studied her face— and my lungs ballooned. She wore the same guarded yet wide-eyed expression as Tully.

"You want to hear what I got to say."

I glanced at Tully. She was starin at the woman too.

"What, Cherrie Mae?" I touched her arm. "What do you have to say?"

Her dark eyes bounced between Tully and me. She licked her lips, and words tumbled out. "'Circumstances may accumulate so strongly even against an innocent man, that directed, sharpened, and pointed, they may slay him.'"

Tully's face screwed up. "Huh?"

"Charles Dickens."

I blinked at her. More car engines started. The whole scene felt surreal.

Cherrie Mae's shoulders flexed back. "They got your brother, Deena. But they got the wrong man."

She said it so firmly. My chin rose. "How do you know?"

"I know."

"How?"

Cherrie Mae's gaze slid to Tully. "Baby, *you* know somethin too?"

Tully froze, then nodded once. This was not a woman she would go up against.

"Well." Cherrie Mae mushed her lips. "Ain't this a turnabout."

I raised both hands. "Will somebody please tell me what's goin on?"

Cherrie Mae waggled a finger. "Tully know somethin. *I* know somethin. She cain't possibly know what I know. So the way I sees it—the three a us got some talkin to do."

2010 Pulitzer Prize

Feature Writing

The Jackson Bugle

Gone to Ground

What happens to a small, quiet Southern town when evil invades
in the form of a serial killer?

By: Trent Williams
October 29, 2010

(Excerpt)

Martha Edgars, the Closet Killer's first victim in the spring of
2008, lived in Amaryllis all her 62 years. Born Martha May Baxley to a
seamstress and a manager at Bradmeyer Plastics, Martha grew into a
boisterous child, then a life-embracing adult. She married Tom Edgars
at age eighteen and doted on him until the day he died.

"Martha never saw a stranger," her neighbor Lawrence Wilkins
claims. "First day me and the wife moved next to her and Tom, she
showed up on our porch with a chicken casserole. Nicest woman you'd

ever want to meet. Do anything for you. We lived next door to her for over twenty years. I was a pall bearer at Tom's funeral." Lawrence hitches his shoulders, the right side of his mouth quirking. "One thing about Martha. Don't tell anybody, but she wasn't that good of a cook."

A year later, fifty-seven-year-old Sara Fulgerson was murdered. Sara had been a widow for eighteen years, her husband, Blake, meeting an early demise from a sudden heart attack. The Fulgersons had no children. Friends of Sara remember her spiraling into depression for the first year after Blake's death. She would be seen nearly every day that year kneeling at the Methodist Church's altar, begging God to help her survive. God seemed to hear her petitions. After twelve months, Sara picked herself up and looked around town for those in need. She found single mothers on the verge of poverty, struggling to care for their latchkey children. Sara volunteered to watch the kids after they came home from school. Three boys and two girls ended up "going home to Aunt Sara" every day after class, where she'd meet them with fresh-baked cookies and hugs. When Sara Fulgerson died, those five children sat on the front row at her memorial service along with Sara's family members.

Six months after Sara's death, Sonya Stelligman, an African-American who played the organ at the Victory Baptist Church, became victim number three. Sonya was 61. She "lived and breathed music," according to her daughter, Marquetta. "Mama was always singing in that loud voice of hers. I can remember that way back to when I was little. In summer with the windows open, neighbors could hear her clear down the street. They loved her voice—a rich alto. They'd come to the house and say, 'Sing *Swing Low, Sweet Chariot,* Sara. Sing *Summertime.'* But me and my brothers, we were just plain embarrassed something fierce by it all." Marquetta falls silent, a faraway look gleaming in her eyes. "Wish I could hear Mama sing now."

Chapter 20

Cherrie Mae

 TULLY PHILLIPS, DEENA RUCKLAND, AND I SAT IN MY LIVIN
room starin at each other.

We'd gotten here in a rush, Deena talkin a mile a minute, Tully
draggin her feet, and me just tryin to keep everbody movin along. I
managed to get us all in my car. I swear, we let Tully go, she woulda
pulled on toward home. I said we could go to her house if she wanted,
but her eyes got all wide. "No, what if Mike finds out?"

Strange thing to say. Why she so scared a her husband? Deena
didn't want to go to her own house cause a Trent maybe showin up. I
sure didn't want to be seein Trent myself.

So we ended up at my place.

I tol Tully to sit in my armchair and put her feet up, but she said
no, thank you. I think she was too nervous to get that comfortable. So
I sat in my chair, and the two a them took the sofa, Deena on the end
close to me, and Tully on the other side. One awkward trio. I'd closed

the curtains at the front window. Neighbors seein the three a us would surely get to wonderin.

Suddenly nobody wanted to say nothin, includin Deena. Clearly she had as much to hide as Tully and me. Another thing I thought strange. Wasn't Deena as convinced as me her brother was innocent?

"All right now, we got to get this out in the open." I gave Deena my best piercin look. "You have some reason to think your brother may a done these murders?"

"Oh, no you don't. *You* came runnin after *me*. You go first."

My eyes bounced from Deena to Tully. The poor young thing sat with her arms round her huge belly, lookin like a deer drug to headlights. I took a deep breath. I brung these women here. Now I had to lay myself bare. What if I couldn't trust em?

I leaned forward and clasped my hands. "First, we gon pray." They hesitated, then bowed their heads.

My eyes closed. "Dear precious Jesus, we need Your help tonight, Lord. We all got things on our hearts. We all scared. But I do believe You brought us together and will protect us. So lead our talkin now, Lord, and most of all, show us what to do. Amen."

"Amen," they both murmured.

We looked at each other.

I crossed my ankles. "All right. First—we got to agree on somethin. Whatever we say don't go nowhere else. No matter how bad we want to tell it. I promise that myself. You, Tully?"

She nodded.

"Deena?"

"Okay." One a her legs started bouncin. "So what do you know, Cherrie Mae?"

"Wait a minute, let's not get ahead a ourselves." Despite my prayer, I was still feelin my way. Once I let out my story, there was no takin it back. "I'll say this first. I do think I know who killed Erika. Which means he killed the rest a our women. And it ain't Stevie."

BRANDILYN COLLINS • 141

Deena's back went ramrod straight. "*Who?*"

I held up a finger. "Tully. You think you know who the killer is?"

She hesitated. "Yes."

I let that sink in for a minute. "Deena, you worried Stevie might a done this?"

She bit her lip.

"We all promised to tell the truth."

Deena looked away. "I . . . thought so. Maybe. But the police have always been after him. And they barged into his house. He didn't know how to tell them no. So I don't know. *Please* tell me—who is it?" Deena leaned toward the younger woman. "Tully! Tell me *right now.* "

Tully's face began to shiver. Whatever she was holdin back, it was bad. Real bad. What could she possibly know bout the mayor? Then Tully jus plain came apart. "It's Mike." Her head fell into her hands. She started to sob.

What?

Deena's mouth dropped open. "Your *husband?*"

Tully just kept on cryin. Her sorrow stabbed me right through. No wonder she was frightened to death, her bein so young and pregnant. Whatever would make her think such a thing? "Tully, baby, it ain't your husband killed Erika. It's Mayor B."

Deena whipped toward me, and Tully raised her splotchy face. "Mayor *B?*" They echoed the name.

They gaped at me, then at each other, and I eyed em both right back. The moment felt so odd, like we was at the Tower a Babel and suddenly speakin different languages.

"Cherrie Mae, you're crazy." Deena held up both hands. "No way it's Mayor B. How can you even think that? Everyone loves him. And he's one person who's never been mean to my brother. He even gave Stevie a job when no one else would. If it weren't for Mayor B, Stevie couldn't support himself."

"Maybe I'm crazy, maybe not." More likely not, what with Erika's ring sittin in Mayor B's drawer. "It's time we tol our stories. And remember, we made a pact."

They nodded. Deena licked her lips. "You first."

So I took a deep breath—and told em. Just laid it on the line—all bout openin Mayor B's drawer and seein the awful pictures. And the ring. About bein with Erika the night she died and knowin that ring was on her finger.

Deena listened like her life depended on it, her mouth cracked open. Tully liked to tie her hands in knots. Halfway through my story she started to cry again—whether from sadness or relief, I didn't know. I had to stop and fetch her some tissues.

"Okay, Deena." I figured Tully needed some time to get herself together. "Your turn. Why you think Stevie might a done this?"

She sprang to her feet and started to pace. "I think . . . What that ring means, Cherrie Mae, I don't know. What I *do* know is, that blood on Stevie's uniform is probably Erika's. He came to my house the night she was killed with fresh blood all over him."

Tully gasped. "You *knew* that?"

Deena ignored the comment. She walked to the window, then swiveled around and headed toward me. That girl didn't miss a step, back and forth, back and forth, while her story rolled out a her. Bout Stevie comin to her door at midnight after tryin to wash off in Turtle Creek, and sayin, "I fixed her."

Chills went down my back when I heard that. "But Stevie wouldn't harm nobody."

"I don't know, I don't *know*." Deena pressed her hands to her temples. "You don't see him let out his anger like I do. He gets tired of people makin fun of him." She swung toward Tully. "Like Mike, you know that? He's teased Stevie for years. Stevie hates him. And Erika teased him too. So when he told me, 'I fixed her . . .' And he's got blood on him. And the next day I hear she's dead . . ." Deena pulled to a halt, her shoulders droopin. "Plus all that built-up anger. And the fact that after every killin he's been all antsy and out a sorts." She stuck her hands in her hair. "I actually wondered before if he could be guilty. Didn't want to really look at it, but in my heart I wondered . . ."

She stopped, sucked in a big breath, then stumbled over to the couch and sank down on it.

Sure enough, a lot a what she said fit. But some was just conjecture. "Stevie—out a sorts after each murder? Who in town wasn't? Maybe the deaths a those women frightened him, especially after losin his own mother."

Deena gave me a long look. "Yeah. Maybe."

"And how bout this. We know the stab wound on each woman was precise and exactly the same. Could Stevie do that?"

Deena wrapped her arms around her stomach like it hurt. "Yes."

"Really? How?"

She focused on her knees. "It's one of Stevie's quirks—his methodical way of doin things. I think it's because he *can't* do much that when he finds a way to get somethin done that works, he sticks to it. He'll use that way over and over. No thinkin outside the box for him. It's why he's good at his janitorial job. Mayor B showed him what to do to get things clean, and Stevie does it by rote. Same method every day—same results . . ."

Deena fell silent.

I glanced at Tully. She was listening intently. Deena leaned over, gaze fixed downward.

I shifted in my chair. "So you sayin with the murders . . ."

Deena lifted a shoulder. "That if Stevie killed these women, the first time was just dumb luck." She winced at her own words. "One knife to the neck, and the woman dies. Next time, he'll do it the exact same way."

Tully stared at Deena, her face full a longin and total despair. I could see she so wanted to believe Deena—but somethin held her back.

"Tully?" I kept my voice gentle. "What you have to tell us?"

The young gal turned away and focused toward the curtains. For a minute I thought she was gon change her mind, not say a word. She brought a fist up to her chin. Her mouth trembled. "He was having an affair with her." She spoke so quietly I could barely hear. "Erika told me she was pregnant with his baby. That she was coming into some 'big money,' and they were going to run away together. Mike said he'd kill her for telling me. And that night she was murdered."

Deena's mouth fell open. "You're kiddin me."

Tully hiccupped a swallow. "And he came home late that night, and he was wearin the wrong uniform, and he left blood on the door."

Mercy.

Tully hung her head.

"Wait, don't stop now," Deena said. "You've got to start from the beginning, tell the details."

After a minute Tully nodded, like she accepted her fate—and started talkin. We heard bout her meetin with Erika, her husband comin home late, the blood, his threats. He'd *choked* her. Even when her words run out I knew there was more.

"Tully?" I tried to say the words calm and quiet. "Mike been hittin you before this?"

Tully focused on the floor, her mouth workin. Deena and I exchanged a look. Finally Tully gave a tiny nod.

"Oh, baby, I'm so sorry."

Deena lightly touched Tully's arm. "Me too." She sounded sad but not surprised. Cain't say I was all that surprised either, knowin Mike's hard reputation.

We sat in silence. I couldn't help thinkin a the baby to come, and what Tully was gon do.

She sighed and edged up her chin. "There's more."

Deena and I waited.

Then come the story a what Tully done. The cotton swab and mailin it to the Amaryllis *police*. By the time she was through my mouth hung open along with Deena's. This was one amazin girl.

Deena scratched her head. "I wonder what the chief will do when he gets that package."

Tully's face blanched. "You don't think he'll have it tested?"

"Why should he? He's got his man. He could conveniently 'lose' the swab."

"You think he'd do that?" My eyebrows rose. "Ignore evidence? I thought more than anything he wants to solve this case."

Deena scoffed. "More than anything he wants to regain his reputation. After three years he's finally made an arrest. How would it look now to admit he went after the wrong man? Another failure. Don't forget, this is Mr. Know-it-all. Mr. I-was-with-the-MBI-for-twenty-five-years."

She had a point there.

Tully shook her head. "He won't ignore it. I won't let him. I *have* to know."

"What do you plan to do if he does? You can't come forward and remain anonymous."

"She got that second swab," I put in.

"That's right." Tully firmed her mouth. "And you know what I'll do? I'll call Trent Williams anonymously. I'll tell him what I've done and that the police are ignoring it."

Wouldn't the chief love that.

"If Adam Cotter tests that swab, it'll be for only one reason." Deena looked from Tully to me. "He thinks it'll point to Stevie."

I rested my head against the chair. My mind was all kinked up. "What I cain't figure is how could all three a our stories be true?"

"I hope *you're* right, Cherrie Mae." Tully laced her fingers like she was prayin. "I can't believe Mayor B would do this, but at least he's not related to any of us."

"But that ring seems the least of the evidence," Deena said. "Tully and me, we both saw blood. We both saw men that weren't actin right."

I rubbed my lip. "Could they have worked together? Maybe Mike used Stevie to do somethin? They both get off work from the factory at the same time."

"No way, Stevie hates Mike." Deena winced at Tully. "Sorry."

"But would Mike *make* Stevie do somethin?"

"No." Tully shook her head. "Mike isn't like that. If he needs something done, he'll do it himself. He'd think it insulting to use someone else. And he'd never trust Stevie to keep quiet about it anyway."

"So . . ." Deena screwed up her face. "Mike changed uniforms after work, thinkin in case he got blood on himself, he didn't want you seein it. Then after the murder he planned to change back and ditch the new uniform somewhere. He could have grabbed a clean uniform out of the storage closet. Maybe Stevie left the closet open while he was cleanin. He has the key. Then maybe Mike ran out of time and couldn't change to his old uniform."

Tully drew back. "What about the blood all over your brother?" Her voice rose. "That's a whole lot more than I found on my door."

"Maybe it's not even human blood."

"Well, what did he do then? Kill a pig on his way home?"

"At least *Stevie* didn't threaten to kill Erika the day before she died!"

"And Mike didn't take a bath in Turtle Creek!"

"Whoa, whoa." I smacked my palms on my legs. "Stop it right now. We don't stick together, who's gon get to the bottom a this?"

They glared at each other. Tully's breaths came in little pants, and Deena's cheeks flamed.

Deena turned away from Tully and folded her arms. "I don't want my brother goin to jail for somethin if he didn't do it. I just want the truth, pure and simple."

Didn't we all. "'The truth is rarely pure and never simple.'"

I pushed to my feet. "We need to write stuff down. Figure out what we know and what we ain't sure of." I gave em both a hard look. "And I know it won't be easy, but you both got to step back and look at this objectively. We let emotions take over, we'll never get nowhere."

I headed into the kitchen, where I fetched a pad a paper. I sure wasn't bout to mess up my notebook full a classic quotes, on the table beside me. I brought the pad back and sat down again. Picked up the pen on top a my literature notebook.

On the first piece a paper I drew two lines, dividin it into thirds. At the top a the columns I wrote the three suspects' names. "Okay now. First we list the evidence we have about each man."

We went over the stories again, me writin down the details. Includin the timeline. We knew Mike and Stevie was out a their houses after 11:00 p.m. Stevie didn't show up at Deena's until midnight—so where had he been since gettin off work at 11:00? Mike came home at 11:50. Where had *he* been? As for the mayor, he had to have left his house sometime that night, 'cause he'd ended up with Erika's ring. But we didn't know what time.

Deena squeezed her eyes shut. "Erika could have been killed between 11:00 and 12:00." She looked at me. "You said you saw her eat a brownie around 10:00 when you left."

No wonder Trent wanted to know that. "True. But I left those brownies with her. She coulda eaten some later. Although she did tell me she was headed for bed."

Wait a minute. "Deena, did Trent say the coroner found Erika was pregnant?"

Deena's eyes rounded. "No. Not a word." She turned to Tully. "Maybe she wasn't."

Hope flicked across Tully's face, then was gone. "But I saw the picture of Mike and her . . ."

"The coroner didn't necessarily tell Trent everything." Deena shook her head. "This might be one of those we're-goin-to-keep-this-quiet details."

I thought that over. "Could you get Trent to press the coroner for more information? Maybe let on he knows bout a pregnancy—see what the coroner says?"

"But then I tip my own hand." Deena sighed. "The thing with Trent is—he's a good friend, but he's also an ambitious reporter. He'd be all over me like white on rice if he thought I knew somethin he didn't."

We fell silent.

Deena ran a finger along her jaw. "Tully, why would Erika be comin into some big money?"

"I don't know. Maybe life insurance for her husband's death?"

"Maybe." I thought bout my own Ben's life insurance. "But that shoulda come before now." On the paper I put a circled question mark near my notes bout the money.

Tully shifted uncomfortably on the sofa. I peered at her ankles. They was swellin. "We need to get you home where you can get those feet up."

She nodded.

Some home. A house where she lived with a man she thought had murdered six women. A shudder rattled my backbone.

"So what do we do now?" Deena shoved off the couch and started pacin again. "I can hardly sit still, thinkin about Stevie in jail."

I rubbed my finger across the paper. "You need to go see him. Visitin hours for men is Sunday, two to four."

"How do you know that?"

"I visited a few young men there in my day. Somebody needed to cheer em up, try to set em straight."

Deena scratched to a halt. "I can try again to get him to talk to me. Maybe now he'll be scared enough to do it."

"That's what I'm hopin. Won't be easy, though. The visitin place there—you got people settin right next to you. Easy to overhear. And he'll probly see an attorney by then who'll tell him not to say a word to nobody."

Deena sighed. "Sunday seems so far away. He'll have to spend all Saturday there."

He'd be spendin a lot longer than that till this got straightened out, but I didn't say so. "As for me, I'm gon take some pictures at Mayor B's house when I clean Monday. I got to get proof a that ring in his office. Just hope it's still there."

Deena paced around. "What then?"

"Tell you the truth, I don't know. I just know I cain't do nothin or say nothin till I got some proof."

"And me?" Tully looked so tired and scared.

"Way I see it, they's nothin you can do but wait." And that would be mighty hard. "See if the *police* put that green or red construction paper in their window."

"Cherrie Mae's right," Deena said.

"But Tully"—I knew she wasn't gon like this—"how bout if you stay with your parents for awhile? You're not safe in your own home."

"I can't. They didn't want me to marry Michael. I'd be telling my parents they were right."

Deena made a face. "Looks like they were."

Tully threw Deena a dark look, then turned back to me. "And they'd want to know what happened. What would I tell them?"

Deena huffed. "That you need your own space away from Mike, that's all."

"It's not that simple."

"Of course it is."

"Wait now." I held up a palm.

"You want not simple?" Deena jammed her hands on her hips. "How about livin with a man you think is a murderer? A man who hits you and has now threatened to kill you. Why would you stay with that?"

Tully's face reddened. "I don't see you turning your back on your brother."

"I don't *live* with him."

"Hush yourselves now!" I stood up, all five feet a me ramrod straight, and gave em both the eye. "Deena, you got to watch what you say. And Tully." My voice went softer. She was such a young thing. "You need to listen. Because you sure ain't safe in your home. You got to think bout that baby."

Her face screwed up, and she started to cry. "I'm scared to leave him. He'll come after me."

"He cain't hurt you in your parents' house. He do somethin in front a them, they'll see him for what he is."

Probly already did. It weren't no secret Judy Starke couldn't stand her daughter bein married to Mike Phillips.

Deena plopped back down next to Tully and laid a hand on her arm. "Come on now, it'll be okay."

Tully sniffed. "You don't know what it's like at home. You just don't know."

Deena and I exchanged a glance. I thought a my Ben and couldn't imagine.

All the more reason for us to band together and *do* somethin bout this.

"Listen now." I put on my best confident air, even though I didn't feel it. "We got to stay in this together. We're a team now, and that means makin a solemn pact. We got to keep in touch, help each other figure out our next moves—and most of all, don't talk to nobody else. We each got a piece a the puzzle. We put em all together, we'll see the whole picture. Thing is, one a us may not like what that picture shows. But we got to go where the evidence leads." I looked Deena in the eye, then Tully. "You willin to do that?"

"Yes." Deena sounded decisive.

Tully nodded. "Me too."

The poor girl still looked like a scared mouse, but I could see a faint hope dawnin.

"All right then. I'm in too." I lowered myself back in my chair. "First thing, let's get each others' home and cell phone numbers. We're gon have to keep in touch."

"I just have a cell, no land line," Deena said.

I wrote down the numbers, one list for each a us. "Here you go."

Mercy, my bones was tired. "I think we all agree we cain't go to the police yet. We first got to see what they do with Tully's swab. Plus I need those pictures I'll get Monday. You both agree?"

"Absolutely." Deena wagged her head. "I don't trust the chief or John as far as I could throw em. And the chief's too fat to throw very far."

That got a tiny smile out a Tully. "Fine with me."

Deena's leg bounced. "Even with those pictures, Cherrie Mae, you're goin to have a hard time convincin Chief Cotter to suspect the mayor. That evidence just might disappear too."

"But I'll have the pictures on my camera."

"Sure. And we can use Trent, if it turns out to be Mayor B. If the media comes down on the Amaryllis police, they won't have such an easy time keepin their secrets. The town will demand to know."

Yes, but . . . "That would mean we'd have to go public. Think bout that. We'd be paintin one big target on our backs for the killer. And in the meantime if the police don't listen . . ."

The reality sank in. We stared at each other.

What had I got myself into?

I pushed to my feet and held out my arms. They was shaky. "I think we better do a little more talkin to God."

Deena stood and helped Tully up. The three a us formed a tight circle, holdin hands, and prayed the good Lord to watch over us.

SATURDAY–SUNDAY
APRIL 23–24, 2011

Chapter 21

Deena

HOW DO YOU WAIT FOR NORMAL LIFE TO START UP AGAIN? Since leavin Cherrie Mae's house Friday night I felt like my feet never quite hit the ground. I just floated, my mind in a haze. All the things Cherrie Mae, Tully, and I discussed swelled and receded in my brain. The more I thought of the different scenarios, the less I knew what was true. I only knew that wherever I went, people crossed the street to avoid me. Saturday I drifted through my appointments— that is, the few people who showed up. Half of them cancelled for some cockamamie reason. How weird to talk to them on the phone— people I'd known all my life. The conversations were so strained. A week ago, I wouldn't have put up with it. Would have demanded, "Okay, tell me why you're *really* not comin." Now . . .

I just plain didn't have the energy.

Did friends avoid me because they believed Stevie was guilty, or because they knew he wasn't and didn't want to be overheard saying so? I wanted to believe the latter. But more likely most folks thought he did it. Why shouldn't they, after Chief Cotter had run his mouth?

On Friday night Chief Cotter and John searched Stevie's trailer, this time with a warrant. I didn't even know about it until Saturday mornin, when Hesta Bradley asked me what they'd found. I nearly dropped my curlin iron. I called the police station right away. Chris Dedmon answered. Yes, he said, they'd searched with a warrant. But he wouldn't say if they found anything.

The not knowin drove me crazy.

Saturday late afternoon Trent came over. He planned on stayin in Amaryllis long enough to attend Stevie's court date on Monday. Then he'd have to head back to Jackson. Life went on, and there were other crimes to cover.

He stood on the porch. I almost didn't let him in the door. "Well, there you are." My tone wasn't exactly friendly.

Trent spread his hands. "Just wanted to see how you're doing."

"You sure didn't seem to care last night. Soon as Chief Cotter got through you were gunnin to ask him more questions. Didn't have the time of day for me." Not that I cared where Trent was. But he said he loved me. So what came first—his work or me?

I crossed my arms. "I suppose you've filed your story by now. The one that's gonna be read all over Mississippi, sayin Stevie Ruckland's the Closet Killer."

"I didn't say that, Deena. I had to report he was arrested."

"Why?"

"Because that's my job."

I glared at him.

"Look—would you just let me in?"

No. Yes. No.

I was bein an idiot. Trent was one of the few people who'd at least talk to me. And the only one who'd bothered to come over.

I stepped aside.

We walked into the livin room in silence. He faced me awkwardly. "Deena, I'm really sorry about all this. I can't *not* cover the case. You have to know that. I need to write the articles as objectively as possible. That doesn't mean I agree with everything Chief Cotter does."

Somethin cracked inside me. My eyes started to burn. "I know."

"So . . . can I least sit down?"

I nodded.

Trent eased onto my couch, as if afraid I'd change my mind. I stumbled into a tired pacin. I didn't know what else to do.

He cleared his throat. "Chief Cotter might've jumped the gun, arresting Stevie."

I stopped in my tracks. "How?"

"I can't see that they have enough evidence yet. Makes me wonder what the D.A. thinks of the arrest. D.A's are known for holding police back until there's enough evidence to convict. They want all their ducks in a row. Right now Chief Cotter doesn't even know if the bloodstains on that uniform came from Erika. I mean, if by some wild event that proved true, Deena . . ."

If that proved true, Stevie was toast.

"Way I look at it, the chief's made a big gamble. He really thinks Stevie's his man, and he wants to get the culprit off the streets. If he waits for DNA evidence to make an arrest—which could take weeks—and another murder occurs in the meantime, the town'll want to skin his hide. So he arrests Stevie, figuring he's got just enough for the judge to deny bond, given all the murders. Then the chief's got a couple months until the grand jury convenes to gather evidence— main thing being the DNA results."

"A couple *months?*"

"Afraid so. They don't meet until July."

July. It was a lifetime away.

Sudden knowledge punched me in the gut. That blood on the uniform *was* Erika's. I was goin to lose my brother. The only family I had left.

My legs went weak. I stumbled to the couch and fell on it. Next thing I knew I was bawlin on Trent's shoulder. He just patted my arm and let me cry. "I'm so sorry, Deena. I'm so sorry."

When I got hold of myself, I pulled away. Staggered to my feet to fetch tissues.

That night I didn't sleep at all. Just stared at my dark ceilin like some zombie. Was Stevie safe? By some miracle, would the judge grant bond on Monday? To think of him stuck in jail until the grand jury met in July! Unless the DNA came back with no match to Erika. But if he *was* indicted he'd sit in jail months longer until his trial came. Then he'd be convicted. If Chief Cotter could gather evidence to charge him with more than one murder, Stevie would be up for the death penalty.

Did my brother do this? Had he really killed those women?

By 5:00 a.m. Sunday I still lay awake, my body rigid with one thought: get Stevie to talk. My visit with him meant everything. If Stevie could just tell me that blood came from someone other than Erika, I'd tell Tully and Cherrie Mae. We could concentrate on Mike and Mayor B. The quicker we managed to prove one of them killed Erika, the quicker I'd bounce Stevie out of jail. I didn't want to wait for Cherrie Mae's photos. Or Tully's swabs. Who knew if Chief Cotter would even pay attention to them?

I dragged myself in and out of the shower. To the kitchen for three cups of coffee. I could barely eat. My face looked ten years older, dark circles under my eyes. By noon my brain had near shut down again. I slumped on the sofa—and fell asleep.

A ringin phone startled me awake.

"Hello?" My voice sounded drugged.

"Deena, that you?" It was Cherrie Mae.

I twisted upright, rubbin a crick in my neck. "Yeah. Just fell asleep for a little while."

The time! My gaze jerked to my watch. One thirty. I had to leave soon to visit Stevie.

"Just checkin up on you." Cherrie Mae sounded worried. "I know you bout to go."

"I'm . . . okay. No, I'm not. It doesn't matter what I am. I just have to make my brother tell me the truth. I'm gonna do that, Cherrie Mae. I'm not leavin that jail till he talks to me. When I get back here we'll know more. I'll call you."

"Hope you right, chil." She sighed. "I do hope you right."

"Have you talked to Tully?" In all my worry over Stevie, I'd given her little thought. How selfish of me. Couldn't be easy bein around a husband she thought was a killer. And who abused her. "If Mike finds out what she did—I'd hate to think what he'd do to her."

"Haven't talked to her. And I ain't stopped prayin since she left here. I wanted to call, but what if Mike answered the phone? I'm not sure Tully's got much freedom when he's off work. Wouldn't want to get her in trouble."

"Yeah. I hear you." I flexed my shoulders. "I need to go, Cherrie Mae. Call you soon as I can."

"I need to be goin myself. Erika's funeral's at two o'clock."

The funeral. I'd forgotten all about it. Good thing I had an excuse not to attend. No one would want me there anyway.

In my bathroom I threw on some makeup. Somewhere between foundation and mascara I managed to convince myself of Stevie's innocence. This was all just a big mistake. I'd get the truth—the whole story—out of Stevie, and put an end to this.

I would.

At 1:45 I slid in my car. Ten minutes later I drove past the pretty park in Bay Springs. Past the town's City Hall and toward the courthouse. Tucked behind the courthouse was the jail, a low-lying, bland buildin of faded red brick. I pulled into a parkin space and gazed toward the entrance. Two people sat on benches near the door. A third fed coins into a Coke machine.

My eyes caught sight of a blue-trimmed sign. "Visitation," it read, with an arrow pointin down the length of the buildin.

I pushed myself out of the car.

For a moment I stood lookin dumbly at my purse. Would they let me take it in? My brain couldn't seem to make a decision. Just whirred like a machine out of gear.

I opened the trunk and shoved my purse inside. Locked the car and dropped the keys in the front pocket of my jeans.

Chin lowered, I shuffled down the sidewalk to the rear entrance for visitors. To my left sat the back of the red-bricked courthouse, where Stevie would be on Monday. I wasn't even sure I'd attend the hearin. Trent had told me Stevie would be handcuffed and shackled. How could I see him like that? Maybe I'd stay home, wait for Trent to call.

I reached the jail's back entrance. Three other people, two black women and one young white man, waited ahead of me, sittin on mustard-colored chairs with steel legs. They glanced at me, then lowered their eyes. I pulled to a halt and stood awkwardly, arms crossed over my chest like it was a winter day.

"You waitin to see somebody?" one of the black women asked.

I nodded.

"Sign in over there." She pointed to a small rectangular table to the left of the door. A piece of paper and pen lay on it. I stepped to the table and leaned down to view the list.

Name: Deena Ruckland.

Inmate: Steven Ruckland.

Relationship: sister.

A few minutes later the door opened and a man stepped out. He smiled at us and checked the paper. "Only four today. All right. Y'all can come in. No purses, no cell phones." His gaze swept over us.

One by one we were checked and admitted inside.

Behind me the steel door shut with a heavy *clang*. The air closed in, suckin away my breath. Already the outside world seemed so far away in this place. I could feel the thud of my heart.

The man led us to a stark, rectangular area with five visitation stations—a lineup of steel stools and gray cubicles with white phones. A shelf you could lean your elbows on. Thick glass separated each visitor from the other side. A piece of wall stood between each cubicle both on the visitor and inmate side. My heart flipped at that. If Stevie and I leaned forward and spoke softly into our phones, no one would hear us.

The jailer pointed the other three people to their assigned seats. He looked at me. "Ms. Ruckland, please sit here." He indicated my stool. Did his eyes linger on me? Checkin out the relative of the suspected Closet Killer?

I sat on the stool and faced the glass.

My mouth dried out. Suddenly I wanted to jump up and run. What if Stevie begged me to take him out of here? What if he screamed at me for lettin him be arrested? *How* could I see him like this?

Then—there he was. Clad in a bright orange jumpsuit. Starin at me through the glass, lookin so lost. My throat jerked. The jailer nudged Stevie's arm and pointed to his stool, then withdrew. Stevie sat. I picked up my phone and gestured toward the one on his side. My brother reached for his extension.

"Hi, Stevie." My words came out breathy.

"Hi."

"How are you?" What a dumb question.

"How do you think?"

"Have you seen a lawyer?"

"Yeah." Stevie made a face.

"What did he tell you?"

"How I'm gonna see a judge tomorrow, and how he'll ask the judge for a bond, and I may or may not get it—probably not. And if I don't I get to sit in here for a lot longer. I don't like it here. The beds are like rocks. I have to be in a cell all by myself. I don't *like* bein by myself all day!" His voice rose. "And I don't like the people here either."

"Shhh." Goose bumps popped down my arms. Maybe bein isolated in a cell wasn't such a bad idea. At least no one could hurt him.

Stevie shook his head hard. "I *hate* Chief Cotter."

"You know I want to get you out of here."

"So do it." He glared at me.

"I'm tryin. But you have to help. Will you do that, Stevie?"

"What can I do? I talk, they don't listen. I don't talk, they don't listen."

"Who's they?"

"Chief Cotter and John. Yeah, that man you married."

"I'm not married to him anymore."

"Good thing."

I licked my lips. Leaned forward and lowered my voice. "Look Stevie, I'm workin on some things. But you have to do your part. Right now, you *have* to tell me what happened last Tuesday night."

"My lawyer said don't talk to anybody."

"*Anybody* doesn't include your sister."

Stevie's eyes slid to his left. "There are people in here."

"Talk real quiet—they won't hear you."

"There's nothin to say."

Please, God, let this work! "How did you get that blood on your uniform?"

"I can't tell you that."

"Why?"

"'Cause I can't tell you that."

"You *have* to tell me, Stevie."

"I *can't*."

I thought of Mike Phillips, the blood he'd left on his own front door. "Did someone at the factory make you do somethin when you got off work?"

"Like what?"

"Like . . . go to Erika's house."

"Nobody made me go to Erika's house!"

"Shh." Sweat broke out over the goose bumps. I felt lightheaded. "Did you go on your own?"

My brother firmed his lips and eyed me. The expression scared me to death. I'd seen it too often when he was little.

"Stevie. *Did* you go to Erika's house?"

"It was *her* fault."

"Who?"

"She was mean to me."

A rock dropped down my stomach.

"I didn't mean to get blood on my clothes. I don't know how that happened. I took off my uniform so it wouldn't get dirty. Then I put it back on—and there it was. I don't like the smell of blood. Made me sick. I tried to wash it off in the creek. Then I put it on the washin machine. I thought I ran it through to clean but guess I didn't."

Scenes of our childhood flashed in my head. Stevie lyin to Mama. Him comin home from school, his lip split by some bully. He hadn't fought back. But in the house he'd trashed his room.

Sittin on that hard steel stool in the county jail, I'd never felt so alone in all my life.

"Stevie." My throat was so tight I could hardly talk. "Did you tell all this to Chief Cotter?" If he had, he was doomed.

"No."

"What did you tell him?"

"That I didn't kill that girl!"

"Okay, shhh." My fingers gripped the phone. Tears filled my eyes. I tried to blink them away, but they ran down my cheeks.

My brother's face twisted. "Don't cry, Deena." He sounded so plaintive, like he used to when we were young and some boy would break my heart. Stevie had always been there to comfort me.

"Why?" I had to say the word twice before he could hear.

"Because I don't want you to cry."

"No, Stevie. Last Tuesday night. *Why* did you do it?"

Indignation flitted across his face. He straightened. "I'm tired of bein picked on."

"What did she do to you?"

His face shuttered. He leaned a forearm on the shelf in front of him and shook his head.

"*What,* Stevie?"

"She says things about me. About . . . what I can't do as a man." Dark red flushed his cheeks. "Like *she* would know. And then she made such a mess. I had to clean it up. I was scared I'd get in trouble. And then the blood got on my clothes . . ."

My brother hunched over and dropped his head in his hand.

What would I have done if the glass wasn't between us? Hug him? Hit him? My stomach churned and my body felt hot. Stevie's life was over. Mine too.

I stared at the gray shelf until it glazed.

A thought rose in my brain. "Did you take her ring?"

"What ring?"

"The one Erika always wore on her little finger. A band of small diamonds."

His mouth firmed. "I didn't take nobody's ring!"

"Okay, okay."

"I didn't! Why are you accusin me of that?"

"I didn't. I just asked—"

"I'm tired of people accusin me of things I didn't do." He jabbed a finger at the glass. "I'm tired of it!" He yanked the phone from his ear and slammed it into the receiver. Jumped to his feet. He was still yellin, but I heard only the muffle of his voice.

A jailer appeared, tryin to calm Stevie down. Which only made him madder. My brother slapped the man's hands away. A second man leapt into sight. The two jailers forced Stevie up against wall, yanked his hands behind his back and snapped on cuffs. They dragged him away.

I sat frozen, the deadened phone still to my ear. It had happened so fast.

Next thing I knew, I was outside, bright sun ablaze on my head, my feet stumblin toward the car.

Chapter 22

Tully

I COULDN'T WAIT FOR THE WEEKEND TO BE OVER.
Mike and I weren't talking much. Oh, I made him supper and washed his clothes. Other than that I tiptoed around him, scared to death. I tried to cling to hope. Steven Ruckland had been arrested for Erika's murder. Cherrie Mae said Mayor B killed her.

So why couldn't I believe one of them was guilty?

Sunday afternoon I sat propped against pillows on the couch, my feet up. At the Methodist Church Erika's funeral had started. Mike hadn't even mentioned it. My eyes were fixed on a TV rerun, not seeing a thing. Mike was outside, cleaning his ratty boat. Said he wanted to go fishing when he was done. Again. Well, good. Better than him being here.

I kept thinking about Cherrie Mae, telling me to go back to my parents'. Like a puppy with her tail tucked between her legs. I couldn't imagine it. How does a grown daughter—a *pregnant* daughter—go back to live with her parents like a marriage never happened? Plus,

Mike would never stand for it. He'd break their door down to get to me. Get himself thrown in jail.

Maybe that wouldn't be so bad.

When the baby came things would be different. At least I'd have another person to think about. A cushion between me and my husband.

The front door slammed. Mike strode into the living room, scowling. The front of his shirt was wet.

I tensed. Muted the TV. "What's wrong?"

"You, that's what."

I couldn't answer.

He pointed toward the street. "I been out there, thinkin the whole time how you ain't hardly said two words to me since Friday night. Then Jeff comes over."

Jeff Gridley from across the street. A day worker at the factory, about five years older than Mike. I never liked the man.

"And guess what he tells me." Mike stuck both hands on his hips.

The tingle started at the back of my neck—the feeling that warns me I'm in trouble.

"We're talkin about Stevie Ruckland's arrest and the town meetin, and Jeff mentions he saw you there."

"I told you I was there. I wanted to hear what was happening."

"You didn't tell me you sat next to Stevie's sister. Or that you followed her out to the parkin lot afterward."

The tingle grew stronger.

"What could you possibly have to say to Deena Ruckland?"

I cringed. "Nothing. Just that I felt sorry for her."

"That all?" Mike's head tilted. He looked at me from the corner of his eye, daring me to lie to him. "Jeff said you looked like you were in a deep conversation. And some black woman was with you too. Jeff didn't see who it was."

"We were both just trying to comfort Deena."

"Who was the black woman?"

"I don't remember her name."

"That so."

I forced myself to look at Mike. My heart rattled against my ribs. He moved closer, his jaw jutting out.

"Funny you don't remember her name, seein as how you got in a car with her and Deena and drove away."

Heat rocketed down my spine.

"You told me you came straight home from the meetin, Tully. I'm givin you one more chance to tell me the truth. Where'd you go with those people—and why? And *who* was the black woman?"

Fear and defiance ballooned in my chest. Both were deadly. I struggled for an answer.

"*Don't* you lie to me again."

"It was nothing! Deena felt terrible, that's all. And I was telling her I felt bad for her. Then the other woman came up—it was Cherrie Mae." Mike shouldn't mind that—everybody loved Cherrie Mae. "We ended up going to her house for a little while to comfort Deena. Then Deena drove me back to my car, and I came home."

Mike's mouth twisted. "When have you ever been to Cherrie Mae's house in your life?"

Not until last night. I kept quiet.

"Why didn't you tell me?"

"Do I have to tell you *every* conversation I have?" The words jumped off my tongue before I could stop them.

Mike strode over and slapped me. My head snapped against the back of the couch.

I raised my hands. "Stop it, Michael!"

"You'll tell me anything I *ask* you to tell me, got that? *I'll* decide what's important. And right now I want to know why you went off with two women you hardly know. What do you care about Deena Ruckland?"

I pressed against the pillows, hands in front of my face. "I just felt sorry for her, that's all. That's *all*."

"Why? Cause you think her brother is innocent? Cause you think *your husband* killed Erika?"

I shook my head.

"You do, don't you?" Mike smacked my hands away and grabbed my chin. "You still think I did it."

"No I don't."

"Then why aren't you talkin to me? Why're you treatin me like some kind of criminal?"

"I'm *not*."

His fingers dug deeper into the sides of my jaw, pushing my mouth in. I whimpered.

Michael leaned down until his face was inches from mine. His teeth clenched. "I. Didn't. Kill. That. Girl. You hear me? I *did not* kill her."

I tried to nod, but his hand held me too tight.

"If I hear anything about you tellin people you think I killed Erika . . ."

"I won't." The words came out muffled. "I haven't."

"Good. Because you will be mighty sorry if you do."

He pushed my head back and let go. Straightened up to glare down at me.

I turned away, his eyes blazing into my back. Sudden anger burst in my chest. I imagined pushing off the couch and screaming it all out—his meanness, my empty heart. How he'd snatched away my whole life, and now I was going to have his baby, and I was *trapped*. And I *hated* him.

The rage blew shrapnel into my lungs. I clamped my mouth shut and held my breath, praying for it to stop.

"You got somethin to say, Tully?" Mike's breaths came out hard.

I shook my head.

"You know what I think? I think not workin's no good for you. Too much time on your hands."

I lay still.

"From now on I don't want you goin *anywhere*, you hear? You stay in this house till the baby's born."

Then what? Little Michael and I would both be his prisoners?

"Wh-what about the doctor? And errands?"

"I'll worry about buyin groceries. And you just went to the doctor, so you're set for awhile."

Mike could only be doing this because he'd killed Erika, and he knew I knew it. He'd have to spend the rest of our lives scaring me enough to keep quiet.

The rest of our lives.

"You hear me, Tully?"

The words caught in my throat. "I hear."

Mike grunted and swiveled on his heel. "I'm goin fishin. Have supper ready when I get back."

The front door slammed. I lay on the couch and cried.

2010 Pulitzer Prize

Feature Writing
The Jackson Bugle

Gone to Ground

What happens to a small, quiet Southern town when evil invades
in the form of a serial killer?

By: Trent Williams
October 29, 2010

(Excerpt)

Six months passed in Amaryllis—then came victim number four,
Alma Withers. At 48, Alma was the youngest so far, and the third
white woman. She was eccentric, almost a recluse outside of her work
as a librarian in Bay Springs. Her neighbors knew her as "Miss Alma,"
a woman who'd never married and loved books more than people. Or
perhaps she was simply more comfortable around the printed page.
One of Miss Alma's eyes wandered, giving her the appearance of
looking through people rather than at them. "That eye of hers is what

made her shy, I think," says her next-door neighbor of twelve years, Beth Ackler. "She and I did have our conversations once in awhile. Mostly she perked up when I mentioned what book I was reading. You wouldn't guess it, but Alma loved to read mysteries. Agatha Christie was her favorite. Now—what a thing to happen." Beth shakes her head. "Miss Alma's part of a mystery herself."

African-American Carla Brewster, age 64, is the most recent to fall prey to the Closet Killer. Like Sonya, Carla attended Victory Baptist Church, serving as a Sunday school teacher for over two decades. She was a tiny woman with a high voice that earned her the nickname "Squeaky" as a child. But she radiated energy.

"Did you know what a prayer warrior she was?" Her long-time friend Selma Raddlers folds her hands in the ancient pose of supplication. "That woman heard from the Lord. God answered her prayers, yes He did."

Selma lets her hands fall, her forehead wrinkling. "I just don't know where He was on the night she was killed."

MONDAY
APRIL 25, 2011

Chapter 23

Cherrie Mae

THE LITTLE CAMERA SAT HEAVY ON ME.

I'd worn a loose pair a pants with a big front pocket to hide it, and a long shirt to hang down over. Wasn't the way I typically dressed to clean. Musta looked a sight. "A slovenly dress denotes a disorderly mind," said Don Quixote. I could only hope my mind wasn't too disorderly. I hadn't exactly been sleepin well the last two nights.

Well hidden camera or not, as I lugged my cleanin supplies out a my car at the Bradmeyers' house, I was sure the thing glowed like neon in a swamp at midnight.

My plan hadn't changed. I aimed to set bout doin my work till Mrs. B left to help Cory and the Baptist crew weed at the cemetery. Then I'd have plenty a time to get the pictures. And I was prayed up. Weren't so much that my task was hard. I just wasn't used to playin detective—and knowin lives rode on it.

I rang the front bell. Mrs. B took a long time answerin. She was dressed in a summer housecoat, hair all mussy and no makeup. Her eyelids drooped. My heart did a flip.

"Hi, Cherrie Mae." Her voice came out croaky.

I gaped at her. "You sick, Mrs. B?" *No, Lord, not today.*

She made a face. "Got the flu or somethin. Woke up with it." She shuffled back. "Come on in. I'll keep away from you."

Took me a couple trips to tote in my vacuum and mop and sundry supplies. The camera got heavier in my pocket.

We stood in the entryway. "I'm so sorry you feelin poorly, Mrs. B."

"Me too." She glanced toward the stairs. "I'll just be up in my room for now. When it's time to do the room you can kick me to the couch."

"You want me to do your bedroom first? Then you don't have to worry bout gettin up again."

"Oh, I'm up and about anyway. I keep coming down to the kitchen for a drink or medicine or something. I feel antsy just lying in bed." A thought flitted across Mrs. B's face. She closed her eyes and slumped. "Oh, dear. I was supposed to help the Baptist women weed at the cemetery today. I'll have to call Cory."

Wonderful. Just wonderful. I couldn't even remember the last time Mrs. B was sick. Now how was I gon get my pictures?

"The best laid schemes of mice and men go often askew." Or was this God, payin me back for my schemin?

Couldn't be. I was schemin for a good cause.

"I'm sure she'll understand." I picked up my bucket a supplies to head upstairs. "I'm gon do your room first anyway. Then if you want to take a nap, you can."

"All right." She eased toward the livin room couch.

I got right to it in the master bedroom, runnin up and down the stairs to fetch my step stool and vacuum. Then I swept the whole upstairs so the noise wouldn't disturb Mrs. B later. By the time I finished all that, I done set myself with determination. First order a business was to get Mrs. B in her bed and keep her there. No way was I leavin that house without the pictures.

I carried the vacuum back downstairs.

"Done, Mrs. B." I hurried into the livin room, where she was spread out on the couch, watchin some ol movie on TV. Her eyes was at half mast. "Now I'm gettin you up to bed where you belong. We're gon take a glass a water, all your medicines, whatever you need." I looked down at her like a nurse to a stubborn patient. "I don't want to see you up again while I'm here. You need your rest."

"Oh, Cherrie Mae, you take such good care of me."

My conscience panged. "Come on now, let's get you upstairs."

I led her into the kitchen, where I fetched her water and cold medicine. "You want a plate a somethin to eat?"

"No, no." She waved her hand, lookin gray.

"You sure?"

Mrs. B nodded. Her whole body sagged. She gave me a blink long enough I wasn't sure her eyes would open up again. "I need to . . ." She gestured toward the stairs and headed that direction.

I followed behind, carryin her things. She took awhile gettin up the stairs. As she crawled into her bed I set the water and medicine on the nightstand. "Anything else I can get for you?"

She laid the back a her hand across her forehead. "Oh, my. I forgot to write you a check."

"Don't worry bout it. I'll get it Thursday."

"No really, I—"

"Mrs. B—no. Just go to sleep. I'm gon shut your doh, and I'll see you Thursday."

I turned away with purpose.

"Thank you, Cherrie Mae." Her voice faded off. "I can always trust you to be kind."

On the way down the stairs I begged God to forgive me for my duplicitous ways.

I hit the downstairs hall and strode right past my cleanin supplies. Now was the time to get those pictures. All I needed was a couple minutes. Then I could relax.

At the entrance to the office I felt a rush a cold air. I stopped in my tracks and looked around. Where had that come from? I saw no windows open. But sure as I was livin there was a chill in that office.

I eyed The Desk Drawer.

Funny thing. Now that the moment was here, and after all my plannin, I didn't want to touch that drawer. Didn't want to even go near it. Much less see those awful death scenes again.

Cherrie Mae, you better get hold a yourself.

My feet took me inside the room. Over to the desk.

I lifted up my shirt and dug in my pocket for the camera. I froze then, listenin for any sound from upstairs.

All was quiet.

I took a deep breath, placed my fingers on the drawer handle, and pulled the thing all the way open. I wasn't wearin gloves, and I'd decided it didn't matter. I'd already left my prints on the file last week. And I couldn't wipe the file clean 'cause I didn't want to take off any prints Mayor B had left.

My camera turned on with a little *drring*. The lens pushed out.

Leanin over the drawer, I searched for the folder. There it was. "Closet Killings." Like it was a hot piece a cornbread, I picked it up with the tips a my fingers and laid it on the desk. Then I checked the green hangin file, feelin the thump a my heart. *Please be here.*

The ring sat in the bottom.

I pointed my camera down toward that ring and clicked a shot. The flash went off. I moved the camera closer and took a second picture. Pulled it farther away for a third. Then took the ring out and held it up for a close-up. After that I laid it on the wood and scurried across the room for a wide shot a the desk with the drawer open, fireplace in the background. Somethin to prove this was Mayor B's home office.

Just for good measure I took a second wide-angle shot.

There. I mighta been breathin a little hard, but I'd done it. Easy as pie. Why had I laid awake nights worryin bout this?

"Fear of danger is ten thousand times more terrifyin than danger itself."

I dropped the camera back in my pocket and hurried to the desk. I put the ring back in the hangin file, ready to close up the drawer. Put the folder back inside. My fingers found the handle to push the drawer shut—then stilled.

My gaze glued to the Closet Killings folder. Holdin all those horrible pictures.

Did the *police* know Mayor B had those pictures? Or were they evidence against him too?

With one hand on the drawer, I weighed my decision. I wanted to be done with this. But I also knew I needed all the evidence I could get.

My head turned toward the hall. All was still. I tiptoed out the office, my ear cocked toward upstairs. Vaguely I heard the sound a the TV in Mrs. B's room.

I looked back at the file. Lord help me, I'd need to do this fast. *Without* lookin at one a those awful photos.

With a shaky arm I pulled up the folder. Laid it on the desk and opened it up. Eyes averted, I slid out the six pictures and lined em up on the desk, two rows a three each. My heart started to gallop. If Mrs. B come down the stairs now, I was done for. And as hard as I tried, my eyes couldn't help but land on the bodies in those pictures. Those poor women. All that blood. Seein them again shot anger through my bones. "Oh, Lord, help me catch the man who done this."

I snatched out my camera. Aimed it at the row a photos, close enough so you could see what was in em, and clicked the button. Then I backed up bout four feet and took a long distance shot a the pictures on the desk.

There. Now I was done for sure. I tossed my camera in my pocket.

That's when the front doh opened and Mayor B's footsteps sounded in the hall.

Chapter 24

Deena

I PACED MY KITCHEN.

The coffee in my stomach gurgled, and sweat prickled the back of my neck. Over and over I checked the clock on my oven. I could swear the hands weren't movin.

Trent had promised to call me soon as the hearin was over. As much as I wanted to be there, I couldn't go. Couldn't risk Stevie seein me and gettin all mad. That's the last thing the judge should witness.

Court session was at 10:00. Trent didn't know how long it would take before they got to Stevie. Depended on how many people had to see the judge and the luck of the lineup.

Yesterday when I got home from the jail, I'd been all wound up. Had to *do* somethin to channel my energy. But with Erika's funeral goin on, I knew the police station would be closed. I waited an eternity until I saw neighbors comin home. Then I barged down to the station, demandin that Chief Cotter tell me what they'd found in my brother's house. John wouldn't even let me in to see the chief. My cheatin ex just shouted me down, tellin me I had no right to even ask. And didn't I care that Erika's funeral had just let out? I nearly slapped him. Which would've put me in the slammer for sure.

I careened out of the station onto Main Street, mad and cryin. I didn't see Carl Cypress until I nearly ran into him.

"Hey, Deena, any news on Stevie?" Carl had a barrel chest and blocky face. Married in his thirties with three kids under the age of five. He managed the late shift at the plastics factory.

"Not yet." I stopped and sniffed. Hugged my arms to my chest. Carl was a good man and had always been nice to Stevie. If it had been anyone else I probably would have pushed right past him. "His hearin's today."

Carl folded his massive arms. "I'm so sorry. I just . . ." He spread his hands.

Not exactly a vote in Stevie's favor, but at least the man was talkin to me. "I know. It's hard to know what to say."

Carl glanced around and lowered his voice. "I haven't said anything to anyone, but Stevie was sure riled up at the end of our shift last Tuesday."

I stilled. "Why?"

"At first I didn't know. He was stompin around, mad, cussin to himself. I asked him what was wrong, and he just told me he was gonna make her pay."

Ants crawled down my spine. "Her, who?"

Carl gave me a long look. I saw compassion in his eyes—and something else. Guilt? "I didn't know then, Deena. I couldn't have known. I asked him who, but he wouldn't answer."

I felt my head nod. So now we had a witness to Stevie's state of mind that night. In a flash I saw Carl on the stand, tellin the court how Stevie had acted, what he said. How many other people would come out of the woodwork to remember this or that? A statement, a look that would help fry my brother.

I looked back toward the police station. "You on your way to tell the chief this important piece of information?"

He started to speak, then stopped. "I wasn't the only one to see him like that. But then—"

"Yeah. Sure." I ran my hand through my hair. Maybe I ought to cut it all off short—clear to my ears. Bleach it white-blonde and steal away to New York with Trent. New look, new life.

"I'm sorry, Deena."

"So's everybody, Carl." My tone went sharp. "That is, the people who'll talk to me at all."

He shook his head. "I don't think Stevie—"

"Well, if you have your doubts, I suggest you keep your insights about last Tuesday to yourself. Maybe you're wrong about what happened that night. Maybe you just might nudge the police to look all the harder at Stevie when they should be lookin elsewhere."

But in my heart I knew the truth. It *was* Stevie. Not Mike Phillips. Not Mayor B. It was *my brother.*

Carl shifted his feet and gazed down Main. "A little later that night I heard Stevie say he had to clean up 'the big mess.'"

The sun lost all its heat. I stared at Carl, Stevie's words clangin in my ears. *"I worked real fast to clean the mess up. But then the blood got on my clothes . . ."*

Had Stevie killed Erika *before* his shift ended? Had he slipped out of work and come back, only to return later to her house to clean up the "mess"?

My fingernails bit into my palms. Half of me didn't want to ask the question. "Did he explain what he was talkin about?"

"No."

My shoulders sagged. *Thank heaven.*

"You know Letty June," Carl said.

I snorted. "Yeah, I know her all right. My brother's best friend."

Carl's head tilted, like he knew just what I meant. "She knew Stevie was mad that night too. And I think she told Chief Cotter."

Of course she did. "That would be just like her." Steam ran through my body. I swear if I saw Letty June on the street I'd smack her down.

"But, Deena—"

"Don't!" I thrust up my hand. "Just don't say anything more, I can't take it." I turned away, sick to my stomach. "Thank you, Carl. For talkin to me."

I couldn't remember drivin home after that conversation. I couldn't remember much about the rest of the day, except goin to check on Stevie's trailer to see how badly the police had ransacked it. After a long search I found my key and walked down there. The inside was a total mess. Looked like my life. I stood there and cried.

No way could I deal with cleanin it. I'd locked the door behind me and left.

Now a day later as I paced my kitchen, my cell phone finally rang.

I rushed over and snatched it up, not botherin to check the ID. "Hello?"

"Hi. Hearing's over." Trent's voice.

"What happened?"

"About what we expected. Chief Cotter was there. The D.A. presented their case. The judge thought it was enough to hold him until the grand jury meets. Gives them all that much longer to get their case together."

My heart sank. "No bail?"

"No." Trent cleared his throat. "They had an additional piece of evidence, Deena."

Oh, no. "They find somethin at his house?"

"They didn't mention finding anything at the house. But they did get preliminary testing of the blood on the uniform over the weekend at that private lab."

"So fast?"

"One of the officers hand-delivered the uniform on Friday, and Chief Cotter must have promised to pay a bundle for immediate processing."

I almost didn't dare ask. "What did they find?"

"It's not good, Deena. The blood *is* human. And the type matches Erika's. It's AB, Rh negative. Of all types, that's the rarest, found in less than one percent of the population."

My gaze fastened on the toaster. Slick and silver, like a knife blade. I turned away and stumbled to a kitchen chair. Leaned over, forehead almost to my knees.

"Erika's rare blood type explains why Chief Cotter arrested Stevie so fast." Trent's tone remained objective. So reporter-like. As if his news hadn't pierced right through me. "The chief would have learned of it through the autopsy report. He was betting the blood on Stevie's uniform would be the same rare type—giving them stronger evidence to keep your brother in jail. If Erika's blood had been more common, the defense could argue a match in type didn't mean much."

"You think he did this?" My voice was barely above a whisper.

Trent hesitated. "It doesn't look good, Deena."

"You said you loved me." My voice caught.

"I do."

"Then stop bein such a reporter!"

"I thought you wanted to know what happened."

"I do, but . . ."

Silence.

"You want me to tell you Stevie didn't do it?"

A sob rolled up my throat.

"Okay, maybe he didn't." Trent sounded nonplussed.

"Say it like you mean it."

"Well, we still don't know for sure."

"So go prove he's innocent!"

"Deena. I'm not a detective. I'm a reporter. I just write what—"

"I don't *want* you to be a reporter." I shoved to my feet and propelled myself around the kitchen. "I want you to be a friend. You know about crime and the courts. So use your knowledge to help someone else for once!"

Our breathing collided over the line.

"Listen to me." Trent's voice was low and tight. "You want the truth? I'm not sure he is innocent anymore. At first I thought no way. But the stuff they've got on him . . ."

I strode into my livin room and threw myself on the couch. Who cared if I was being irrational? I couldn't stand for Stevie to be guilty. And so he wasn't. And so I had to help him. "*Don't* remind me what they've got on him. Think what they *don't* have."

"The DNA tests will prove whether or not that blood is Erika's. All you can do right now is wait for that, Deena. If it's not hers, this will be over. If it is, you'll have to accept it."

You. Not *we.* Nothin in his words about stickin beside me.

"I'm sorry to have to tell you all this."

I stared at the blank TV, rememberin the moment Stevie banged on my door six nights ago.

"Deena?"

"What."

"I have to return to Jackson now."

"Of course you do."

"I wish I didn't. Wish I could be there with you."

I slumped back against the couch, my anger drainin away. I was too tired for it. "I'd be lousy company."

"I know a lot's been happening. But have you thought more about coming to New York with me? I'm moving in a month."

He was asking about this *now*? "How can I go to New York and leave Stevie here?"

"He's in jail. There's nothing you can do to change that."

"I can go visit him."

"Really? After what happened the last time?"

My mouth clamped shut. A new wave of despair washed over me. Trent had a point. Still, did he have to be so callous about it? "I just won't ask him any questions that'll get him upset."

"I know life in Amaryllis can't be easy for you now. You could break free of that."

My eyes closed. What was it with this guy? "But I wouldn't be free, can't you see that? No matter where I am, my brother's still in jail. He still may be a murderer. And *that*, Trent"—my voice broke— "is goin to keep me in chains no matter where I am."

I clicked off the line.

Part of me wanted Trent to call back. He didn't.

For a long time I stared out my front window. My thoughts rolled around and around, no place to land. Was Cherrie Mae at the Bradmeyers' house now? Had she gotten the pictures of Erika's ring in Mayor B's file? That had to mean somethin.

But Mayor B would have some explanation. That ring was nothin compared to the victim's blood on my brother's clothes.

It *was* her blood, wasn't it. In my heart, I knew.

And how had Tully gotten through the weekend? I checked my watch. Too early to call. When Mike left for work I'd phone her.

"The blood type matches Erika's." Trent's words rang in my head. *"The rarest of types."*

Then whose blood was on Tully's swabs?

Chapter 25

Tully

I HUDDLED IN MY ROCKING CHAIR IN THE NURSERY, GAZING at the room. Everything was ready for little Michael. A month ago my mom and the ladies at the Methodist church had given me a baby shower. The crib was set, with its blue blanket and a mobile. Disposable diapers sat on the shelf of the changing table, next to a closed-lid trash can. The little dresser was filled with outfits, everything from newborn to eighteen months. It was all so pretty.

My hand went to my stomach.

Mike was in the living room, watching some sports station on TV. He'd barely spoken to me since we got up. I'd tried to act like nothing ever happened, but a black cloud hung between us and neither of us could find our way through it.

My thoughts turned to the swab hidden in my drawer—and sudden panic rose in me. What if Mike went through my things? If he found that . . .

My body went hot.

I was crazy for keeping that swab here. I needed to get it out of the house. Let Deena or Cherrie Mae keep it. But how could I do that? Mike wouldn't let me go anywhere, and he probably had Jeff and his wife, Becky, across the street spying on me. I could just imagine him telling them how I was trying to do too much. How I needed to keep off my feet—

The doorbell rang.

My head cocked, listening.

The TV muted. Mike's footsteps thudded against the carpet. The front door clicked open.

"Mornin, Mike." A man's voice. "Tully here?"

"Why?" Mike sounded suspicious.

"I need to talk to her."

"What for?"

I pushed to my feet, heart hammering.

"We just need to talk to her."

"Maybe I don't want you talkin to my wife."

I waddled out of the nursery and around the corner. Down the hall. In my doorway stood Officer Ted Arnoldson in uniform. Mike turned and glared at me.

My stomach hit the floor. Was this about my pact with Deena and Cherrie Mae? The swab? Couldn't be that. How could they know?

"Mornin, Mrs. Phillips." Officer Arnoldson gave me a tight smile. He stood over six feet—taller than Mike. His blond hair looked mussed, like he'd been in a hurry. "I'd like you to come with me down to the station." His ice blue eyes drilled into me.

"*What?*" Mike's faced flushed.

I bunched the neck of my T-shirt. Could he see my bruises through the makeup? "Why?"

"We need to talk to you. I'll bring you home soon as we're done."

"My wife's not goin anywhere with you." Mike flexed back his shoulders.

I couldn't answer. My knees were about to give way.

"Mrs. Phillips, you need to come down to the station."

"What *for*?" Mike stepped toward the officer.

"It's business between her and the police."

Mike's hand raised. "I'm her husband."

Officer Arnoldson stiffened. "Mr. Phillips, move back."

"You tell me why——"

"Move. Back."

"You are *not* takin my wife!" Mike swung the door to shut it.

Officer Arnoldson shoved his foot in the threshold. "Stand back now! Or I'll put you in cuffs."

"For *what*? Protectin my wife?"

"Wait, Mike." My voice shook. "Don't get in trouble. I'll go."

"You're not goin anywhere."

"It's okay."

"No, it ain't!" Mike swiveled toward me, his back to Arnoldson. "What have you done?" he hissed.

I shook my head, my throat stuffed with cotton. Whatever this was, I couldn't let the cop go now—and leave me alone with my husband.

"Mr. Phillips, move aside." The policeman reached for the mike at his lapel, ready to call for backup.

"It's okay, I'll go." I tried to move around Mike.

"No you're not." He pushed me back.

"Hey!" Officer Arnoldson stomped through the doorway.

Mike swung toward him. "You stay outta this."

Arnoldson clamped a hand on his arm. "You assaultin your wife in front of an officer?"

My husband jerked away. "Get off me!"

"Mike, stop!" He couldn't get arrested. Not now. What if they did know about the swab and told him? "I'll come right back."

"Step away." Arnoldson pointed a finger in Mike's face. "Or I'm takin you in."

The vein in Mike's temple throbbed. He glared at the policeman, chest heaving.

Michael, don't.

Mike's tongue ran across his bottom lip. His eyes shifted to me, full of rage. He'd kill me for this.

With a slow blink, Mike leaned back. He sneered at Arnoldson. "You gonna tell me what this is about?"

"I don't need to." The policeman motioned me toward his car. For the first time I noticed it sitting at the curb. What would the neighbors say? The news would be across town in a heartbeat.

I didn't dare look at Mike. Head down, I shuffled out the door. He and Arnoldson argued some more, but I barely heard above the blood pounding in my head.

Somehow I made it down the sidewalk. Arnoldson opened the front passenger door of his car. I fumbled into the seat. He closed the door—and I swear all oxygen sucked away.

Not until we started off did I glance back at Mike. He stood on the porch, arms folded, body rigid. A look to kill in his eyes.

Chapter 26

Cherrie Mae

 MAYOR B'S FOOTSTEPS SENT MY BODY INTO A FREEZE. I gawked at the pictures lyin out in rows, the open drawer.

The footsteps headed my way.

I flung myself to the desk.

The steps slowed. Mayor B must be starin at my cleanin supplies in the hall, wonderin what I was doin without em.

"Eva? Cherrie Mae?"

He sped up again.

With a heave a both arms I whisked the photos and the empty folder across the wood and into the open drawer. They landed askew on top a the hangin files, no time to set em all straight. I slid the drawer closed.

"In here, Mayor B." I snatched up his ashtray and spun around. He appeared at the office doh. He carried two blue folders in his hand.

We stared at each other.

Suspicion creased his forehead. "What're you doin?"

I raised the ash tray. "Just emptyin this." My heart skittered round like a cornered muskrat.

He eyed me. "Where's Eva?"

"She still feelin poorly. I made her go to bed. I cleaned your room first so she could rest. Look like it's flu, leastways a bad cold." I picked up the waste can by the desk and started toward the kitchen, where I'd empty it and the ashtray. My ankles liked to shake my feet clean off.

Go upstairs, Mayor B! I had to get back in the office and straighten that drawer. The way the man was lookin at me, I half expected him to check it soon as I left the room. But I couldn't just stand there and wait for him to leave.

His gaze followed me as I passed him into the hall.

"You might want to look in on her, see if she need anything." I walked on toward the kitchen, head up, like my whole world hadn't gone spinnin. My fingers nearly dropped the ashtray.

"What anxious moments pass between the birth of plots, and their last fatal periods." Joseph Addison wrote that almost three hundred years ago. I knew exactly what he meant.

I rounded the corner, still feelin Mayor B stare after me. He was gon check that drawer. I knew it. And I'd be a dead woman.

How fast could I run to my car?

In the kitchen I emptied the waste can and ashtray. Washed out the glass dish and dried it with a paper towel.

Where was Mayor B?

By the time I got back to the hall my heart had nearly broke my ribs. Mayor B was nowhere in sight.

I leaned toward the staircase and gazed up. The master bedroom was open. Voices murmured.

Relief sagged me like a rag doll. I hurried into the office and set down the two items. Reached for The Desk Drawer.

Upstairs a doh closed. Did I hear footsteps on the carpet?

I swiveled and headed back out the office toward my cleanin supplies. Mayor B's heavy tread sounded at the top a the stairs. I reached
for my vacuum cleaner. Started rollin it toward the livin room. Mayor
B hit the wooden floor a the hallway, still carryin the blue folders.

"She all right?" I turned back to him.

"Pretty sick. Bed's where she needs to be." He gave me a piercin
look.

"Mm-hmm." I headed on toward the livin room, feelin his eyes at
my back.

Nothin I could do but keep on cleanin. I plugged in the vacuum
and set to work. Any minute I was sure Mayor B would stalk into the
room. Grab my arm. Where *was* he? In the office? The kitchen, gettin
lunch?

Lord, You got to help me.

Seemed like it took a lifetime to sweep that carpet.

Finally, as I unplugged the vacuum, Mayor B appeared, a sandwich
on a plate in his hands. "You clean the office yet?"

Have mercy. My voice was gon shake. "I usually vacuum and
dust in there toward the last. You want me to go ahead and do it
now?"

"No, that's all right. You can just kick me out when you get
to it."

Was the man playin with me? "Okay."

I headed to the TV room. For another good hour I kept cleanin—
and prayin. My hands never stopped their shakes, and my mind ran a
hundred directions. Meanwhile Mayor B didn't leave his office, far as I
could tell. Never had he stayed home so long on a work day.

He *had* to be playin with me.

By the time I was ready to clean the office I knew I was done for.
The man was sittin in there, jus waitin for me to come in and try to
work. He'd roll out that drawer, say in a voice to kill, "What you been
doin, Cherrie Mae?"

I reached the doh to the office, my knees tremblin. The mayor sat at his desk, studyin papers from the folders he'd brought home.

"I'm ready to clean in here now."

He leaned back and took his time lookin round the room. Ran his finger across the top a his desk, then inspected it for dust. "Know what? It doesn't even look dirty in here. Just leave it till Thursday."

My pulse stopped. I had to get in there and fix that drawer. Maybe by some wild miracle he hadn't already seen it. "You sure? Won't take me long."

"I'm sure." He smiled at me—most chillin smile I ever seen in my life. "Go on home, now, Cherrie Mae. We'll see you Thursday."

I eyed him another second. My tongue ran around my dry lips. "All right. Thank you."

Quick as I could, I moved my cleanin supplies out a that house and into my car. I drove away in a hurry, thankin God I'd got out with my life. For now.

But night would come all too soon.

2010 Pulitzer Prize

Feature Writing
The Jackson Bugle

Gone to Ground

What happens to a small, quiet Southern town when evil invades in the form of a serial killer?

By: Trent Williams
October 29, 2010

(Excerpt)

The ancient legend of the amaryllis flower drips with blood.

In Greek mythology Amaryllis was a shy virgin nymph who fell in love with Alteo, a conceited shepherd with the strength of Hercules and the beauty of Apollo. Alas for Amaryllis, her love was unrequited. Alteo desired only one thing—a beautiful flower that had never before existed. In despair, Amaryllis consulted the Oracle at Delphi as to how to find such a bloom. The Oracle instructed her to stand at Alteo's door every night dressed in white and pierce her heart with a golden arrow. For thirty nights she stabbed her own heart, spilling her blood. When Alteo finally opened his door he found a crimson-petaled flower that had sprung from Amaryllis's blood. Only then did he recognize her beauty and fall in love with her.

The modern-day flower we know by the nymph's name grows in abundance around the Amaryllis Methodist Church on South Street, thanks to volunteer gardener Harvey Bayless. In his suspenders and faded blue baseball cap, Harvey, age 71, carefully tends the church garden throughout the year. The amaryllis bulbs, which can grow to four inches wide, lie dormant through the winter and push through the soil to bloom in March and April. Their colors are spectacular, some red, others orange. Harvey's favorite color is that of the "apple blossom," tinged pink and white, with green in the center.

Every three to four years Harvey digs up the bulbs.

The reason, he explains as he weeds the garden around the church, lies with the bulbs' tendency to sink deeper into the soil a little each year. "The bulbs like to have a bit of their tops exposed," he says in his heavy Southern drawl. "Leave 'em alone too many years, and you'll find 'em sunk too low, hidin'. You could say they've gone to ground." He makes a sound deep in his throat as he ponders his choice of words. "Sort of like that killer we cain't find."

And so, once the amaryllis are done blooming in that third or fourth year, Harvey will carefully remove the bulbs from their homes. But not too soon. He first allows time for the leaves to continue growing. "You got to allow the foliage to replace the bloom in the bulb," he adds. He tends the uprooted bulbs over the cold months, replanting them in February.

Harvey was unaware of the legend behind the amaryllis flower. Upon hearing the story he stops weeding and rocks back on his heels, one dirt-streaked hand finding his jaw. For a moment he is silent. His gaze lifts from the garden to roam down the street toward the house where Alma Withers, victim number four, lived. "Kinda makes you wonder, don't it."

After another spell of solemn rumination, Harvey takes off his cap to wipe his forehead, then doggedly returns to work.

Chapter 27

Tully

I'D NEVER SET FOOT IN THE AMARYLLIS POLICE STATION. And I sure didn't know about the scary little room where Chief Cotter took me. Didn't look much bigger than a prison cell. Dull gray walls. No windows.

John Cotter stood behind me. Two against one. He carried a beige folder.

My mind churned.

"Have a seat." The chief's gray eyes took in my white face, then dropped to my neck. My shoulders pulled up. He studied me for a minute.

A rectangular wood table backed against the wall with three chairs around it. On the table sat a tape recorder. Would they tape everything I said?

I lowered myself into a seat at one end. No way would I sit in the middle of these two cops. The chief sat down next to me.

My pulse fluttered.

John Cotter remained standing, watching me. "You need some water?"

I nodded.

He laid the folder on the table, then strode out. My eyes fastened on the smooth beige. What was in there? The folder had a tab. Nothing written on it.

Officer Cotter returned with a full glass. "Here you go."

My mouth tried to say "thanks," but nothing came out.

He closed the door and sat down at the other end.

The air closed in. I took a long drink, then sat straight-backed, hands clutched in my lap. A voice in my head whispered I didn't have to answer their questions. Didn't have to talk to them, period. At any time I could ask them to take me home.

To Mike.

My fingers curled into my palms.

Chief Cotter clicked a button on the tape recorder. A red light came on. "Don't worry about this." He waved a hand. "Just normal procedure." He leaned his big arms on the table and spoke toward the recorder. "Monday, April 25th, 11:15 a.m., Amaryllis police station. Present are Chief Cotter, Officer John Cotter and Tully Phillips."

He looked to me. "Reason we brought you down here, Mrs. Phillips, is we heard some information that leads us to believe you may know somethin about Erika's Hollinger's murder."

I stared at him. The swab? *How* could they know?

"I know this is frightenin to you. But you got nothin to be scared about. Just tell us the truth, that's all we ask. Looks like you've been wantin to do that anyway."

Air had to fight its way down my windpipe.

The chief pulled the beige folder toward himself and opened it. Inside sat the envelope I'd sent him last Friday.

My heart stopped.

He pointed to the envelope. "You ever seen this before?"

I licked my lips. "What is it?"

The chief gave me a look. "I received this in the mail on Saturday. Postmark was Friday, from Bay Springs. When I saw the content and the note, we immediately began investigatin who'd sent it. Soon as the Bay Springs post office opened this mornin I gave them a call. Asked if anyone happened to remember processin the envelope. Turns out someone did since it was sent to me, no return address, soon after a murder in our town. The employee said the envelope had been pulled from the mailbox outside the post office. The letter sat on top of the other mail, as if it had been dropped in there toward the end of the day."

Chief Cotter watched me for any sign of recognition. I waited him out.

"Mrs. Phillips, I know you tried to be anonymous. I can understand that. But of course we needed to know who sent the envelope. When I questioned the worker at the post office, the person mentioned steppin outside of the building around five o'clock and seein a young pregnant woman walkin away from the mailbox. We went on a hunch the young woman was from Amaryllis, since the employee didn't recognize her. Well, there aren't a lot of young women near deliverin a baby in this town. When we showed the employee your senior picture in the high school yearbook, that person said it was you."

The plastic gloves. My boxy printing. The envelope and stamp sealed with water from the faucet. I'd been so careful.

"Mrs. Phillips." The chief tried to sound gentle. "We know you sent the swab. It's really important you tell us about it."

I focused on the envelope, feeling the two men watch me. The room felt so hot.

"Tully," John Cotter said. "You're not goin to get in trouble."

I already *was* in trouble. More than they could know.

The chief tapped the folder. "Take us back to last Tuesday night. What time did your husband get home from work?"

"I came home at the regular time. You got that?"

I bit my lip. "I don't know."

"You don't know?"

My head shook. "I was already in bed."

"But you weren't asleep, were you?"

I kept quiet.

"Because your husband was late. And you were worried."

They were just guessing. They couldn't really know. Unless they'd heard Mike threatened to kill Erika.

How would they know that? "Why should I be worried?"

"Does your husband usually come home on time?"

"Yes."

"But he didn't that night."

Say nothing, Tully.

"I take it that's a yes." The chief leaned back. "So Mike comes home late. What happened then?"

My eyes closed. In my mind I heard the shower running, Mike's uniform dropped on the floor . . . "Was she pregnant?" The words blurted out of me.

"Who? Erika?"

Shame washed down my throat. I'd done it now. Bad enough I couldn't keep my husband, but for these men to find out . . .

"You askin me if Erika was pregnant?" The chief's voice edged.

I raised my chin and gave him a defiant look.

His eyes narrowed. "Was your husband having an affair with Erika?"

The words sounded so harsh. Chief Cotter's face blurred.

"Tully." John Cotter leaned forward. How could these two men gang up on me like this? "The autopsy did show Erika was pregnant. That fact has not been revealed to the media. So how do you know that?"

"She told me."

"Her own mother didn't know. Why would she tell *you?*"

I pushed back from the table. "I don't want to talk to you anymore."

"Wait now." Chief Cotter held up his hands. "We'll take you home soon, I promise."

"I want to go home *now.*"

He shook his big, fat head. "We still need some answers."

"I know my rights." My heart jittered. How could I talk back to the *cops?* "I don't have to be here."

"You're not bein charged with any crime, Mrs. Phillips."

"Then take me—"

"Yet."

My mouth snapped shut. I stared at him.

He scratched his jowl. "Look. We're tryin to be easy with you. All you have to do is tell us the truth. Fact is, we got a witness who's one hundred percent sure about seein you at the Bay Spring mailbox—"

"So I mailed a letter. That's not against the law."

"Tully." The chief planted his arms on the table. His chair creaked. "You sent us a swab with blood on it that you 'found,' saying it could be connected to Erika Hollinger. The minute we got that swab on Saturday I had one of our officers drive it to the private lab we used to test other evidence in this case. They processed it over the weekend. You want to know the results? Same blood type as Erika Hollinger. The rarest blood type there is, found in less than one percent of the population. That's quite a coincidence."

My veins went cold.

"With that swab, we got enough to arrest you right now."

What? "You said I wasn't in trouble."

The chief cocked his head. "And you won't be. *If* you talk to us. All you have to do is explain how you came by that blood. And before you answer, remember the lab will be runnin it through a DNA test. If that test comes back with a match to Erika, you'll have no wiggle room at all."

Wasn't he such a clever man. I wanted to knock his face off.

"One more thing. I've already got an officer runnin down a judge for a search warrant of your home. Anything interesting we might find when we get there? You might want to tell us now."

Pictures of policemen trashing my house flashed through my mind. Going through my drawers, finding the other swab. What about Michael's dresser? Was *he* hiding anything?

"Now." No gentleness in the chief's voice anymore. "You ready to start over?"

I shook my head. "You've already arrested Stevie Ruckland for Erika's murder."

"Actually, we have a theory about that." The chief raised his forefinger. "Stevie and Mike work the same factory shift. Get off at the same time. Somehow they both got a rare type of blood on them Tuesday night—blood that's apparently Erika's. They must have conspired in the murder."

"No way. They don't even like each other."

"We know Mike and Erika dated at one time. Now we learn from you they were havin an affair."

"I never said that."

"And apparently she was pregnant with his baby. I got this right so far?" The chief's eyes cut holes in me. "Erika wanted Mike for herself. She tells you she's pregnant, that she's takin Mike away from you. You confront your husband. He goes into a rage—and kills her."

My mouth opened. How could he guess so *right*?

"But he doesn't want to get caught," the chief continued. "Mike's too smart for that. So he gets Stevie Ruckland involved. Stevie'd be an easy target."

"That's not true!" No way would Mike trust Stevie Ruckland.

So why did they both have Erika's blood on their clothes?

Maybe it wasn't her blood at all.

"Tully." John Cotter rapped his knuckles against the table. "We need you to tell us what happened Tuesday night. Then you can go home."

Sweat trickled down my shirt. I looked from John to the chief, searching for a way to get out of this. They stared at me, their faces grim. They'd trapped me for sure. Chief Cotter had me before he even sent Ted Arnoldson to pick me up.

My gaze dropped. Don't tell—and I get arrested. Do tell—what then?

"I *can't* go home now." The words choked.

"You afraid of Mike?" Chief Cotter's voice softened.

I focused on a grain swirl in the table, light oval with dark in the middle. Almost looked like a winking eye.

"Mrs. Phillips?"

I rubbed the swirl.

Everybody in town was going to judge me. I didn't just marry the wrong man. I married a *murderer.*

"Tully, please. Talk to us."

"Tuesday night he was almost an hour late coming home from work." The sentence slipped out—so easy. And here I still sat. And the world still turned.

Chief Cotter grunted. "What'd he say when he got home?"

"Nothing. I pretended to be asleep."

How long did it take to tell the story that had changed my life? Time went on hold, my finger rubbing that grainy place on the table. I admitted everything, while the cops sat like stones and the tape recorder ran. I started with going to Erika's house, then Mike's threat to kill her. How he acted when he came home late, and our fight. Finding the blood, making the swabs. Mailing one off.

"Why didn't you send them both?" John Cotter asked.

I looked him in the eye. "In case you messed the first one up. Or ignored it."

He glanced at his father. The chief just smiled. Then turned serious again. "Mike been abusin you before this, Ms. Phillips?"

My gaze drifted toward the wall. I nodded.

"Why didn't you report him?"

Like it was that simple. "Where would I go?"

They chewed on that for a minute.

John Cotter sniffed. "You have any idea where that picture you saw of Erika and Mike went? We didn't find it when we searched her house."

I stilled. Why hadn't I thought about them finding that picture? "No."

Chief Cotter was silent—and I knew what he was thinking. Mike had looked for the picture in Erika's house that night. And destroyed it.

"We did find the digital on her camera yesterday." The chief watched my face. "It's taken us awhile to process everything from her house. Apparently Mike forgot about the camera."

This was really happening. My husband had really been there that night, no way to deny it. Dread curled in my stomach.

"Anything else to tell us, Tully?"

"No."

No way would I tell them about Deena and Cherrie Mae. But Cherrie Mae needed to get her own pictures down here fast. If they were even important anymore.

"Where's my daughter?" My mother's voice cut through the door. "What are you doing with her?"

I jerked up.

"Where's Tully? *Why* is she here?"

Footsteps sounded. I heard Ted Arnoldson answer but couldn't make out the words.

"No, you can't—Tully, honey!" The door pounded. "You don't have to talk to them! Come out of there!"

Chief Cotter shoved back his chair and yanked open the door. "Mrs. Starke, calm down. Your daughter's fine."

"Why do you think she has anything to do with the murders? Is it Mike, did he hurt her?"

"Did he hurt her?" Why would she ask that?

My mother pushed into the room, cheeks flushed, and her usually perfect hair a mess. Her dark eyes landed on me. "Are you all right?"

"She's fine." Chief Cotter stepped in front of my mom. "Now you need to let us finish, then you can talk to her."

"But I—"

"Judy, stop it." Chief Cotter pointed at her. "This is police business."

Tears filled my eyes. My mom had come. She really cared. Suddenly I realized how much I'd needed her the past few days. The past year. I wanted to throw myself in her arms. "I'm okay, Mom. Really."

Her eyes glassed up. "I'll wait for you. I'll be right out here."

I nodded.

Chief Cotter closed the door and returned to his seat. He gave me a soft look, like a parent to a child. "When we're done here, Tully, you need to go home with your mother. You'll do that, won't you?"

Tears fell down my face. I didn't *know* what to do.

"You can't go back to your own house. I don't want you alone with Mike, even for a minute."

"What's going to happen to him?"

"We'll bring him in for questioning. And we'll search your home. You don't want to be there while that's goin on."

I nodded.

The chief shifted in his chair. "Is there anything we're gonna find in our search that you want to tell us about?"

"I told you about the other swab."

"Any unregistered guns in the house?"

I shrugged. "The one Mike has is registered."

Why was he asking this? "Are you saying you won't arrest Mike unless you find something else?"

"I'm not sayin that at all."

"Then why do you want to know?"

"Tully, leave it be. We'll take care of this."

Sure, like they had for the last three years. I shivered. After this, they *had* to put Mike in jail. If they didn't, no use staying with my parents. He'd come after me, no matter where I hid.

Someone knocked on the door. Chief Cotter got up and opened it. Officer Chris Dedmon stood in the hall. They spoke quietly. I heard Dedmon say "search warrant."

The chief nodded. "Thanks."

Dedmon disappeared. The chief stayed in the doorway. "Mrs. Phillips, thanks for your time."

"Did he say he got the search warrant?"

"Yeah. We'll be out there soon."

Michael would hate me forever. Our life together was over. My head hung. I stared at my huge belly, carrying our son. *My* son. Michael would most likely be in jail when he was born.

"Come on, Tully, I'll help you up." John Cotter stepped to my side. "Your mother's waitin for you."

I lifted my chin. "Don't take my cell phone or computer. You hear? The phone and computer are *mine*. Michael never uses them. He doesn't even know how to turn that computer on."

"I can't promise you—"

"You *do* promise! They've got nothin to do with the murder. They're *mine*. If you don't promise me, I'll make my mother take me back home right now."

I pasted a defiant look on my face, my heart quavering. Truth was, I'd hide in the locked car while my mom went in the house and got my stuff. She'd do that for me. She'd take on Michael and not bat an eye.

Officer Cotter exchanged a look with his dad. I glared from one man to the other.

The chief shrugged. "Don't worry about that, Tully."

Right.

In the lobby Mom rushed over and clung to me. I hugged her hard, wishing I could scream. I couldn't make a sound.

"It's okay, it's okay." She smoothed my hair.

"She needs to go home with you, Mrs. Starke," the chief said.

"That's just where I'm taking her."

Hadn't we come full circle. Mom again in charge of me. For once I was glad.

Without a word I let myself be led outside to Mom's car. Not until we were driving away did I tell her. "We have to make a stop at my house."

Chapter 28

Deena

THANK HEAVEN MY SALON WAS CLOSED ON MONDAYS.

I slumped on my couch, starin at the coffee table. No energy to move. I didn't want to leave my house, couldn't bear to see anyone. My brother had just been arraigned for Erika Hollinger's murder. Soon Chief Cotter would find a way to pin the other five killings on Stevie. How was I supposed to live with that? Go back to work tomorrow and cut folks' hair like everything was just the same? If anyone would even set foot in my shop now.

What if I lost all my clients? How would I pay my bills? I'd lose my home, my car. I'd already lost my brother.

I leaned over, hands diggin into my temples. This was a nightmare.

My cell phone rang in the kitchen. I pushed off the sofa and hurried in to answer it. The ID read *Tully Phillips*.

I clicked on the line. "Tully, how are you?"

"They just arrested Mike for Erika's murder." Her voice sounded dead. "They think he made Stevie help him."

"What?"

Her story spilled out. My mouth hung open as I listened.

"I'm at my parents' house now," she said. "I wanted to call you soon as I got here, but my mom took forever going back to work. She didn't want to leave me alone. First I had to tell her about the blood and the swabs. I didn't say a word about you and Cherrie Mae, or she'd have wanted to know all that too."

My brain whirled. Maybe Mike *had* made Stevie help him . . .

"Half hour after we got here Chief Cotter called." Tully's voice caught. "They went to my house with a search warrant and to pick up Mike for questioning. They were hoping he'd confess. But Mike asked for a lawyer and wouldn't talk. The chief wanted me to know he'd been taken to jail. He's there at least until his hearing a few days from now."

I sank into a kitchen chair. That jail wasn't very big. They'd better keep Mike away from my brother. "What do we do now?"

"I don't know."

I stared out the window to my backyard. If Mike did this he'd have threatened to kill Stevie if my brother talked. No wonder Stevie had clammed up. Rage kicked up my spine. I hoped Mike *fried.*

Tully started to cry. "They found that picture of Mike and Erika on her camera. But not the printed one. Mike must have looked for it that night and got rid of it."

We'd never thought about that camera. What *else* had we missed? "When did they find it?"

"Yesterday. So they probably would have brought Mike in for questioning anyway, even if I hadn't sent the swab."

Poor Tully, second-guessing herself. "You did the right thing. You gave them the evidence they needed."

Easy for me to say. I hadn't turned in evidence on my brother.

Tully shook a shaky breath. "Where's Cherrie Mae?"

"Probably workin. I haven't heard from her."

"So you don't know if she got the pictures?"

"No."

"We have to call her. Can you do it? I remembered your number from making hair appointments, but I don't have hers with me. All I got out of my house is my purse, cell phone, and computer. I don't even have my *car*. And now the police are *trashing* the place!"

"I'm so sorry." Like they did Stevie's trailer. I knew what Tully would face. "I'll call her now."

"Then let me know right away. *Please*."

"Okay. We'll talk soon." I ended the call and ran to my purse to rummage for the phone list. Found the piece of paper and punched in Cherrie Mae's number.

Please answer.

"Hello, Deena?" Cherrie Mae sounded out of breath.

"Where are you?"

"Just finishin my second house. I'm carryin my stuff out to the car. I got the pictures. But I'm toast, Deena, he caught me."

Oh, no. "You mean Mayor B?"

"He come home, and I couldn't get the pictures put away right. I think he knows I been in that drawer. If he don't already, he will soon as he opens it. But the way he acted—he knows."

I heard a car door slam.

"I'm scared, Deena. That man gon come after me. I'm scared to be by myself after dark. I got one more house to clean, then I'm puttin the pictures on my computer and takin em down to the *police*."

"Mike Phillips has just been arrested for Erika's murder."

A pause. "What you say?"

I told her Tully's story.

"Oh, have mercy. Poor Tully. Lord, help us all. Now they done gone and arrested *two* wrong men."

"But the blood. It's got to mean somethin."

"I don't know what it mean." Her voice rose. "But I'm tellin you—Mayor B's guilty. I knowed it by his face. The way he looked at me today when he thought I'd been in that drawer. He played with me, Deena. Downright played with me. Sent ice through my veins."

"You think—"

"I got to get those pictures down to the *police right now.*"

I'd never heard Cherrie Mae so riled up. "What about—"

"I'll tell my next customer somethin's come up and I'll do her house later. I got to get home and put those photos on my computer."

"Can you print them out?"

"Ain't got no printer. I'll take my computer down to Chief Cotter. Leave my camera home as back-up, just in case something happens to the ones on my laptop. 'In this world you got to hope for the best and prepare for the worst.'"

Those pictures would totally mess up the cops' theory about Mike and Stevie. Far as they were concerned, those two made much better suspects than Mayor B. "Don't leave the camera in your house, Cherrie Mae. That's the first place the police would come lookin."

"You right. I'll give the camera to you. You got a computer? You could make copies too. The more the better."

"No. But Tully does."

"All right then. I'm gettin home now. Then I'm gon make the *police listen to me—whether they want to or not."

"Okay. Call me before you go to the station."

"I will."

I hung up and immediately called Tully to report what happened. Then I put down the phone and stared out my window, picturin an avalanche rushin toward all three of us. When it hit, who would be left standin?

Chapter 29

Cherrie Mae

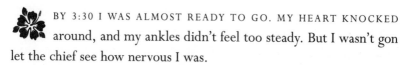 BY 3:30 I WAS ALMOST READY TO GO. MY HEART KNOCKED around, and my ankles didn't feel too steady. But I wasn't gon let the chief see how nervous I was.

I sat at my kitchen table, takin one last look at the pictures on my computer. I hadn't gotten a close enough shot a the ring to show the initials inside the band. Still, these should be okay. Surely nobody else had a ring looked just like that one.

While the computer shut down I called Deena and told her I was set.

"Okay." She sounded a little out a breath. "I'm nervous. Keep us posted."

"Where are you?"

"At Tully's house. I picked her up and brought her over here so she could get her car and some clothes. The place is messed up a little but not bad. Nothin like they did to Stevie's trailer. I think they were careful, so Tully wouldn't have to be on her feet, putting the whole house back together. I'm helpin her straighten up."

The computer clicked off. I shut the lid. "She not stayin in that house by herself tonight, I hope. Tell her to stay with her parents. We still got a murderer out there."

"Don't worry, I've already given her that speech. She's not fightin it. She's too upset to do much of anything."

Poor Tully. *God, help that girl.*

"Maybe you two ought to stay at her house just till I'm done with the *po*lice. I'll come over and we can have a meetin."

"Sounds good. But wait—we have Tully's computer. Bring your camera over here first so she can copy the pictures. She says it'll go fast. Plus you can leave the camera with us. We'll have two backups."

"Okay. Be right over."

When I pulled up to the curb outside Tully's, two neighbor women was across the street, talkin. Glancin at me and her house. No doubt gossip was flyin round Amaryllis. The *po*lice here—twice—and now Mike arrested. They had to be wonderin what I was doin here. I raised a hand and waved as I got out the car. They waved back. I could feel their eyes gawkin at me as I hurried up the sidewalk, totin my computer.

Inside Tully's house I set down my laptop and hugged her hard. She looked pale and worn. Deena didn't look much better. At least they was too tired to be fightin with each other. I figured they done formed an odd kind a bond—both of em with a loved one arrested for the same murder.

"Misery acquaints a man with strange bed-fellows."

We gathered round Tully's table, her computer bootin up. I gestured toward it with my chin. "You're lucky the chief didn't take it."

She gave me a sly look. "Oh, he'd have liked to. I made my mother come over here and get it before we went to her house."

"What did Michael do?"

"I stayed in the car with the doors locked. At first he wouldn't let Mom in, but he wanted to know what had happened with me. She barged around and got my computer and purse, and when he wouldn't let her out with them, she told him the police were right behind her, and he'd best let her go if he knew what was good for him."

Mercy. "Your mama got spunk."

Tully's mouth curved in a wistful smile.

I turned on my camera and stuck the connector into her laptop. "You don't have a printer, do you?"

She shook her head. "I wish."

"Me too." I made a face. "The *police* gon have to keep my computer till they can print out copies."

Deena sniffed. "You'll never get it back. Make em print copies while you're there."

I'd try. Who knew how things would shake down.

Grim silence fell over us as Tully went through her download program. Didn't take her long.

"There. Done," she said.

"Don't look at em, Tully." I didn't want her seein those dead women.

"Don't worry." She pressed her palms against her cheeks. "You think Chief Cotter will listen to you, Cherrie Mae?"

"Don't know. I'd like to think he'll want to hear evidence anybody brings. But things look so convenient for him now."

Lines pinched Tully's forehead. "What if all of this fits together? What if all three of them did . . . something?"

Deena make a *tsking* sound. "Then Mayor B would be the brains behind it. I can hardly see Mike or Stevie makin that man do anything. He holds their *jobs* in his hands."

We looked at each other.

Deena's eyebrows raised. "I haven't told you what Carl Cypress said. According to him, on the night of Erika's murder Stevie was all upset about somethin near the end of their work shift. He was stompin around, and he told Carl he was gonna 'make her pay.' Carl asked him who and what he was talkin about, but Stevie wouldn't answer. And then my brother said he had to 'clean up the big mess.'"

Tully's eyes widened. "What big mess?"

"I don't know. But what if Mayor B killed Erika before that factory shift was over, and then made Stevie go clean up the crime scene?"

Hmm. "But then who was Stevie talkin bout, he gon make her pay?"

"Don't know. I thought it was Erika because she's always taunted him."

"Maybe the 'big mess' was just something at work," Tully said. "After all, that's his job—cleaning."

"Yeah, maybe. It's just . . . the timin."

I mulled that over. "We got to add that to our notes—whatever it means." I pulled the papers from our first meetin out a my purse. "Here. You two look these over while I'm gone. Add anything new to em. We can talk bout it when I get back." My gaze fell on the first page where I'd circled a big question mark around Erika "comin into big money."

A thought flashed in my head.

"Tully, you think Mike really did plan to go away with Erika? Cause if he did, why would he kill her?"

Tully shook her head. "I think she was lying. I don't think he would have left me. He was too excited about our son." Pain flicked over her face.

"Then maybe the part bout money comin to her was another lie."

"Probably. Maybe she lied to Mike about the money, too, trying to bribe him away from me. And once he took off with her and learned the truth, she figured it would be too late. Sounds just like her."

Deena sighed. "But all this focuses only on Erika. Don't forget there are five other murders."

She was right bout that. This whole thing was a mess. I held out my arms. "I need to go. First we got to pray."

They grasped my fingers, and I led us all in prayer that God would give me the right words. And most of all that he'd lead us to the killer a those six women. Fast.

I pushed back my chair. "All right then. Be back when I'm done."

Chin held high—like I was confident as a fat cat—I left Tully's house and headed for the *po*lice station.

Chapter 30

Cherrie Mae

ON MAIN STREET, I STRAIGHTENED MY BACK AS I CLIMBED out the car, my purse hangin from one arm. My hands was sweaty-slick on my computer.

Inside the station I spotted Ted Arnoldson first. He was sittin at a desk talkin on the phone. I caught the words *evidence* and *test*. Ted nodded at me, then turned away, lowerin his voice. The air in that little lobby crackled with energy. The *police* had to be trippin all over themselves, tryin to figure how to get *two* suspects for one murder.

Just wait till I got through with em.

The chief's office doh was closed. Muffled voices sounded behind it. I strode over and knocked. Ted looked over his shoulder at me and held up a finger—*wait*. I paid him no mind and knocked again. Next thing I knew Chief Cotter stood in the threshold, starin down at me. Behind him I could see John Cotter, sittin in a chair in front a the chief's desk.

The chief nodded, and his beefy jowls shook. "Cherrie Mae." He glanced at my computer, faint curiosity in his eyes.

"I got to talk to you. It's important."

He breathed in, makin his nostrils flare. "We're pretty busy right now. Can you come back?"

"Nope. It cain't wait."

"What's this about?"

"Erika's murder. I got new evidence."

John Cotter rose. I heard Ted Arnoldson hang up the phone, felt his eyes at my back.

"New evidence, huh." The chief rocked from his heels to his toes. "You remember somethin about bein at her house that night you forgot to tell me?"

"Nope." I looked around. "Can we sit down? I got somethin to show you."

Chief Cotter scratched the back of his head. "What is it?"

"You done arrested the wrong men for Erika's murder, chief. Or at least you need to arrest a third."

He gave me a look. So did John Cotter. And I knew Ted was starin at me.

"You tellin me you got *another* suspect for me?"

My courage wavered. I didn't like the way the man looked down at me. What did he see? Some five-foot African-American cleanin woman he could wave away with a flip a his hand? Sure was different from a week ago, when he *needed* my information.

I firmed my mouth. "That's exactly what I'm sayin."

The chief sighed. "All right." He sounded dubious. "Let's go in there." He pointed to the little room where they'd questioned me last Wednesday. "We'll make it quick, okay?"

Mm-hmm.

I opened my laptop and pressed the button to turn it on. The chief spoke in low tones to his son. John Cotter left the office and went to his own desk.

Adam Cotter hurried down the short hall toward the interrogation room. I followed, balancing my open computer in both hands like one a the wise men bearin his gift.

In the room with the doh closed we settled at the table, Chief Cotter to my left at the end. His chair squeaked as he sat down. "Okay, Cherrie Mae. What you got?"

The recordin machine sat before us on the table. I surveyed it. "Aint you gon turn that on?" They'd had it runnin for my interview last week. All important interviews was taped.

The chief pushed up his bottom lip, frustration crossin his face. "Sure." He leaned over and hit the button with his fat finger. Settled back in his chair. "There."

"Ain't you gon say who's present?"

He looked at the ceilin. "Monday, April 25th. Present: Chief Adam Cotter and Cherrie Mae Devine." He held out his palm—*go ahead.*

This wasn't goin right. The chief was bein way too dismissive. And I hadn't even tol him who the new suspect was yet.

Maybe *dismissive* wasn't the right word. Chief Cotter acted just plain distracted. He had no time for this. I knew where his mind ran. He was stagin scenarios a Mike and Stevie killin Erika. And how they could have killed the other five women too.

My computer finished bootin up. I moved the mouse to bring up the pictures.

"So *what* is it?" He drummed his fingers against the table.

"I'm gettin to it." My hand almost shook.

Up came the first photo—Erika's ring in Mayor B's green hangin file. Suddenly it looked so small and insignificant on my monitor. Why hadn't I printed the pictures out somewhere? I just knew the *police* were gon take my computer and destroy everything on it. Some little "slip-up."

I enlarged the picture to fill the screen.

"Cherrie Mae, you're takin my time, and I really am busy right now."

Indignation stalked round my chest. This man was here to serve the town. We weren't here to serve him. I huffed upright in my chair, arms folded. "You want my information—or should I just take it to the newspapers? I got Trent Williams' cell phone number."

A dark look crossed Chief Cotter's face, followed by one a forced patience. "Now, Cherrie Mae, no need to go callin Trent. I'm listenin."

"Good. Get me a Bible and some cigarettes—and I'll talk."

The chief gawked at me, then chuckled. "Since when did you start smokin?"

"The cigarettes is for you. You gon need em."

He drew his head back, then recovered. "I'll be fine."

"I still need the Bible."

"We don't have a Bible in the station, Cherrie Mae. Now if you got somethin to tell me, get on with it."

"Fine then. Pretend you do. And I'm layin my hand on it." I stretched my hand above the table, palm down. "I swear on the Bible everthing I'm tellin you is true. And you know Cherrie Mae don't take the Bible lightly."

He dipped his chin. "Duly noted."

"Okay." I shifted in the chair. "Member last week you wondered bout Erika's ring? It was missin? Well, I found it."

"Really."

"Yup. And you ain't gon believe where. I didn't want to believe it first myself. But evidence is evidence." I turned my computer around and pointed to the picture. "That's it. Got Erika's grandmama's initials in the band, so I'm sure it's the same one."

The chief leaned forward, frownin. I pushed the computer close to him. He stared at it, then looked at me. "Where'd you get this picture?"

"Took it myself. That's the top drawer a the desk in Mayor B's home office."

The chief's beady eyes rounded. *"Austin Bradmeyer?"*

"Yup. I got more to show ya." I clunked my chair closer to the chief so we could both look at the computer together, then worked my mouse to bring up the other pictures. "Here's a close-up a the ring. Here it is on the desk, taken some distance away. See—that's Mayor B's office."

Chief Cotter examined each picture, tongue-tied.

"He also got a file in that drawer a the murder victims, you know that? A close-up shot a ever one a the six women, includin Erika."

The chief's eyes snapped up to me. "You got proof of that?"

I showed him the photos a the six gory pictures spread out on the mayor's desk.

When I had nothin more to show, the chief blinked at the computer for a long time, then leaned back in his chair. He studied the far wall. "Who knows about this?"

I hesitated. "A couple other people. They got copies a the pictures."

"Who?"

"Don't matter who. What matters is what you gon do bout it."

The chief studied me. "Tell me, Cherrie Mae. How come you to open a drawer in Mayor B's desk?"

"Why's it matter? Point is I did—and that's what I found."

"Someone give you some kind a tip? A reason to go lookin?"

"Nope." I wasn't gon get into this. The chief had enough to do without investigatin my snoopin. But he sure was lookin at me funny. I come in here with evidence against Mayor B, and suddenly *I* was feelin like a suspect.

He breathed in. "When'd you take these pictures?"

"Late this mornin."

"Today?"

"Yup."

He poked out his cheek with his tongue. "Well, now, that's inter-esting." He got up and went to the doh. Opened it and stuck his head out. "John."

"Yeah."

"You need to come in here. Bring that piece of evidence from the Phillips'. And a glove."

The chief waited in the threshold until his son stuck a small paper bag and latex glove in his hand. He brought em back to the table and sat down. John Cotter followed, closin the doh and sittin on the other side a me. I glimpsed some writin on the bag, but the chief turned that part away from me.

"Reason it's so interesting"—he pulled on the glove and unrolled the top a the evidence bag—"is within the last two hours, durin a search of Michael Phillips's house, we found this."

He reached into the bag with his gloved hand and pulled out Erika Hollinger's ring.

2010 Pulitzer Prize

Feature Writing
The Jackson Bugle

Gone to Ground

What happens to a small, quiet Southern town when evil invades in the form of a serial killer?

By: Trent Williams
October 29, 2010

(Excerpt)

"Why?" the residents of Amaryllis ask themselves daily. "Why here, in our quiet little town? Why these particular victims, who had no enemies?" The questions reverberate through the Main Street businesses, the churches and homes. They are whispered at the dinner table, in bed, and on front porches. The drive to understand, to make sense of the nonsensical, runs crucial to the human psyche. After each murder the questions have swirled harder.

Twin sister to *why,* is *who.* The citizens of Amaryllis long to believe the Closet Killer is from another town. Maybe someone slipping over from Bay Springs or Heidelberg. Someone even from the next county—perhaps from the large "city" of Laurel, population 18,000. In the midst of the upheaval and fear, distrusting one's own neighbor is too traumatizing. Friends and families need to pull together for comfort and strength, not point fingers. But with each new murder in the town's boundaries—and with no other similar crimes anywhere else in the entire state—the "someone else" theory has begun to deflate.

"Maybe the killings are done now," Theodore Stets says from behind the counter at the drug store on Main. "Five women—maybe he's had enough. He'll just stop." His tone turns from wistful to grim. "'Course then, we might never know who it was."

Could he live with never knowing, if the murders stopped?

Theodore wipes imaginary dust from the counter. The furrows in his forehead deepen, as if he questions the wisdom of speaking his mind. "Thing is, as odd as it sounds, now we still have hope. Oh, in a way everybody suspects everybody, but not really. I don't *truly* think the killer is my good friend from grade school, my brother or neighbor, the guy I sit next to in church every Sunday. But the whole town can't be right about that. The culprit *is* going to be somebody's brother or father, neighbor or friend. And what's a person to do with a shock like that? Finding out the truth about someone you believed in all your life? You think Amaryllis folk have trouble trusting now. Imagine what it'd be like having your whole world turned inside out."

Chapter 31

Deena

TULLY AND I MOVED TO HER LIVIN ROOM, WHERE SHE could put her feet up. I pulled down the shades. Tully took the couch while I perched in the worn armchair. First I added the new information to our notes. After that I had to get up, move around. We went over everything we'd written down—and didn't come up with a single new insight. Tully was too worried about her husband bein in jail, and what the rest of her life would look like. And I couldn't stop thinkin about Stevie.

And *what* was takin Cherrie Mae so long?

Meanwhile Tully's phone wouldn't stop ringin. No doubt people all over town were hearin about Mike's arrest and wanted details. Tully checked the ID and most of the time let it ring. Then Trent called. Tully gasped. "I don't want to talk to *him!*"

"Don't answer. Besides we agreed we wouldn't tell him anything unless Cherrie Mae's meetin with the police goes belly-up."

Tully bit her lip until the ringin stopped. "There'll be other reporters. I'll have to hide." Despair crossed her face.

Then her mother called. Tully picked up. Judy Starke's voice shouted over the phone loud enough for me to hear.

"*What* are you doing there? I called and called the house—"

"I had a friend bring me over. I needed my car and some clothes. I'll be back tonight."

"*Tonight*? You need to get back over there *now*. What if Mike comes back?"

Tully's eyes closed. "Mom, he's not coming home."

"You never know—"

"He's *not* coming. He's arrested. In jail. Because of what *I* told the police."

"Tully, this is not your fault. He's in jail because of what *he* did."

"I don't want to talk about this right now. I'll see you later." Tully hung up the phone. She stared at the floor.

Poor thing looked so young. She *was* young. What it must be like to be Tully Starke Phillips, caught between a controlling mother and an abusive husband. Who just might be a killer.

"You are goin back there tonight, right?" I faced her from across the room. "You can't sleep here alone."

She nodded.

Another ring—this time from my cell phone. I picked it off an end table and checked the ID. "It's Trent." I pushed the *talk* button. "Hi."

"I just heard Michael Phillips has been arrested for Erika's murder."

"News travels fast."

"What do you know?"

I gazed at Tully. "Not much. Probably just the same talk you have."

He blew out air. "I called the police station to confirm, and Ted Arnoldson actually talked to me. He said they searched the Phillips' house and he found something akin to 'a smoking gun.' But he wouldn't tell me what."

My eyes widened. Tully looked at me in alarm—*what?*

"I have no idea what they found."

"Man. Wish I wasn't in Jackson."

"You could always come back."

"Can't. I got stuff here. Do you know Tully Phillips very well?"

Tully's eyes still locked with mine.

"I cut her hair, that's about it. Why?"

"Just wondering if you could persuade her to talk to me. I called her house but she doesn't answer. Called her parents' house too, just in case she's there."

"Maybe she doesn't want to talk to a reporter."

"But it's *me*."

"Trent, you're not callin as a friend. You barely know her. You're callin as the crime writer for *The Jackson Bugle*. Her husband's just been arrested—she's got to be upset."

He sighed. "Yeah, well. I'll keep trying. Phone me if you hear anything, and I'll run it down."

"All right." I hung up.

"What?" Tully sat up straight. "What'd he say?"

"You know anything about the police findin a 'smokin gun' when they were here?"

Her face whitened. "I didn't think they found much of anything. But then I didn't talk to any . . ." She bit her lip. "What could it be?"

"The picture, maybe. Of Mike and Erika."

"But they already had it on the camera. That's not news."

"It is if the hard copy's in *your* house. Last you saw it, Erika had it—just a day before she was killed."

Tully's breaths got fluttery. A sick look twisted her expression. "Oh . . . I'm . . . going to—"

She shoved off the couch and lumbered fast as she could toward the bathroom. A toilet lid slammed open. I couldn't listen to the sound of her throwin up—or I'd be right behind her. The world was already tilted. I wanted to get *off*.

Eyes squeezed shut, I sagged into the armchair and slapped my hands over my ears.

Chapter 32

Cherrie Mae

 AT SIGHT A THAT RING MY STOMACH DROPPED TO MY TOES. Was it the same one?

Chief Cotter laid it on the table.

I leaned over it. "Do it have the initials A.K.L. inside the band?" But I could already see em, catchin the light like they was winkin at me.

"It's Erika's ring, Cherrie Mae."

I straightened up, thoughts collidin in my head. "How'd it get there? In the Phillips's house."

"Mike Phillips, how else? He must have taken it the night of the murder. Since you'd just seen it on Erika—if you remember your statement."

My lips tightened. "I remember just fine. I also remember takin a picture a this here ring at Mayor B's house not three hours ago."

John Cotter nudged my computer toward himself to view the picture.

The chief lifted a shoulder. "Maybe it wasn't the same ring. I couldn't see the initials in any of your photos."

"Mm. Funny how it was with pictures a all the Closet Killer victims. Which I don't think you gave to Mayor B."

The chief nodded. The man was tryin to keep a poker face, but it was slippin. I glanced at John Cotter. He was goin through all the pictures, his forehead creased.

I leaned back in my chair. "You both know somethin funny's goin on here."

Chief Cotter picked up the ring and put it back in the bag. "I'll admit on the surface it doesn't look good. But we'll take it from here." He slipped off the glove. "I thank you for bringin me these pictures."

Mayor B *did* know I'd been in his desk drawer. He knew he had to get rid a the evidence before I tol somebody. But he didn't know I had proof, did he. "That ring had to be planted in Mike Phillips's house."

Lord, don't let it be by one a these two men.

"We'll look into it."

"Which officer found it?"

"I said we'll look into it."

The chief and I stared hard at each other.

He pushed back his chair. "We're done here."

"Can you print out copies a the pictures? I want to take my computer home."

"That'll take awhile. Leave it here for now. We'll get it back to you soon."

"Don't you make em disappear."

The chief huffed. "We're not gonna do that."

The timin a the search at the Phillips's house would a been perfect for Mayor B. All he had to do was get that ring over there somehow . . .

I shook my head. "That ring was *planted*."

"I *said* we'll look into it."

John Cotter pushed my computer toward me and got up. As he opened the doh, I heard sounds from the lobby. A man greetin Ted Arnoldson.

The voice belonged to Mayor B. "Chief in?"

My heart took off out a my chest.

"Yeah, down in the room. He's talkin to someone right now."

This was no coincidence, the mayor showin up. He'd heard they was done searchin Mike Phillips's house, hadn't he. And he wanted to make sure that ring had been found.

"Hi, Mayor." John stepped out a the room. Clearly he didn't want Austin Bradmeyer to see me. They were gon handle this new wrinkle their own way, without Cherrie Mae Devine around. Just what kind a story would Mayor B cook up when they interviewed him without me present? I could imagine him trashin me. Callin me a snoop and a liar, denyin everthing.

John started to close the doh.

"Hi, Mayor B," I called out. Puttin a grim tone into my voice. I shoved my computer lid halfway closed.

John froze. Chief Cotter made an irritated sound in his throat. Footsteps approached. Mayor B appeared, lookin from John to me to the chief. His cheeks blanched.

Silence gripped the room.

Mayor B forced a smile. "Y'all havin a party without me?"

"Nah." The chief tried to sound nonchalant. "Cherrie Mae was just leavin."

Mayor B licked his lips.

"Actually, it's a good thing you come along." I kept my eyes on the mayor. "Since we was talkin bout *you*."

"Oh." He laughed, but it came out nervous. "Sounds serious."

"Cherrie Mae's just teasin you." Chief Cotter snatched up the evidence bag and glove, and stood. "Come on in my office, Austin. What can I do for you?" He started headin out the room.

Mayor B looked from the bag to Chief Cotter. Curiosity battled fear on his face.

"No, I ain't teasin, and I think he got a right to know." I stayed put in my chair, not bout to let this meetin come to a close. "Don't you want to know, Mayor B?"

Austin Bradmeyer stepped past John into the dohway. The chief jerked in my direction. "That's enough, Cherrie Mae."

"No, no, she's right." The mayor leaned against the threshold, tryin to look casual. "Three people meetin about me in the police station? I'd say I have a right to hear what's goin on."

Chief Cotter glared at me, then turned back to Mayor B. "I also have the right to follow up with you privately. And that's—"

"I told em bout the pictures you got, Mayor B. And Erika's ring."

The chief's face glowed red. "That's—"

"Wait, wait." Mayor B stepped inside the room, forcin Adam Cotter back. "What pictures? What ring?"

Well. My jaw moved to one side. I fixed a look on Chief Cotter. Now he had the man headin for a lie. And that tape recorder on the table was still runnin.

John eased back into the room.

I looked back to Mayor B. "The pictures a all our murdered women. And you know what ring."

Mayor B's forehead wrinkled. "Cherrie Mae, *what* are you talkin about? I don't have any pictures from the crime scenes. And I sure don't have any ring."

The chief and his son exchanged a glance.

"Where in the world did you supposedly see these things?"

"In your office desk. Top right drawer."

"In my *desk drawer?*" Mayor B shut the doh and walked toward the chief's vacated chair. Folded his arms and gazed down at me. "Why, that can't be. You'd have to be snoopin in my desk, and surely you don't do that."

I scooted around in my chair to face him. Chief Cotter edged back toward the table, holdin the evidence bag and glove low at his side. He glanced at the turnin tape in the recorder.

"If people knew you did that, Cherrie Mae"—the mayor shook his head—"seems to me you'd lose a lot of customers."

Chief Cotter didn't move, but I could feel sick surprise rollin round inside him.

"Mayor B"—my back was ramrod straight—"I seen those pictures in a file in your drawer just this mornin. *And* I seen Erika's missin ring."

His expression darkened. "You are *lyin*. And I have no idea why." He threw a look at the chief. "Adam, you can go to my house right now and search that desk if you want. You won't find a thing."

Chief Cotter held his gaze. "You never had any photos of the victims?"

"No. Why would I?"

"And you didn't have Erika Hollinger's ring?"

"Why in the *world* would I have Erika Hollinger's ring?"

"Is that a no?"

"Of course it's a no!"

Chief Cotter drew in a long breath. He looked anything but happy. "Cherrie Mae, open up your computer."

Mayor B's eyes snapped to my laptop, as if it had sprung out a nowhere.

I lifted the top and moved the mouse around, turnin off the screen saver. The photo a the crime scene pictures spread across the mayor's desk filled the monitor. I turned the computer toward Mayor B. He leaned down and peered at it.

Color drained from his face like somebody done pulled the plug.

I sat still as death, my heart bangin.

"Show him one of the ring," Chief Cotter said.

I slid the computer where Mayor B, the chief and I could see it. John took his seat at his end a the table, surveyin the mayor's face. One by one I brought up the ring pictures. First in the bottom a the hangin folder. Then the close-up. Then sittin on the desk.

Mayor B plunked down hard in the chair.

My voice would barely work. "I took these today. You knew I'd been in that drawer, Mayor B. That's why you wouldn't let me back in your office to clean."

He ran his tongue over his lips. "I . . . there's got to be an explanation for this."

Chief Cotter grunted. "I'm listenin."

"Well, surely somebody put those things there. I didn't know they were in my house."

"They been there since at least last Thursday, when I first seen em."

"*What* were you doin in that drawer, Cherrie Mae?"

John Cotter scratched the corner a his mouth. "The bigger question is—why are they in *your* drawer?"

"I have no idea." Mayor B looked from John to the chief. They both stared back. The mayor spread his heads. "Look, what *is* this? You gonna let somebody come in here and tell these lies about me? I've been mayor of this town for fifteen years. Been a loyal member of the Methodist Church long before that."

Settin in church don't mean much, if you're heart ain't right.

Chief Cotter buffed the side a his head. I could tell he was upset. "Cherrie Mae, thank you for comin down."

I studied his face. He made a small gesture toward the doh with his head.

They intended to interrogate Mayor B the rest a the way without me. Fine. I'd done my part. Avertin my eyes from Mayor B, I picked up my purse and stood.

"You can close the door behind you," Chief said.

My head nodded. I stepped out without lookin back. Felt like I was leavin part a my life behind. Somebody I'd once thought could be trusted—couldn't. And whatever happened here, I'd never clean the Bradmeyers' house again. Who knew bout my other clients.

In the lobby I stopped to take a long, deep breath. Ted Arnoldson sat at his desk, files spread across it. He was starin at me. And the anxious look on his face . . .

"Ted." I ducked my chin.

"Sounded like some meetin in there."

Just how much had he heard? That room was a little ways down the hall. I clicked back in my memory to when Mayor B shut the doh. "I reckon so."

He waited for me to say more. Uh-uh.

Ted picked up a pen and twiddled it between two fingers. "I heard you say something about Erika's ring."

"Yup."

Seconds ticked by. "Well, Chief just showed it to you, didn't he?"

"Yup."

"We just found it at Mike Phillips's house."

"Which officer found it?"

"I did."

Oh, Ted. "Where was it?"

"In the cushions of the couch. Must have dropped out of Mike's pocket."

"Mm."

That pen kept twiddlin. I stared at his nervous fingers. He put the pen down.

"You look puzzled about something, Cherrie Mae."

Ted Arnoldson was a young officer, years a his career still ahead. Why'd he done it? "Not puzzled. Just . . . sad."

"Sad?"

Our eyes locked.

He looked away.

Dear Lord, how many people's lives do I have to wreck today?

I stepped closer, put my purse on his desk. "You want to tell me bout it, Ted?"

"Tell you about what?"

"Why you let Mayor B talk you into plantin Erika's ring in Mike Phillips's house."

His mouth creaked open. *"What?"*

I waited.

"You're out of your mind! Why would you say such a thing?"

"Why you think I brought my computer in here?"

He screwed up his face. "I don't know."

"Well, maybe you better wonder bout that. You bein a cop and all. You're supposed to notice the details."

"Okay, Cherrie Mae." He acted like he was playin along with a child. "Why did you bring your computer in here?"

"Cause it has pictures on it. Of a file in Mayor B's house. In that file were photos a all the murder victims. And at the bottom was Erika's ring."

Ted stilled like a wax doll.

"If I was a bettin woman, I'd wager he got those pictures through you too."

The officer's gaze drifted from me to the interrogation room. Fear played out on his face.

I flicked a glance toward the little room. "That's what they talkin bout in there. My pictures. Mayor B's gon have to come clean too. Don't think he won't give you up. Besides, the chief already knows you the one who 'found' that ring."

Ted swallowed.

"'It's the nature of truth to struggle to the light.'"

He ignored my quote. "I *did* find it."

I shook my head. "Tell em the truth quick as you can. Maybe the chief will go easier on you if you go to him first."

Defiance hardened Ted's expression.

"Ain't you worried bout what Mayor B's sayin right now? He could be layin all the blame on you. I was in there, I heard how the man can lie."

Which is why I couldn't believe Ted had anything to do with the actual murders. Mayor B surely gave him some story bout needin those pictures—and havin the ring.

The officer snorted. "They won't listen to him."

"Chief and him go back a long way. Longer than the chief does with you."

Ted's shoulders fell. He closed his eyes like he wanted to block out the world.

"Come on, young man. Get yourself in that room right now. Tell Chief Cotter the truth with Mayor B sittin there. That's what I done— confronted him before he got the chance to spin tales bout me."

The officer slumped forward, pressin two fingers between his eyes.

"You want the chief to think you were involved in Erika's murder?"

"He'd never think that."

"Then why would you help somebody plant evidence?"

Ted's head wagged back and forth. "It was just a convenience."

"A convenience?"

"To help convict the right man." His voice was so low I could barely hear him. "Mayor B saw that ring drop from Mike's shirt pocket at the factory. What harm would it do to 'find' the ring in Mike's house so we could use it as direct evidence? The mayor just wanted the murders solved. Like everyone else does."

I didn't know which was crazier, the mayor's story or that Ted believed it. Except—who was I to judge? Before I opened that drawer in Austin Bradmeyer's office, I'd never believed he could murder anybody either. Jus went to show how respected he was in Amaryllis.

Lord, help this town.

"Why'd he want the pictures in the first place?"

"To remind him of the murders, he said. So he could help catch the guy. After Erika's death he wanted hers too."

I had to chew on that for a minute. "When did he want the other five pictures?"

"I don't know. Maybe ten days ago."

"How come you didn't just tell him no?"

Ted pulled in a ragged breath. "I needed the money."

Mayor B *paid* him? This was an even bigger mess than I thought.

Ted fell against the back a his chair, starin at the ceilin.

"Ted, go tell the chief. Now. You know you cain't hide from this."

He moaned. "I'll lose my job."

He jus might lose more than his job, fiddlin with an investigation, takin bribes. Ted knew that.

"Go. The longer you wait, the worse it'll be."

"I can't."

"I ain't leavin till you do."

His mouth twisted. "*Go*, Cherrie Mae. I'll handle it."

"You want me to knock on the doh myself?"

"No!"

I stood back from his desk, arms folded. "You got ten seconds. Then I'm knockin."

He sneered. "You're nothin but a meddler."

"Mm-hmm. Ten."

"Cherrie Mae—"

"Nine."

"I *can't* do it!"

"Eight. Get up, Ted."

He swiped his hand across his face.

"Seven."

Slapped his hands on his desk.

"Six."

He pushed back his chair, then hung there.

"Five. Four. Three."

"Stop, I'm going!" He shoved to his feet.

"Two, one."

Ted was breathin in little snorts. Stiff-headed, he walked round the desk toward the room. My heart turned over as I watched him.

At the last second he looked back at me. I nodded.

Ted knocked. Opened the doh. "Chief, I need to talk to you."

Chapter 33

Deena

TULLY LAY ON HER COUCH, LITTLE LEFT IN HER BELLY TO throw up. I'd gone back to pacin. Every second hung like an eternity. We weren't even talkin anymore. Nothin new to say, and we both had too much to think about.

We waited for Cherrie Mae.

How her news could change our lives. Would it, *could* it somehow prove to me my brother wasn't a killer? Could it show Tully her husband was innocent?

At 4:30 I heard a car outside the house. I trotted over to peek through the blinds. "It's her!"

"Oh, thank heaven." Tully slapped a hand against her heart.

"Stay there, I'll let her in." I bounded to the front door and opened it wide. Cherrie Mae slipped inside, lookin a little gray around the gills. Her purse hung from her arm. I shoved the door closed and locked it. "What happened, what happened?"

She wiped her forehead. "I need some water."

"Where's your computer?"

"They kept it."

"I told you."

"I'll get it back." Cherrie Mae started toward the kitchen.

"I'll get the water, Tully, you stay on the couch." My words knocked into each other, tryin to get out of my mouth. I wanted to rage and listen and squeeze the answers out of Cherrie Mae all at once.

I splashed water into a glass and herded Cherrie Mae into Tully's livin room. "Just tell us everything, we're goin crazy waitin. Here, take the chair, I can't sit anyway."

She sank down and took a few gulps of water. Set her purse on the floor.

"Did you hear the police found something here?" Tully's eyes glistened. "Something really important."

"Oh, did I. Erika Hollinger's ring."

We both gaped at Cherrie Mae. *"What?"*

"That was *my* reaction."

Tully paled. "But that's . . ."

Cherrie Mae waved her hand. "Jus hold on. Let me tell you everthing."

And she began her story.

Tully lay still, her eyes fixed on Cherrie Mae and her hands balled up at the base of her neck. I stood with my back to the window, arms wrapped around my chest. Cherrie Mae took us through showin the chief her pictures. Seein him pull Erika's ring out of an evidence bag. The arrival of Mayor B himself. His lies. And Ted Arnoldson.

"Ted?" I couldn't help it. His name just blurted out. I sure knew how to pick men. I'd once had a crush on Ted, then married John Cotter.

Tully looked sick. "So there's Ted and Mayor B in the station, talking to each other like nothing ever happened."

"Oh, they was both cool, all right." Cherrie Mae shook her head.

"But Ted didn't stay cool when I got the truth out a him. One thing, though—I underestimated the chief. He didn't *want* to listen, but he did. I don't think he's gon try to cover anything up. And now he got the mayor to deal with." She pushed up her bottom lip. "Man cain't be happy."

Maybe. I still wasn't so sure the chief—or John—could be trusted. "So what now?"

"I don't know." Cherrie Mae set her water glass on the floor. "Question is—what did Mayor B tell the chief bout why he wanted the ring planted? Same story he gave Ted? Which wouldn't implicate him for Erika's murder, just messin with the evidence."

I thought about that. "And Stevie wouldn't be off the hook yet."

"Or Mike," Tully said.

Cherrie Mae scratched her head. "Well, anyway, I still think Mayor B killed those women. Man livin his life in front a everbody, nobody guessin the truth. Includin his own wife. Thought he could get away with it because a who he is. And he just might a planned from the beginnin to frame somebody else soon as he could."

Yeah, but . . . "Then why didn't he plant Erika's ring in Stevie's trailer?"

Cherrie Mae shrugged. "Maybe he didn't hear bout that search soon enough. All the officers was with Chief Cotter at the town meetin. Mayor B probly didn't have time to get to Ted. But when he heard bout Mike . . ."

"What did he care—Stevie or Mike?" Tully's words came out thick. "Long as he could pin it on somebody else. And Ted Arnoldson, at my front door to take me down to the station. Did he know *then* what he planned to do? How could he look me in the eye? How could he face Mike? How could he face his own *conscience*?"

"And to do it for money." I made a face. "How much money's he gonna have when he loses his job?"

Tully shifted on the couch, her face creasin. Cherrie Mae studied her. "You feelin all right, baby?"

She put a hand at her lower spine. "It's just my back."

We fell silent. My mind whipped questions around like a hurricane blowin straw. I sank down on the end of the couch, beyond Tully's feet, and looked to Cherrie Mae. "We still don't know what the blood means—on Stevie or Mike. Are they completely innocent? Or did Mayor B involve them somehow?"

"The *police* cain't know till they get the DNA results. That'll take another week or two."

"So . . . meanwhile they stay in jail?"

"I guess they'll have to. Even if Mayor B confessed to all the murders and swore up and down he did em alone, the chief would still have to keep em both till he sees the DNA. Confessions can lie, but DNA don't."

"Mike won't be coming home, then." Tully closed her eyes. In relief? Sadness? Guilt? Maybe all three.

"No, baby. Leastways not yet. You go stay with your parents. You'll have some time to sort things out."

Tully played with the neckline of her T-shirt.

I ran a hand over my face. "What do we do now? I have to do *somethin.*"

Cherrie Mae checked her watch. "Been an hour since I left the station. I'll call, see what's goin on." She dug in her purse and pulled out her cell phone. "I got their number in here somewhere." She pushed a few buttons.

I sprang up and hurried over to her. "Hold the phone out so I can hear." It started ringin.

"Police station, Officer Dedmon." The words sounded clipped.

"Hi, Chris, this is Cherrie Mae. Didn't know you was workin today."

"Just got called in. What can I do for you, Cherrie Mae?"

"I need to know what's happened to Mayor B and Officer Ted."

"I'm not sure I can give out that information."

"Now, Chris, you listen to me. I been a good citizen and tol what I seen. Now I'm worried for my own safety. I need to know if Mayor B's gon be a free man tonight."

A long sigh blew over the phone. "Why is this happenin, Cherrie Mae? What is goin *on* with this town?"

Cherrie Mae and I exchanged a look. This wasn't Officer Chris Dedmon talkin. This was Chris, deacon of the Baptist Church where she attended. Where she was a mentor to everybody.

"Hard to say." Her voice gentled. "I just know we got to keep prayin."

I mouthed to Tully, *Can you hear?* She nodded.

"So, Chris, tell me what's happened."

"They've both been arrested."

Tully widened her eyes.

"What for?"

"A list of things havin to do with tamperin with evidence and bribes."

"Not murder."

"Murder? No."

"Nothin about that at all?"

"They're not killers, Cherrie Mae. They just got stupid, is all. Thought plantin evidence would help us get the bad guys quicker."

Bad guys meanin Stevie and Mike. The thought blew through me.

"Then why'd Mayor B have those pictures in his house?"

"He said to be reminded of the murders, cause he wanted em solved. Ted shouldn't a given him those pictures, but the mayor havin em wasn't a crime."

Cherrie Mae tapped a finger against her chair. "Will Mayor B stay in jail long?"

"Probably not. I imagine his wife'll bail him out."

Cherrie Mae's jaw moved back and forth. "And Ted?"

"He'll get out too if he can make bail. He won't have a job to come back to, though."

"I'm real sorry bout Ted, Chris. Makes me sad."

"Me too." He sighed again. "Me too."

They ended the call. Cherrie Mae stared at the phone in her hand. "Mayor B's gon come after me. I just know it."

"You think he'll get out of jail today?" I hated how scared she sounded.

She drew a quick breath. "I don't know. I shoulda found that out."

"Well, just in case—stay with me tonight. You can sleep in my guest room."

"Ain't you got to get up and go to work tomorrow?"

I snorted. "If I have any clients left. Doesn't matter. Stay anyway."

She nodded grimly. "Yup. Believe I better do that."

I edged back to the couch and sat down. None of us spoke. Dread swirled in the air.

"'Silence is of different kinds, and breathes different meanins.'" Cherrie Mae said the words half to herself, starin at the floor. She looked beat down and tired.

I blinked at her. "That some quote?"

"Charlotte Bronte."

Tully's gaze wandered from Cherrie Mae to me, but her mind seemed far away. "Tully." I patted her foot. "This'll . . . work out. Somehow."

She teared up. "Mike was there, Deena. In Erika's house. I know he was. I know that blood is hers."

Her pain vibrated into me. "I could say the same thing about Stevie."

In my head I heard Carl Cypress relatin my brother's words the night of Erika's death: *The last thing I heard Stevie say was that he had to clean up 'the big mess.'*

Cherrie Mae hefted back in her chair. "Way I see it, solvin this thing rests on us. First, we have the most to lose. Second, Mayor B's still lyin. No way he's gon admit to killin. And by now he got hisself a lawyer so the *po*lice cain't question him no more."

Tully swallowed hard. "How are *we* supposed to solve it? I can hardly think straight."

"I know. But we will, with the good Lord's help. We got to. Fact is, we know things. With all our pooled information—the proof is there. Somewhere. We just ain't seen it yet."

Made me tired—and all the more scared—just thinkin about it.

"Problem is," Cherrie Mae sighed. "With proof Stevie *and* Mike *and* Mayor B all killed them women—we're plain back to square one."

Chapter 34

Tully

BY THE TIME CHERRIE MAE LEFT, MY MIND HAD NUMBED out. I couldn't even cry anymore. She said she was headed home to eat supper and pray. She'd be over at Deena's before it got dark. "And, Tully." She patted my cheek. "You talk to your parents now, hear? Tell em all that's been goin on with you. And don't be afraid to tell em bout Deena and me. I know we have a pact, but this ain't the time for you to be keepin things from your parents. If you don't give em the whole story, they cain't understand your confusion right now. 'Sides, they surely heard bout Ted's and Mayor B's arrests by now anyway. Might as well tell em what you know." She looked to Deena. "You agree?"

"Yeah."

Deena stayed to help me pack a suitcase. Only as I gathered my things did I think to check the drawer where I'd hidden the second swab. The police had taken it. Of course.

What was Ted Arnoldson thinking right now, sitting in the county jail? Was he sorry for what he'd done? And how far away were they keeping him from Mike?

Two men accused of the same crime *plus* a police officer *and* the town mayor—all in that jail. Bay Springs must think Amaryllis had gone crazy.

Deena lugged the suitcases out to the car for me. Said she didn't want me lifting anything. I dragged behind her, remembering the day Mike and I had moved into the house. How happy I'd been to live with my new husband, on my own. No longer having to listen to my mother.

Now here I was, running back to her.

"You've got your list with all the phone numbers now," Deena said after she shut the trunk of my car. "Call us tonight if you need anything."

I needed a lot of things. Like a new life. "Okay."

She put her hands on my shoulders. "Listen." She brushed the hair off my neck. "No matter what happens with Mike—even if he's completely cleared of any charges—don't be afraid to admit you made a mistake. I know where you're at, more than you think. I was married once too, remember? And he turned out not to be so nice a guy. Was runnin around on me. I got to where I couldn't take it anymore and finally divorced him. You can hold your high after goin on from your mistakes. But you can't hold your head high if you live with those mistakes and never do anything about them."

I looked down and nodded.

She stepped away. "Okay. See you soon. Keep your cell phone on. We'll call you if anything comes up."

A few minutes later I pulled up to the curb of my parents' one-story brick house.

My mother hustled out, my father behind her. She was still dressed in her tailored gray business suit, her heels clacking on the sidewalk.

She opened the car door and practically pulled me out. "Oh, I'm so relieved you're here! Come on, we'll get your things inside for you."

"Hi, honey." My father gave me a hug, then stood back to study me. His brown eyes were warm, concern playing around his mouth. "You doing all right?"

Another nod.

He looked at me as if he knew better. "Go on inside and sit down. I'll get your stuff."

Mom had chicken and rice baking. The smell filled the house as I walked in the front door. Can't explain why, exactly—but at that moment something inside me gave way. The house of my childhood wasn't cold and judgmental. It was warm and comforting. I could stay here. I *would* figure out what to do.

"Pop up the footrest on the couch till dinner." Mom nudged me toward the living room. "We've got another half hour or so."

My father toted my suitcase down the hall and into my old room. He returned and settled on the love seat next to Mom. "Tully." His voice was gentle. "Please tell us what's been going on. We love you. We want to help."

The tears came back. They blurred my eyes and choked my throat. Mom fetched me a tissue. I wrung it one way, then another, until I got myself under control.

"Mike's been hitting me."

"I *knew it*," my mother hissed under her breath.

I flicked a glance at Dad. His jaw had turned to rock. "Go on."

"Not a lot. Just . . . sometimes. I kept thinking he'd stop, but . . . And now with a baby coming . . ."

"I will strangle him with my bare hands." Mom's teeth clenched.

"Hush, Judy." My father frowned at her. He looked back to me. "How is he mixed up in Erika's murder?"

For the first time I thought of all the Amaryllis gossip they must have heard since Mike's arrest, the probing questions. Waiting to hear my story couldn't have been easy on them.

I started at the beginning, with Erika's phone call. Mike coming home late the night of her murder, and how he'd choked me the next morning. My mother cried out at that, and my father visibly shook. We all had to get ourselves together before I could continue. I told them about my meeting with the police. And finally, everything about Deena and Cherrie Mae.

I wiped my forehead. I felt so tired. "You can't tell anyone the things I know from Cherrie Mae or Deena. The three of us are still trying to figure it all out."

My father focused on the carpet, as if searching for what to say first. "This is all so crazy. Mayor B bribing an officer?"

"And maybe killing those women." My mother shook her head.

"But that's just speculation."

"Then why did he have the ring?"

I listened to my parents' reactions—and a stunning thought hit me. My head snapped back. Mayor B had the ring because he *was* in Erika's house that night. But if Mike killed Erika, why was the mayor in her house at all?

Mike's words echoed in my head. *"If Erika was pregnant—which I wouldn't doubt, knowin her . . ."*

Was she having an affair with Mayor B too?

My gaze drifted out the window. Erika and Austin Bradmeyer . . .

Then, *slam*—a second thought. A picture of what could've happened that night.

Breath left me. If that picture was right, Mike didn't do it. He *didn't kill Erika*. The hope of that idea left me weak.

"Tully?"

Vaguely, I heard Mom call my name.

"Tully."

"Huh?" I blinked at her.

"What are you thinking?" Her voice was tight, so frightened for me.

"N-nothing." I pressed my hands to my temples. "It's just . . . my brain is so full."

The oven timer dinged. Supper was ready. Somehow I made it through the meal, barely tasting it.

"Tully," Mom said at the table, "you know you're welcome here. Come back. We'll help you with the baby. And I know that look in your eyes. You're beating yourself up because you think you've failed. Well, you *haven't*. You've got lots of years to live yet. It's not too late to start over."

I looked at my plate, forcing back tears. "I know. Thanks."

After supper I fled to my room, saying I had to rest. I lay on my old bed, hoping, praying. Trying to think through it all. My brain dredged up facts from the notes with Deena and Cherrie Mae. I imagined Mike going to Erika's last Tuesday night. The pictures in Mayor B's drawer. Remembered what Stevie said when Deena visited him in jail. I heard Erika sneering how she was coming into "big money." Thought of Ted Arnoldson taking Mayor B's bribe . . .

Wait.

I sat up. Stared at the floor.

Ten days.

DNA.

My mind whirled.

I shoved to my feet, then swayed. Where was my purse with my cell phone? I had to call Deena and Cherrie Mae. Had to see them.

I knew what happened. I *knew*.

Chapter 35

Cherrie Mae

HALFWAY BETWEEN HOME AND DEENA'S HOUSE, I HEARD A voice shout in my head: *"Go see Eva Bradmeyer."* I was bout to cross Main, checkin for traffic on the old brick street. My small packed suitcase sat in the backseat.

"What?" I said aloud. My fingers tightened on the steerin wheel.

"Go see Eva B."

"You crazy?"

The command echoed inside me. Guilt came not far behind. I knew that Voice. Had heard it plenty in my lifetime. Now here I was, tellin God he was crazy.

"I'm sorry, Lord." I crossed Main, tryin to fool myself into thinkin sayin sorry was enough. Cause absolutely last thing I wanted to do right now was face Eva B.

But the words beat on: *"Go see her."*

Shakin my head, I made the next right turn toward the Bradmeyer house.

I pulled up to the curb, thinkin why would Eva B even answer the doh? Her husband sat in jail thanks to me. Plus she'd been sick. She was either in bed with the covers over her head, or she was talkin to a lawyer.

My finger pushed the bell. My arm was shakin.

I fixed my gaze on the little peephole in the doh. Surely if she got as far as seein my face, she wouldn't let me in.

Footsteps sounded.

A long moment passed. Then the doh flung back. Eva B stood there in her robe, hair messy, cheeks and eyes red. Unsteady on her feet.

"I can't *believe* you're on my porch." Her voice came out high and strangled. "Get out, Cherrie Mae! Get your feet off my property. And don't you *ever* come back!"

She started to close the doh. Something made me stick my foot in the threshold. "Wait."

The heavy thing hit my foot. Eva B shoved harder. "Get *out* of the way!"

"No, Mrs. B. I got to talk to you." I *did*? And jus what was I gon say?

"No. Go away!" She tried to close it again, but she was too weak. I held up my hand against the doh and nudged it back.

"I don't *want* to talk to you, Cherrie Mae! I don't want to see you ever again!" Tears spilled from her eyes.

My heart liked to turn over. This woman and I'd been friends for years. Now I'd betrayed her.

I forced myself into the house. "You need to hear what I got to say."

She sobbed. "I don't want to hear it. I don't!" Mrs. B swayed. I caught her elbow. She wrenched away and swayed some more. "Get *out*."

But her words sounded as feeble as a newborn lamb. Poor thing looked like she had no strength left in her. I took her by the arm. "Come on. You need to sit down."

"No. Go." But she stumbled toward the den as I led her, too spent to fight. "I don't . . . I can't . . ."

We reached the couch. I nudged her down. She half fell into it.

Eva B's body folded in half. Her hands covered her face as she cried. "*Why*, Cherrie Mae. Why did you do it?"

I perched alongside her, searchin for what to say. Hatred and need rolled off her in waves. If I hadn't been the one who told on her husband, she'd be weepin on my shoulder. Now she just wanted to hit me.

"I'm gon get you a tissue." Up I rose and hurried into the kitchen. Came back with a whole box a Kleenex. I pressed one into her hands.

"You lied to me." Her shoulders drew in. She rocked forward and back, forward and back. "Putting me in bed, acting so worried about me. All the while you just wanted to get me out of the way so you could take pictures. Isn't that right?"

How to deny it? "Yes'm. Fraid I did."

"But Austin didn't *do* anything."

She rocked and rocked, tryin to comfort herself. Tryin to tell herself her husband was completely innocent—when deep inside she knew it wasn't so. Only then, when I saw the conflict inside her, did I know why I'd come.

"Mrs. B, listen to me—"

"I don't *want* to listen to you."

But she wasn't tellin me to go. Truth was, she needed to know what *I* knew. She needed to understand.

I waited till she calmed a little. In time her rockin and cryin slowed. She still wouldn't look at me. "You snooped in my husband's private things."

"Yes."

"Why?"

I thought back to that day. "Can't tell you why, exactly. It's like my hand just went to that drawer. And first thing I saw was the file a those pictures. And the ring."

"You didn't have to look in the file." Her voice was thick. Accusin. "You had to *search* to find that ring."

Oh, this was hard. "Yes."

"*Why?*"

This time the question sounded different. Like it wasn't meant for me, but for her husband.

"Austin's given his *life* for this town." Eva B's hands balled the tissue. "Employs people. Donates to charity. He wouldn't do this. He couldn't *do* this."

"I know. I cain't quite believe it either."

"But you told the *police*. You went running right to them!"

I stared at the coffee table. Had I vacuumed round there just this mornin? Seemed like days ago. Suddenly my mind went back to the McAllisters' home last year, cleanin the hardwood floh under Ed and Verna's bed. I saw myself pull out that lacy little thong. Remembered the look on Verna's face . . .

Oh, have mercy. *Have mercy.* I should a known.

Took some time to pull myself together. I tried to find the right words. "Eva, I had to. Do you realize that ring was planted in another man's house? Mike Phillips could go to jail for the rest a his life. I couldn't let that happen."

Truth was, I hadn't known bout that ring bein planted till I got to the *po*lice. But I wasn't bout to get into that now.

Eva B. sat quiet for a long time. Her hands shredded the wet tissue in her lap. I pressed a new one into her fingers.

"Maybe Mike really did it," she finally said. "Maybe he *is* the killer, and Austin just wanted to catch him. You ever think of that?"

I sighed. She was still not wantin to see. Well, how could she? Hadn't been that long since she heard. She was still in shock.

"Listen, Eva. I got to warn you bout the *police*. They gon be comin to talk to you."

She gave a bitter laugh. "*You* warn *me?*"

"It's bout the ring. See, I know Erika had that ring on her finger when I visited her, up to ten o'clock the night she died. The autopsy says she could a died as soon as eleven o'clock. Somehow in that time that ring got from her house to this one."

Mrs. B took to shreddin the second tissue.

"They gon want to know was your husband home with you that night."

"He's already *said* he was home."

"I know. But *you* know he wasn't."

Her fingers stilled. She turned her head to glare at me, eyes puffy. "Yes. He. Was."

"Eva. You cain't lie to the *police*. They gon find out. And when they do, you'll be in big trouble. Look at Ted Arnoldson, sittin in jail right now."

"He interfered in an investigation!" Too late, she realized what she'd said. She jerked away to face her lap again. The fingers went back to tearin.

"And that's what they'll say bout you if you don't tell 'em the truth."

"He was here. All night."

"No, he wasn't."

"He *was*."

"Maybe most a the night. But he left for awhile, didn't he? I'd guess it was earlier rather than later. Maybe he told you he needed to check on somethin real quick at the factory. You didn't think nothin bout it."

She shook her head hard.

"Then when he made that statement bout bein home all night, you just kept quiet. Maybe you figured it was a slip on his part. And it didn't matter anyway."

Eva B's hands went into a frenzy. Then all a sudden they dropped into her lap. She slumped even more. Her gaze went to the coffee table and hung there.

A minute drug out.

"How did you know?" She barely whispered it.

I pictured that thong under Ed McAllister's bed. Now I could see why Erika was so much younger than the other women. Mayor B hadn't meant for her to be one a his victims at all, had he? He was simply havin an affair with her—until she did somethin to provoke him. Had he gone over to her house that night *knowin* he would kill her?

Maybe so. He left no fingerprints. Unless he wiped em away. Or had he made Mike and Stevie clean up that house?

I lifted a shoulder. "Like I said, I know Erika had that ring on when I was with her."

Mrs. B. nodded. She clasped her hands, one thumb rubbin over the other. "I just thought it was like he told me—he needed to do something at the factory before it closed. I still think that. How he got hold of Erika's ring, I don't know. I'll find out when he gets home."

So she still wasn't lettin herself see the whole picture. *"It is no use, lyin to one's self."*

"How soon will he come home?"

Her jaw firmed. "Soon as I can bail him out."

I started to press her for exactly when that would be but couldn't do it. From the look on her face she wouldn't answer anyway.

I'd made the right choice, sleepin at Deena's tonight.

I patted Mrs. B's arm. "Anything I can do for you before I go?"

"Haven't you done enough?"

Well. Suppose I deserved that.

I rose. "You have my cell phone number. Call me if you need me."

"I *won't* need you, Cherrie Mae."

I lowered my chin in a nod. How bad I felt leavin this woman. All alone here and sick. Not knowin what to think bout her husband. And here I stood before her—a friend. But with my mind set on bringin her husband to justice for the murders he done.

Some friend.

Eva Bradmeyer didn't bother to get up as I headed for the doh. She waited till I was bout to step into the hall, then called out. "By the way, Cherrie Mae!"

I turned back, my heart heavy. "Yes, ma'am?"

"You're fired."

2010 Pulitzer Prize

Feature Writing
The Jackson Bugle

Gone to Ground

What happens to a small, quiet Southern town when evil invades in the form of a serial killer?

By: Trent Williams
October 29, 2010

(Excerpt)

The meager facts about the murders cast paltry light on the kind of person who would commit such crimes. The victims, although all women, were not sexually assaulted. They were killed with knives from their own kitchens and with one quick stab to the carotid artery. No torture here, certainly no overkill as tends to be found in crimes of passion. These murders, in fact, display a decided lack of passion, as if the killer merely wanted to get the job done as quickly as possible. Chief Cotter at one time speculated that the precision of the wounds may point to a perpetrator with some medical background. However, the chief's later pursuit of a suspect (who didn't pan out) proved he had shoved that theory aside—at least for the time being.

If one follows the legends of Hollywood and TV talking heads, the culprit will prove to be a white male, a loner, and psychotic. But according to the FBI, these general "profiles" of serial killers are myths. History has shown they are not all social misfits. Some of the most well known modern-day serial killers in our nation have been husbands, even fathers, employed and sometimes active in church. Neither are multiple murderers always white males. Sex is not their sole motivation—as clearly shown in the Closet Killings. And, contrary to belief, some serial killers can and do cease their activity for myriad reasons.

Theodore Stets's wish that "five is enough" is not beyond the realm of possibility. The town can only hope.

Chapter 36

Deena

AS I WAITED FOR CHERRIE MAE TO ARRIVE, OF ALL PEOPLE who should I see on my street? Letty June. Walkin down the sidewalk in front of my house like she owned the place. If I hadn't been starin out my front window, I'd have missed her. Now I glowered at her like she was a wild animal skulkin by. What on earth was she doin here? Her house was a good four blocks away.

She'd come to gloat, that's what.

I scanned the parked cars on the street. They were always lined up out there at night, but I didn't see any I couldn't recognize. Had she walked here?

Before I knew it, I'd flung open my front door and stalked out to the porch. "What're you doin in front of my house, Letty June?"

She spun toward me like she'd been stung. Her mouse brown hair stuck out in its outdated curls, and her fat face scowled. "I'm out for a walk. It's a free country."

"You come to gawk at my brother's trailer, is that it? Wanted to see if the cops left anything standin?"

"What are you *talking* about, Deena Ruckland?"

I stomped down my two front steps. "I know you went runnin straight to the cops the other day. Just had to tell them how mad Stevie was at work the night Erika was killed."

"He *was* mad. And they needed to know."

"What difference does it make?"

"What difference? He was mad enough to kill somebody."

"How would you know what it takes to kill somebody?"

She stuck her hands on her bulgy hips. "You can't be blamin me for what your brother did."

"And you're just so sure he did it, aren't you." My legs shook. This woman represented every person in town who wanted to pin the murders on my brother. Who wouldn't *think* to give him any benefit of the doubt. "You've never given Stevie any slack since the day you first set eyes on him. That make you feel strong, Letty June, pickin on the weak? That make you feel *big*?"

Cuss words rolled out of her mouth. "I don't have to take this from you." She turned around and started hoofin it down the street.

"You're gonna look as stupid as you are when Stevie's acquitted!"

Letty June whirled back. "He deserves everything he gets, Deena! You know what he did to me Tuesday night? Hmm? He took a five-gallon drum of slippery cleanin fluid and dumped it near the women's bathroom, then said he would tell Mayor B *I* did it. *Then* he dumped more in my personal locker."

My head snapped back. Stevie did *that*?

Well, so what? What had she done to provoke *him*? Besides, what did that have to do with provin he's a murderer?

Vaguely, I registered the sound of a car comin down the road. "I'm sure you deserved it, Letty June."

She flung her head about. "*He* deserves to be sittin in jail. For the rest of his life."

I raged two steps toward her. "Get away from my house right now before I run you down."

Letty June smirked. "Oh, great. *Two* killers in one family." She pivoted and strutted away.

Fury shot through me. I started after her.

Cherrie Mae pulled up to the one empty spot at the curb. Letty June passed by the car as the engine turned off.

I slowed, still seein red.

Cherrie Mae got out of her car, head turnin from Letty June's hunched back to me. Letty June glanced around, then kept on walkin, nose in the air.

Cherrie Mae shut the car door. "Deena?"

I had to look stompin mad. My cheeks were hot, my breath comin like a mad bull's. I shot Letty June one last witherin look. She wasn't worth it. Wouldn't she love to go runnin to the police if I so much as touched her.

"It's nothin." My teeth still clenched. "*She's* nothin."

Cherrie Mae threw Letty June another look. "Let's get you in the house." She pulled a suitcase and her purse from the backseat of her car and hurried toward me. "And let's lock the doh."

A faint smile pinched my lips.

Inside—with the door locked—I showed Cherrie Mae to my guest bedroom, where she put down her things. "Thank you." She looked around at the light blue walls and quilt on the bed. "It's pretty."

Settled in the den, each of us with a Coke, she told me about seein Eva Bradmeyer. Now *that* was a story. Cherrie Mae had way more courage than I did. Made my fight with Letty June seem petty. I told her about it anyway.

Cherrie Mae made a sound in her throat. "Stevie's not the only person who's had run-ins with that girl. Why she got to be so mean?"

"In league with the devil, for sure."

My thoughts went spinnin back to my visit with Stevie at the jail.

"It was her fault."

"Who?"

"She was mean to me."

I blinked at Cherrie Mae. "What if he was talkin about Letty June?"

"Huh?"

"Stevie." I focused on my lap, strugglin to reason through it. "In jail he kept sayin 'she was mean to me, she made me do it.' What if he wasn't talkin about Erika at all? He could've been thinkin about what happened at the factory."

Cherrie Mae worked her mouth. "Maybe. I'd a had to hear y'all's conversation."

I played it again in my head. "It fits. I mean, you had to be there. It's the way he said it. Stevie wouldn't answer my questions directly. He'd go off in a tangent."

"But why would he even be thinkin bout Letty June when he's sittin in jail for murderin Erika?"

I shook my head. "My brother's mind . . . But really, it *does* fit. When the cops questioned him, they probably told him people at work had seen how mad he was. And how did he explain that? He'd have known it was Letty June who told them. He'd have blamed his bein in jail on *her.*"

Cherrie Mae scratched her jaw. I could see her mind workin.

My body heated up. This was important. Felt right . . .

"You know what"—I looked around for my cell phone—"I should call Carl Cypress. He's the one who told me Letty June talked to the police. I got so mad, I cut him off. Now I wonder what he was . . ."

Where was my phone? I pushed off the couch and knocked around, searchin for it. Found it in the kitchen.

I had to look up Carl's number. He answered after a long three rings.

"Carl! It's Deena." I walked back into the den, hovered near the TV. Cherrie Mae perched on the couch, her gaze fixed on me. "Remember when we were talkin about Letty June outside the police station? You told me she talked to the cops about Stevie. Then you started to say, 'But, Deena—' I cut you off. What were you goin to say?"

"Oh, yeah. I was gonna tell you the rest of the story. I think he was mad *because* of Letty June. I think she played a trick on him, just before their shift was over. She spilled a bunch of cleaner, knowing he'd have to stay late and mop up the mess."

"*She* did that?"

"I think so. Because as she left work I saw her cackling to herself, like she'd just pulled off some major prank. And then I saw the mess at the women's bathroom—the one near the side door that all the workers use? I felt sorry for Stevie, but I couldn't help him clean it. I was backed up in my paperwork and had to stay late to finish. When I finally came out of my office, Stevie was still there on his hands and knees, stripped down to his underwear. Soppin up the cleaner with rolls of paper towels and cussin. He was startled when he saw me. I think he thought he was the only one there."

"In his *underwear?*"

Cherrie Mae bugged her eyes.

"Well, it was either that or get his uniform full of soap. Plus, like I said, he thought he was alone."

His uniform . . . Mike Phillips went home that night with the wrong uniform . . .

"You didn't see anyone else around when you left, Carl?"

"No."

"What time did you leave?"

"Around 11:30."

Eleven-thirty. And Stevie was still workin. He showed up at my house at midnight. *After* he'd stopped to wash in Turtle Creek.

He had no time to kill Erika. My brother had *no time* to kill her.

"Thing is, Deena, after I heard Stevie had been arrested, and about the blood on his clothes, I didn't know what to think. He wasn't seen running home until 12:30."

No, it wasn't that late!

"That could have given him time to get to Erika's house. I thought . . . if he had, was I to blame? I'd seen him mad. Hadn't said anything to him, tried to calm him down. What if he'd left work still raging, and then took it out on Erika?"

"Why would he do that? Why not go after Letty June?"

Carl hesitated. "Because she's married. All the victims were single."

"Oh, come on, Carl."

"I didn't know! I really didn't. And I just—"

"Did you tell the cops all this?"

"I had to. They interviewed me yesterday, since I manage that second shift."

"And you told them everything, about Letty June and the spilled cleaner?"

"Yes."

The witness who'd said Stevie ran home at 12:30. I had to find out who that was.

"Stevie got her back though," Carl said.

"Huh? How?"

"He spilled cleaner in Letty June's locker. Made quite a mess. She didn't find it until the next day."

So she hadn't been lyin about that part.

My brother's voice rose in my head: *"I fixed her."* Could that have meant what he did to Letty June? Not Erika?

"Thank you, Carl. Thanks very much."

"Hope I've helped." Compassion rang in his voice.

"You have. More than you know."

I ended the call and stared at Cherrie Mae. She leaned forward. "What he say?"

Half in a daze, I walked to the couch and sank into it. Told her everything.

Her eyebrows rose high. "Stevie took off his uniform. There was a time when he was *separated* from his uniform."

"Yeah, but you know what? I even *asked* Stevie if he'd taken off his uniform for any reason. He told me no."

"He musta been lyin."

"Guess so. Then we've got Mike comin home with a different uniform than he left with. Could he have somehow gotten Stevie's?"

Cherrie Mae frowned. "But the timin . . . We know Mike left work at 11:00, or at least before 11:30 cause Carl said nobody else was around then."

"But he didn't get home until 11:50. Which definitely gives him time to be at Erika's . . ."

We looked at each other.

"You think he *did* help Mayor B somehow?" I whispered.

Cherrie Mae looked chilled to the bone. "He must have. Stevie couldn't a done it. But Mike had the time."

My mind bounced all over the place. I didn't know which trail to follow first. "I have to find out who the witness was who claimed Stevie came home at 12:30. That person is *wrong*. If the time was put sooner, and added to Carl's statements, the cops would have to see Stevie didn't have time to commit the murder."

"What if you told the *po*lice Stevie came to your house at midnight?"

"I would if I thought they'd listen. But they won't. They'll just say 'why didn't you tell us before, Deena?' They'll accuse me of tryin to give my brother an alibi."

"Maybe Trent knows who the witness is."

Of course! "I'll bet he does. With his network through this town?"

"Would he tell you?"

Would he? I thought of his invitation to go to New York. How he'd said he loves me. *Shouldn't* he tell me, if he cared that much?

But then—he'd demand to know why it was so important. And if I told him Stevie had shown up here at midnight, Trent would be ticked that I'd kept that from him.

I gazed at the cell phone, still in my hand. "I don't know."

"It's worth a try."

"Yeah."

I raised my phone to dial Trent—and it rang. I peered at the ID, then clicked on the line. "Tully?"

"Yeah, it's me." She sounded breathless. "I figured it out. Mike didn't do it."

"What? How?"

"Is Cherrie Mae there?"

"Yeah."

"Good. I'm coming over."

I locked eyes with Cherrie Mae. *"Mike didn't do it."* Tully sounded so excited. But the things we'd just discovered would knock her for a loop all over again. Now Stevie looked totally innocent. While her husband looked more guilty than ever.

Chapter 37

Tully

I SAT DOWN TO POUR OUT MY THOUGHTS TO DEENA AND Cherrie Mae, wanting to shout. Do somersaults and cartwheels. But all I could do was perch on Deena's couch. She was on the other end, Cherrie Mae in the rocking chair. They looked . . . what? Almost worried. Maybe because the exhaustion and excitement made me so shaky.

Mom hadn't wanted me to leave, of course. "I don't want you driving back here alone when it's dark. And it's practically dark now."

"Don't worry. I'll call you. We'll figure it out." I slammed out the door.

On Maxwell Street I'd had to park my car halfway down the block. I was panting by the time I reached Deena's house.

"Okay, here it is." I drummed my fingers on the couch. " I should have seen it before."

Cherrie Mae and Deena exchanged a look.

"Remember Erika telling me she was 'coming into some big money'? Then—think about it—Ted Arnoldson gets in trouble for accepting a bribe from Mayor B."

Deena screwed up her face. "Mayor B was bribin Erika too?"

"No. But what if Erika was blackmailing him?"

Cherrie Mae leaned forward. "Why?"

"Because she was pregnant with his baby."

Deena drew in a breath.

"And of course he didn't want anyone to know. Erika must have threatened to tell the world if he didn't give her a bunch of money. Meanwhile she told Mike the baby was *his*. She wanted him to go away with her—on Mayor B's dime. She had the perfect setup."

Cherrie Mae shook her head. "Mm-mm. 'Let the winged Fancy roam; pleasure never is at home.'"

Deena and I looked at her. She shrugged. "I think you right bout Erika and Mayor B." She looked to Deena. "Didn't get a chance to get to that part when I was tellin you bout seein Eva."

My mouth opened. "You saw Mrs. B?"

"Yup. I told her the *po*lice gon come knockin on her door to see if Mayor B was at home all last Tuesday night. And that she shouldn't lie. Cause I know he wasn't. She finally admitted it. He left home soon before the factory closed."

"You're kidding!" There was the final piece of my puzzle. "And he went to Erika's, right? He planned to kill her because she was blackmailing him. Kill her the same way he'd killed his other victims."

"*That's* why he done it." Cherrie Mae pressed a hand to her cheek. "I never thought bout blackmail. I just thought maybe they argued, and things got out a hand."

"No, I think he planned it. I started thinking about what Ted told you, Cherrie Mae—how Mayor B asked for the pictures of the first five victims ten days ago. That was just a few days before Erika was killed. That's no coincidence. But why would he take such a chance, bribing a police officer?"

Deena's mouth hung open. "Yeah, why?"

"Because he was so paranoid about killing her exactly like he did the others. He wanted to study those pictures, make sure he didn't slip up. It was enough that Erika was so much younger. And that the autopsy would show she was pregnant. This could *not* look like a murder outside the Closet Killings. Because no one had ever suspected Mayor B of *them*. To help even more, he took Erika's ring so he could plant it somewhere. But then once Erika was dead, he got even more paranoid. He wanted *her* picture to check his work. When you discovered the file in his drawer, Cherrie Mae, he must have come unglued. He had to get rid of that ring as fast as he could. The search of our house was perfect."

Deena folded her arms. "So where does Mike fit in? How'd he get Erika's blood on him?"

"He went to her house after work to confront her. And she was already dead."

Deena blinked.

"Can't you see how he'd totally panic? How he'd be afraid to tell anyone? If the cops knew he'd been at Erika's house, he'd be their first suspect."

Cherrie Mae frowned. "He'd a had to go inside, though."

I nodded. "He was too mad to just leave when she didn't answer the door. Maybe he went around back. Found that door unlocked. He went in, saw her in the closet. Maybe he touched her to see if she was dead. That's when he got the blood on his hands. Then he took off."

"It works." Cherrie Mae shot Deena a meaningful look. "That part works."

"Yeah," Deena said. "Maybe it does."

Maybe? "What do you mean '*that* part'?"

Silent messages flowed between Deena and Cherrie Mae. Did they look skeptical or relieved? I sat up straighter. "What's going on?"

Deena focused on Cherrie Mae. "So . . . Mike left the factory about the time Stevie was discoverin the mess Letty June made."

Cherrie Mae nodded. "And at some point after that, when he thinks everbody's gone, Stevie takes off his uniform."

I twisted my head toward her. "What are you talking about?"

She hesitated. "Tully, we learned somethin just a little while ago."

"What?"

Deena went over what Carl Cypress had said. I couldn't take it in—too much to process. "But how does that fit with everything I just told you?"

We fell silent.

Deena gasped. "I think I know!" She closed her eyes for a moment. "Okay, so Mike goes to Erika's. He finds her in the closet. Maybe he really tries to help her. Like pulls her out to see if she's still alive. Her blood ends up all down the front of his uniform. When he sees she's dead, he runs out. Maybe he thinks clear enough to wipe away any prints before he leaves. But he can't go home covered in blood. And like you say, he's panicked. The scene at Erika's doesn't take long, and when he left the factory Stevie was just about to clean up the mess. Mikes drives back to the factory, thinkin maybe Stevie will still be there and the door will be unlocked. He plans to sneak into the men's locker room and get a clean uniform. But maybe he can't find one. Then he notices Stevie's uniform on the floor. Mike snatches it up and puts it on, then runs out, still panicked, leavin his bloodied clothes behind. Stevie comes back to put his uniform on—and it's all bloody."

Deena's gaze bounced from me to Cherrie Mae. "*That's* why, every time I asked Stevie about the blood on his uniform, he kept sayin, 'I can't tell you that.' He didn't mean he *refused* to tell me. He meant he truly didn't know."

I stared at her, trying to picture it all. It seemed right, but it couldn't be. "Mike wouldn't have set Stevie up like that."

Deena held up a palm. "He didn't mean to set Stevie up. He just did what he had to do."

"But later, when Stevie was arrested *because* of that uniform. You're saying Mike knew—and said nothing."

The words hung in the air. Deena looked away.

My vision blurred. I'd found a way to make my husband totally innocent. A man I could believe in. Now he was tainted again.

Cherrie Mae shifted in her chair. "Tully, I understand why you sad bout that. But it all fits. You have any other explanation why Stevie got that blood on his uniform?"

I gazed at my lap, blinking back tears. Who was I kidding? Mike wasn't totally innocent, as much as I wanted him to be. He wasn't a killer. But he *did* have an affair with Erika. He did think that baby was his. And he'd lied to me. Hit me. Choked me.

My throat cinched. I pressed two fingers against my mouth. "No."

I could feel them exchanging more looks. Like they were so much older and wiser than me. Like I should just admit the truth about my rotten husband.

Cherrie Mae leaned over and laid her hand on my arm. Her skin felt paper-thin and dry. She patted me, and I could feel the love in her touch.

"Look," Deena said. "I don't like what Mike did to my brother. But I can . . . understand it." Her words didn't come easily. "Mike was backed against the wall. If he admitted that uniform was his, *he'd* be in jail."

Which he was now anyway, thanks to someone setting *him* up. How ironic. Cherrie Mae probably had a quote for that.

An awkward minute ticked by. Deena turned to look out the window. Darkness had fallen. She got up and closed her curtains.

Cherrie Mae plopped her hands on the arms of the rocking chair. "Well, guess where that leaves us. Back with nobody but Mayor B."

Deena crossed her arms. "Yeah."

A picture of Mike in jail flashed in my mind. And Stevie—he'd been there three days now. Both men innocent. Both surely scared to death. "We have to prove all this."

Deena wagged her head. "We need to go see Chief Cotter together tomorrow mornin. Lay out everything. But first we have to figure out how we *can* prove it."

"Chief Cotter already has some of the evidence," I said. "Like Carl's statement about Stevie staying late to clean. And he knows Erika's ring was planted. We just have to help him put it all together."

"Yeah." Deena sighed. "But our dear mayor's denyin doin anything *but* plantin that ring."

"Wait just a minute." Satisfaction coated Cherrie Mae's voice. "I know how the chief can break Mayor B."

Just like that, I knew what was coming. We both said the answer at the same time.

"DNA."

Deena stared at us.

I could just picture taking the man down. I couldn't *wait*. "Mayor B knows Erika's baby was his. They found that baby in her autopsy. They may even be running its DNA already. He knows if they take a sample of his DNA, it'll be a match. That'll prove the affair and give him motive to kill Erika. Add that to the fact he planted her ring in our house . . ."

"Mm-hmm. And who knows what they gon find if they check his bank accounts." Cherrie Mae rocked in her chair. "If he done give her some cash already, they'll see the withdrawals."

Deena cupped her jaw. "What if the baby wasn't his? I mean, we know Erika was a liar. What if the baby really was Mike's, and she was lyin to Mayor B? The DNA won't lead to him."

I sat too stunned to speak.

Cherrie Mae waved her hands in the air. "Wait now. Mayor B don't know bout Mike bein with Erika too. If he did, he wouldn't a let her blackmail him. We just got to make sure the *police* don't *let* him know."

Deena tilted her head. "You don't think Chief Cotter told him when he was in that interrogation room?"

"No time. It was just minutes I was there talkin to Ted Arnoldson. Then Ted goes in and confesses. Besides, that wasn't their focus. Chief Cotter had Mayor B in a lie—that's what mattered."

Cherrie Mae was right. "Mayor B will cave, because as far as he knows, the DNA *will* lead to him. Even if it doesn't, by that time they'll have his confession."

"Okay," Deena said. "But Mike will have to admit to goin to Erika's that night. And they'll want to know why. Which means he'll have to tell them about the affair."

"That's all right." Cherrie Mae nodded. "The *police* will keep these men separate. That's the way it works. They'll talk to one, not lettin the other know what's goin on. In the end the whole truth can come out."

"Mike *will* admit it." For once I wouldn't let my husband intimidate me. I'd confront him with everything I'd figured out. Tell him if he didn't tell the cops, I would. "Maybe he's already thinking of coming clean. Better to admit finding someone dead than being blamed for the murder."

My cell phone rang from inside my purse. Deena's head snapped around, looking for it. "Sit, Tully, I'll get it." She brought my purse over.

Mom was on the line. "Tully, it's 10:00. Time for us to go to bed. And it's dark. I don't want to be worried about you coming home."

"I know. I . . ." There was no way I could leave now. The three of us still had so much to talk about. I pulled the phone away from my mouth. "Deena, can I just sleep here? I'll stay on the couch."

"No, no, take the guest room," Cherrie Mae said. "I'll take the couch."

Deena nodded. "Do it."

I told my mother I was staying. She wasn't happy. "Don't worry, I'm not alone. I'm with Deena and Cherrie Mae." And Mike was still in jail.

"We'll take good care of her!" Cherrie Mae called.

"All right." Clearly Mom still didn't like it. "Call me tomorrow when you're back at the house."

"I will."

I ended the call. Leaned over and set my phone on the coffee table.

Cherrie Mae checked her watch. "It is gettin late. Had no idea." She pushed to her feet. "I need paper, Deena. We got to sit here if it takes all night and go through everthing we need to tell the chief tomorrow."

Deena went to fetch the paper. She returned with a small notebook and a pen, and gave them to Cherrie Mae. "One thing I'd still like to know." She sat back down on the couch. "Who told Chief Cotter they saw Stevie runnin home last Tuesday at 12:30? That person's a half-hour off. And that's an important half hour."

Cherrie Mae folded back the cover of the notebook. "You were gon call Trent. Think he's up this late?"

"Oh, he's up." Deena reached for her phone. Then hesitated. She regarded the cell, worry crisscrossing her face. Her eyes flicked from me to Cherrie Mae. With a sigh she raised up the phone to punch in the number. Then abruptly set it down.

She spread her hands. "Before I call Trent . . . there's somethin I need to tell you."

Chapter 38

Deena

"WHAT IS IT?" TULLY'S VOICE SOUNDED DEFENSIVE. SHE WAS clingin like crazy to her husband's innocence and didn't want anything to rock it.

I waved a hand. "It's just . . . when I talk to Trent, he might say things . . ."

"Things you haven't told us?"

"No, no. Not at all. It's about Trent and me. Thing is—he's asked me to marry him."

Shocked silence.

"He's goin off to New York in about a month to write for the *New York Times*. They came after him because of his Pulitzer Prize. He wants me to go with him."

Tully gaped at me. "Are you going?"

"I don't know. I mean, I don't really . . . My first thought was no. But with all this goin on there's been times when I thought runnin away from Amaryllis wouldn't be so bad."

Cherrie Mae screwed up her face. "Do you love him?"

"No."

"Then why you even thinkin bout this?"

"Because . . ." I tossed my head. "Look, I don't want to get into this right now. I just want you to know if he says somethin about New York—that's what he's talkin about."

Tully's eyes narrowed. "If he loves you so much, doesn't he talk to you? Hasn't he already told you everything he knows about this case? So what haven't you told us?"

"No, he hasn't."

"Why not?"

"Because . . . he's always the reporter first. He won't tell me about anyone who talks to him confidentially. But he sure does try to pull out of me what I know."

Tully flicked her eyes. "I can see why you'd want to marry him."

I glared at her. As if *she* should talk.

"Well, good." Cherrie Mae smacked the notebook against her knees. "Thanks for tellin us, Deena. We'll keep your secret. Now go on, call him."

Cherrie Mae—ever the peacemaker. I gave Tully another long look. She blinked away.

I dialed the number. "I *will* get this out of him." I hit the volume on the phone a few times so they could hear and held it a short distance from my ear.

The line started to ring.

"Deena." I heard Trent's voice. He didn't sound happy. "I was just going to call you."

"Oh?"

"Yeah. Remember the last time we talked? I asked if you knew Tully Phillips well enough to convince her to talk to me? You told me no. Then guess what I hear tonight when I'm calling all around, trying to pull information from whoever I can. I hear your car was out in front of Tully's house. This afternoon. You were seen going into her house with her. And guess what time, Deena. Before I called you. When I was asking you for help with her, you were *standing right in her house*."

"Well, I—"

"Why'd you lie to me? Is that any way to treat me?"

Was *this* any way to treat the woman he loves? "I just . . . I couldn't tell you. She didn't want me to. She was so scared, she wouldn't talk to you."

"Just where does your loyalty sit? With her or me?"

Wait just a minute. "Where does *yours* sit? How come with me you're always the reporter first?"

"Because that's what I do."

Well, wasn't he just special. I glanced at Cherrie Mae. She shook her head.

Trent sighed. "Will you help me get to Tully tomorrow?"

He wanted to play games? Fine, I'd play too. "Absolutely." I shot Tully a dark look.

"Okay. Thanks. What did she tell you?"

"Nothin, really. She was just upset. The cops searched her house when she wasn't even home. She didn't know if they'd found anything. All she knew was that suddenly Mike was arrested."

"But you think you can get her to talk to me?"

"I'll try. Really. I'll remind her you're the one with the Pulitzer. She's better off in your hands than in some other reporter's."

Silence, as if Trent was trying to figure whether I was sincere or sarcastic.

"So, Deena. Is there anything *else* you know about this case that I should know?"

"I might. But you have to tell me one thing first."

"What's that?"

"Who told Chief Cotter they saw Stevie runnin home last Tuesday night at 12:30?"

"Why's it matter?"

"Because I just want to know."

"You must have a reason."

"Trent, *who* was it?"

"I don't know."

I made a face. "I think you do."

"*Why* is it so important?"

"Because the time's not right!"

Oh, great. Now I'd done it.

"Really. How do you know it's not right?"

I swallowed. "Stevie said it wasn't."

"You told me Stevie wouldn't tell you anything."

"Well I . . . he eventually did."

"When was this? I know you haven't been able to see him since your jail visit."

I squeezed my eyes shut. When I opened them Tully was surveying me, her mouth set to one side. I'd jumped on *her* for trying to excuse the behavior of her husband. Now look what I was takin.

No. I *wasn't* her. And I would not take this. "Trent, tell me."

"No."

"Do you know the answer?"

"Maybe."

My tone chilled. "Fine. Then I won't help you, either."

A long moment passed.

"You know a lot more than you're telling me, don't you, Deena?" Trent sounded so disappointed.

"Maybe I do."

Cherrie Mae fluttered her hands at me and mouthed *get off the phone.* My cheeks heated up. "Fact is, I've figured out a lot of things, Trent."

"Deena," Cherrie Mae whispered. *"No."*

"Like what?"

I clenched the phone.

"Deena!"

"What, Trent?"

"What have you figured out? You could really help me here."

Too bad. He'd get no reply out of me.

Tully circled the air with her finger—*get off!*

More silence. I could hear my heart beat.

"Okay, Deena." Trent sighed. "I get it. I see why you really called."

Okay, so I'd tried to use him. Hadn't he done the same with me? "Good for you."

I punched off the line and threw the cell on the couch. Stabbed Tully and Cherrie Mae with a look of defiance. "Well. Didn't that go smooth as butter."

Chapter 39

Cherrie Mae

WE HAD TO SOLDIER ON WITHOUT THE ANSWER WE wanted from Trent. Wasn't really Deena's fault. The man had a burr under his saddle before he even answered the phone.

First thing I had to do after that call was calm Deena and Tully down. They was all worked up, tired and overexcited, and takin everthing plain too personal.

Deena turned off her phone with a flourish, declarin she wasn't talkin to nobody else tonight. She tossed the cell on the coffee table, next to Tully's. Stuck both hands on her hips. "And guess what else. I am *not* marryin that man."

Tully opened her mouth, as if to agree it was a good choice. I gave her a look. Her lips closed.

We took a bathroom break, poured glasses a water, and settled down to work. I could feel tiredness creepin over me. On the couch, Tully was stiflin a yawn. Hard for a pregnant woman not to get her sleep.

"All right." I picked up the pen. "So we all agree first thing tomorrow mornin we head down to see Chief Cotter."

Tully nodded.

"I'll cancel my clients." Deena gave a grim chuckle. "Won't the Cotter men be so happy to see us. Especially me."

"Deena, you're gonna have to tell them Stevie came to your house Tuesday night—in bloody clothes." Tully spoke the words like Deena just might back out a the deal.

"I know. I will."

I buffed my forehead. "All right. So. Let's write down everthing we gon say, and how we gon help Chief Cotter prove it."

We worked, and the time passed. We went over every detail. What Mike did, everthing Stevie did, what Erika told Tully bout comin into big money, what Eva B. told me bout her husband leavin their house Tuesday night. And on and on. Midnight came, and we kept talkin. We made a detailed timeline a what we thought happened Tuesday night. Mayor B killin Erika, then goin home. To our best guess, he'd taken her ring, thinkin he'd plant it somewhere later. Mike leavin work and findin Erika dead. Goin back to the factory and puttin on Stevie's uniform. Stevie findin his uniform filled with blood, and reluctantly puttin it on.

"Wait." Tully frowned. "Why wouldn't Stevie just get a clean one?"

Deena and I looked at each other. She shrugged. "Maybe there weren't any."

Tully looked half convinced. We talked bout it some more, then moved on.

We wrote down quotes about the cleanin fluid mess from Carl Cypress and Letty June. I filled page after page in the notebook till my hands cramped. Finally sometime after 1:00 we was done.

And everthing—all the evidence we knew about—fit. The chief would have to listen. Cause half this stuff he'd already heard. We was just givin him the rest a the puzzle pieces.

I laid my head back against the chair, truly tired. I could barely think. "Anything else?"

Tully heaved a deep sigh. Her eyelids was droopin. "If there is, I can't think of it now."

Deena yawned. "Me either."

Our work was done. May the good Lord be with us tomorrow. And tomorrow would come all too soon.

"Time comes stealin on by night and day."

Deena checked that all the doors was locked. She pulled a sheet, blanket and pillow out a her hall closet and fixed em up for me on the couch. "Just to let you know." She pulled open the drawer on her side table. "I got a gun in here."

I peered down at the thing. "It loaded?"

"You bet. Got a second one by my bed, just like it."

Hmm. I preferred my billy club. But I'd left it at home.

At least I wasn't *at* home. Was Mayor B still in jail? If his wife got him out, would he be headin to my house tonight?

I fetched my suitcase and purse from the guestroom and waved Tully inside. "Go on to bed now. You need it."

Tully turned off her cell phone, lying on the coffee table. She and Deena both disappeared into their rooms. I shut down my own phone and put it back in my purse. Settled down on the couch. It was dark in the room, the pulled curtains keepin out any street light. My body plain sank into the cushions.

In minutes I was asleep . . .

Next thing I knew I'd jerked awake.

What was that noise?

My body went rigid. I lifted my head off the pillow, listenin. It was comin from the back doh. In the kitchen.

I heard the doh open. Close with a whisper.

Somebody stood on the other side a the wall. Breathin.

Chapter 40

Tully

I WOKE UP LYING ON MY RIGHT SIDE, A PILLOW BETWEEN my knees. How long had I been asleep? My body felt like lead, but my brain wouldn't turn off. Scenes of Mike in jail flashed. His hard, bare cot. The fear that must be eating at him. Once Chief Cotter starting looking into our evidence tomorrow, how long would the investigation take? A few days? Weeks? Months? My baby would be born by then. And in the end, would I be with Mike?

No way. I couldn't trust him anymore.

Then I'd divorce him and go back to live with my parents? I couldn't imagine that either. And I sure couldn't afford to keep our house by myself.

Would Chief Cotter even listen to us in the first place? Why should he? He was set. He had his suspects.

The whole town would look at me as a killer's wife. My son would be shut out. No friends, no invitations to birthday parties. We'd have to move away.

Tears flooded my eyes. I didn't want to go on. I just wanted to sleep for a very, very long time.

I shifted my legs, trying to get comfortable. It felt strange sleeping in my clothes. I longed for my own bed, in my own house. But Mike wasn't there. And even if he came back—the man I married had ceased to exist.

My bladder felt full. I shifted again, not wanting to get up. The bathroom was across the hall, and I didn't want to wake Deena or Cherrie Mae.

Sure, Tully, like you can fight this. In the last two months I'd had to get up at least once a night.

With a sigh I tossed back the covers and pushed out of bed.

Chapter 41

Cherrie Mae

 FOOTSTEPS SKULKED ACROSS DEENA'S KITCHEN, SO QUIET I barely heard em.

Mayor B.

Had he been to my house first and found it empty? On the way back, maybe he noticed my car sittin out front. *Why* hadn't we thought to put my car in the garage instead a Deena's?

The footsteps stopped.

What was he doin? I stopped breathin, listenin with all my might.

They started up again, headed toward the hall. Any minute now I'd see him.

Down the hall near the guest bathroom Deena had turned on a night-light. It glowed a pale green.

A dark form shuffled into view.

I lay on the couch, froze solid, my heart bangin out my chest. Would he see me in the dark?

He reached the dohway to the livin room. Stopped. His head turned my direction.

My pulse stopped. For the longest minute a my life I felt his eyes starin at me. Tryin to see through the blackness.

His breath whooshed. In, out. In, out.

Abruptly he swiveled left, goin down the hall. His right hand stuck out a ways from his body. Holdin somethin silhouetted against that green light.

Knife.

His fingers clenched the handle. I could see the short blade. A parin knife. Just like the ones he used on the others.

My nerves sizzled.

Tully. She was in the first bedroom. He'd think *I* was in there.

He'd stab her once. Hard and fast. Be out a here before I could turn on one a the cell phones nearby, make a call.

Deena's gun. I had to get it.

Holdin my breath, I eased off the couch to the carpet. The smallest sound, and he'd turn around. I'd never shot a gun before. If Mayor B came runnin at me, how fast could I get in that drawer, snatch out the gun and shoot?

Not fast enough.

I peered down the hall. He was walkin slower now. Maybe checkin out the two closed doors.

On hands and knees, I edged toward the end table. An eternity passed before I reached it. My fingers fumbled to grab hold a the knob.

His footsteps stopped.

I jerked my head round. What was he doin? How far was he from Tully's bedroom doh? Two feet? Five?

I felt the knob brush my fingers. I gripped it hard and slowly pulled.

Wood slipped past wood—too loud. I stopped. Had he heard?

I peered down the hall. His head was up, cocked.

He turned toward me.

Beyond him, Tully's bedroom doh opened. All air sucked out a my chest.

I yanked open the drawer, scrabbled for the gun. Grabbed it out. "Tully, get *back!*"

Somebody screamed. Footsteps pounded.

I jumped up and around the coffee table, both hands on the gun. Where was he? Where was Tully?

My feet ran toward the hall. At the far end Deena's door flew open.

Mayor B was almost at me.

In that final split second everything slowed. Where was Tully? Had he stabbed her? What if I shot at him and hit Deena?

I jerked the gun down toward his knee and pulled the trigger.

"Aahh!" He stumbled, then crashed forward. I jumped out the way.

The hall flooded with light.

Chapter 42

Deena

MY HAND FELL AWAY FROM THE HALL SWITCH, EYES BLINKIN in the sudden light. I gripped my gun. A man writhed and groaned on the floor near the livin room, his back to me. He held one of his legs.

Cherrie Mae spun toward me, a gun in her hand. "Where's Tully, where's Tully?"

No. I ran toward the open guestroom door. "Tully?" Flicked on the light. She lay sprawled on the floor, pantin. Petrified. "You okay?"

She managed a nod.

I ran back out.

Cherrie Mae stood over Mayor B, gun pointed at his head. Utter fear and despair pinched her face. A parin knife lay in the middle of the hall.

The man gasped his agony.

I started to shake. "What happened, what happened?"

"Cherrie Mae!" Tully's fear echoed.

I swiveled back to her, craziness flyin out of my mouth. "She's okay, Cherrie Mae's okay. She shot him, he's down, she's up. Can you get to your feet? Let me help you."

I jumped into the room and threw the gun on her bed. Pulled her up. She was tremblin as much as I was.

"Get out here!" Cherrie Mae's voice. "I cain't take the gun off him. You got to call 911!"

I rushed out of the guestroom. Only then did it start to sink in. The Closet Killer had come *here*. For Cherrie Mae? But we'd caught him. We *caught* Mayor B.

I started down the hall. For the first time I looked—really looked at the back of the man's head. His body.

A jolt ran through me. I stopped.

Tully's footsteps sounded behind me. She gasped.

Cherrie Mae looked at me, her eyes over-bright. The gun in her hand shook wildly.

My limbs locked up. "No." I leaned against the wall.

Cherrie Mae swayed. Panic clutched her face. "Deena. You got to call 911."

I couldn't move.

The Closet Killer rose to his knees. He turned his head toward me and shot a look of pure venom. The poison spilled through me, jarred my thoughts upside down. He hadn't come here for Cherrie Mae.

He'd come here for *me*.

"Stop!" Cherrie Mae screamed. Her chest rose and fell with each breath. "Get back down. Or I swear I'll shoot you in the other leg."

He stayed where he was.

"I *mean* it!"

Sweat shone on his forehead. He collapsed on the floor.

I felt Tully leave the space behind me. She ran into the guestroom, then back out. "Where's my phone, I can't find my phone!"

Where was my gun?

"Phones are on the coffee table." Cherrie Mae's teeth clenched. "Deena, help me. Get over here and call!"

Somethin inside me broke. I let out a yell, ran to the Closet Killer and started kickin. I got his ankle, his back, the leg where he was shot.

"Aahh!" He tried to push away from me, his hands grabbin for my foot. I kicked him in the head.

"Deena!" Cherrie Mae screeched.

"How could you do it?" I got him in the shoulder. "How *could* you? You lied to me, you lied to everybody. Actin like you're servin the town. You're nothin but a liar." I kicked him in his ribs. "Liar." In the hip. *"Liar!"*

"Deena, call 911!"

He lay still, groanin. I fell back.

"Deena, come on!"

Panic rose as reason returned. Was I insane? What if he'd caught my foot? Pulled me down?

Where was the knife? I searched the floor, saw it between me and Tully, out of his reach. She kicked it farther away.

"Deena, *come call!*"

My mind exploded. "I can't! How do I get around him, what if he grabs me, he fooled me and everybody, and I didn't know, I didn't *know*. I don't want him touchin me ever again, I want him out of my house now, out, out—"

"To fair request, silent performance maketh best return!" Cherrie Mae shot me a crazed look.

"Huh?"

"Hush up and *do it*!"

My head cleared. "Okay. Okay."

Slidin against the wall, I edged around the murderer. Past Cherrie Mae and into the livin room. Snatched up my phone from the table. I turned it on, punched the numbers.

"9-1-1, what is your emergency?"

"It's—" My tongue stuck. "Deena. Ruckland. We caught the Closet Killer. We shot him, he's alive."

"The Closet Killer?"

"Yes. It's Trent. Trent Williams."

I dropped the phone and wailed.

IT COULDN'T HAVE TAKEN MORE THAN A FEW MINUTES for the police to arrive. But it felt like forever. Cherrie Mae kept the gun on Trent. I fetched the other one off the guestroom bed, inched around the horrible man, and hurried over to Deena.

She took the weapon from me, then stood beside Cherrie Mae and aimed it at Trent. "Try movin now, Mr. Pulitzer-Prize-Winner. Mr. Marry-Me-and-Go-to-New-York."

Her body trembled. My shaking had stopped, now that I knew the cops were coming. Cherrie Mae seemed to be holding up okay. I stood between her and the front door.

Trent lay moaning, breathing in gasps. Between being shot and Deena's kicks, he was hurt bad.

Cherrie Mae looked dazed. Trent didn't fit with anything we'd believed. "Why, Trent?"

No answer.

"*Why?*"

His hands clenched. "I didn't kill Erika."

She stared at him. "Caught in this house with a knife in your hand—and you *denyin* you didn't kill those women?"

Deena snorted. "Yeah, like you weren't here to kill *me*." Her voice bent.

"I didn't kill Erika." Trent's face was pale, his expression cold as ice. Not the slightest hint of conscience.

And then I knew. The final pieces of our puzzle rearranged. We'd spent so long thinking all six murders were committed by the same person . . .

Sirens sounded in the distance.

Deena's head cocked. She'd heard them too. "Fine, Trent. Who killed her, then?"

He said nothing.

I swallowed. "Mayor B."

Cherrie Mae's eyes flicked to me.

I rubbed my face. So tired. And I needed to sit down. "That's where I went wrong. It's why Mayor B wanted the pictures of the other women ten days ago. He'd never *seen* those victims. He needed to kill Erika because of the blackmailing, and he had to make sure it looked like the other murders."

"But . . ." Cherrie Mae shook her head.

The sirens screamed near. Cars screeched to a halt.

I hurried to open the door.

THURSDAY
April 28, 2011

The Jackson Bugle

Pulitzer Prize Winner Confesses to Crimes He Wrote About

Amaryllis. Trent Williams, 32, crime reporter for *The Jackson Bugle,* allegedly confessed Wednesday to the murders of five women, whose deaths provided the backdrop for his 2010 Pulitzer prize-winning feature, "Gone to Ground."

According to Chief Adam Cotter, in a statement to police, Williams, who grew up in Amaryllis, spoke "in a toneless voice with no remorse" about his childhood dream of one day owning a successful business—a dream that never came true. In his late twenties, after seven years of covering crime for *The Jackson Bugle*, Williams said, he saw his life as "headed nowhere" and "wanted something big to boost" himself to fame.

His alleged murders of five women, all living alone in the town of Amaryllis, occurred over a period of three years. His method was always the same—a single stab with a paring knife to the throat, severing the carotid artery. The victims were all found in their bedroom closets, causing the serial murders to be known as the Closet Killings. "I was done after five," Williams said. "I had my prize. I was on the way to New York."

In chilling hindsight, Amaryllis police point to Williams's feature about the murders, in which he wrote about the vagaries of sociopathic serial killers and the difficulty in detecting such criminals due to their ability to present a normal persona.

"I just never would have guessed," said Theodore Stets, owner of Amaryllis Drugstore. "Trent was our hero for writing about the murders. Plus he wasn't living here anymore. Most people thought it was someone still in town."

Williams was meticulous in planning his crimes. He allegedly told police that before a murder he would rent a car—from a different company each time—and make the one hour and thirty minute drive to Amaryllis at night. For every crime he disguised himself with a different toupee, which he later discarded. The murders themselves, he said, took only minutes. Wearing gloves, he would break into the house's back door, grab a paring knife from the kitchen, and stab the victim as she slept. When asked why he took the time to move the bodies to a closet, he reportedly shrugged, "It provided an added interesting twist."

Williams said he chose his victims because they were "widowed or divorced with no children at home, so who would miss them?"

At his arraignment Wednesday Williams was held without bail, awaiting "a certain" indictment from the grand jury in July, said Cotter. Williams could face the death penalty.

In a further development that has stunned the town, the recent sixth murder in Amaryllis of Erika Hollinger, made to look like one of the Closet Killings, has now been deemed to be the work of a different suspect. Amaryllis's mayor of fifteen years, Austin Bradmeyer, has allegedly confessed to that crime.

"We've gathered a lot of evidence to sort these crimes out," said Cotter, who added he's barely slept in days. "And we're continuing to do so. In light of the growing evidence against Austin Bradmeyer, and the statements of two other men who had formerly been arrested for Hollinger's murder, the mayor did break down and tell us what happened."

Cotter continued, "I have to mention the help of three women in town—Cherrie Mae Devine, Deena Ruckland, and Tully Phillips—who not only caught Williams when he broke into Deena's home, but also helped gather information on Erika's death."

On Monday night the three women were staying at Ruckland's house when . . .

SUNDAY
<u>JULY 31, 2011</u>

Epilogue

Cherrie Mae

WHOO, IT WAS HOT OUTSIDE. MY AIR CONDITIONER WAS runnin at top speed and still barely keepin up. I had the front curtains closed against the afternoon sun. Deena and Tully sat on my couch. Me, the ol woman, was now the one with her feet up. Just five weeks after deliverin her healthy baby boy, Tully was already back down to her original size.

The resiliency a the young.

In a small carrier in the corner, baby Michael slept. Cute little thing, round-faced and dark-haired. Looked like his mama.

The first few days after Trent's arrest now seemed like one big jumble. Chief Cotter had a mess to sort out. First he had to interview me and Deena and Tully. We told him everthing we'd figured out. Then Mike had to come clean bout goin to Erika's house—which he did. He even admitted he'd had the presence a mind to search for the picture a the two a them, which he ripped up and flushed down her toilet. He wiped his prints away before he ran out a the house.

Gettin Stevie to tell the truth was harder. That boy was just too scared. But eventually he managed.

The chief never would tell us who the witness was that claimed to see Stevie runnin home at 12:30. But "the person," as the chief put it, "did realize the time could be wrong when faced with all the other evidence."

Hm. Just as well we didn't know who it was.

In the past three months, after all the chaos and news stories died down, Tully, Deena, and I hadn't seen much a each other. Tully was busy havin a baby and tryin to figure out her life. Deena had her hands full settlin her brother back down and tryin to make sense a Trent Williams. Actually, the whole town was still tryin to make sense a that. Everbody was hurt. Everbody. Trent had been our hometown-boy-made-good. Our pride.

Mayor B had hurt us deep too.

Both men had been indicted by the grand jury. Word was, both planned to plead guilty to their crimes, hopin to avoid the worst possible sentences. Trent wanted to avoid the death penalty. Mayor B hoped to get out a jail someday. Even if he did, he wouldn't be goin back to a wife. Mrs. B was divorcin him, I'd heard, both cause a the murder and Erika's baby, which DNA proved was his. Eva B still wasn't talkin to me. Maybe some day we'd be friends again.

As for me these past months? I was just plain wore out.

So Tully, Deena, and I was happy to see each other today. But it was more than just to catch up. We had a major issue to discuss. In honor a our meetin I'd made some cream-cheese muffins and lemonade. Best to have somethin in your stomach when you bout to make an important decision.

We ate and gabbed, then got down to business.

I wiped my mouth. "So who's first? You, Deena?"

"Sure." She spread her arms like she had a big pronouncement. "I vote yes to the book."

Goodness. That was quick.

"I've thought a lot about it." Deena leaned forward. "Cherrie Mae, you want to retire. Tully, even with your parents' help, you need all the money you can get as a single mother. Me, I'd just like to buy a few things. Like a new car. Updated equipment for the salon. Also I want to help Stevie some. His trailer could use fixin up."

Stevie was back workin at the factory. With Mayor B gone, Carl Cypress was runnin the place.

Tully nodded. "How is your brother?"

"He's okay. Sure doesn't trust the police. But he's calmin down. I think he's beginnin to see it's better to tell the truth." Deena looked at her lap. "Course I could say the same thing about myself. I mean if we'd done that right off, maybe he wouldn't have ended up in jail at all."

Maybe. Who's to say? But I couldn't disagree about the truth part.

Deena sighed. "Also, I think writin this book will help me. I mean, this thing with Trent just totally threw me. I still don't get it. To think you know somebody—and then realize they're not at all who you thought . . ."

Bad enough that Deena's childhood friend killed five women. But then to try to kill *her*. Not until after Trent's arrest did his final words on the phone to Deena become clear. *"I get it. I see why you really called."* He'd thought she'd figured out he was the Closet Killer. And he couldn't let her bring him down.

"Yes, baby." I gave her a sad smile. "I think it will help you sort it out."

Tully and I waited for her to say more.

Deena lifted a shoulder. "That's it."

So. One vote yes. We sat on that for a minute.

I turned to Tully. "How bout you?"

She hesitated. "I say yes too."

I couldn't keep the surprise off my face. She'd always been the quiet one. Private. I didn't think she'd want the world peerin into her life durin the worst days she ever had. "Look like you ain't as sure as Deena."

"I wasn't at first. Then I talked to my parents about it. They're happy to have me and little Michael living with them. But they know eventually I'll want to get out on my own. I need to save for that. But how to save when I'm not working?"

Deena nodded. "You're sure, then, about the divorce? You're not goin back to Mike?"

"I . . . no." Tully plucked at her shirt. "He betrayed me with Erika, even if she did lie about the baby being his. Maybe she didn't know *who* the father was. Anyway, now I can see Mike's not the kind of husband I want, or the kind of father little Michael needs. He'll always be my son's father, but not to live with. If he'd acted like he'd changed . . . But he still blames me for his arrest. When he got home from jail I was in our house, hoping . . . I don't know what I was hoping. And he hit me. Left bruises on my face. That was it. That's the day I packed up and moved to my parents' house for good. *And* marched myself down to the police station to report him. Didn't take him long to violate the restraining order. That's why he's in jail now until his trial. My lawyer thinks he'll get more time when his case comes up."

"Maybe so," Deena said, "if you testify against him."

"Oh, I plan to. I'm going to tell them *everything.*"

Poor Tully. That would be hard on her. "Baby, I'm sorry. I'll be prayin for you ever day."

"Thanks, I need it." She lowered her eyes. "I've been goin to church again and . . . well, that's important. I don't think I can do this without God."

Amen to that.

"Anyway." Tully took a breath. "At first I couldn't bear to think of writing all this stuff for the world to read. That just . . . I couldn't do it. But by now our story's *already* everywhere. Think of all the national reporters who've been to our town."

Yup, finally they'd come. *After* the murders was over. They all wanted to talk to us bout how we'd helped solve the crimes.

"Now other people are wanting to write our whole story," Tully said. "If *we* write it, we control it. Yes, we have to show the good and the bad. But at least we'll know it's the truth."

Well. Two yeses. We'd all agreed a decision to go ahead had to be unanimous. Seventy-five thousand dollars apiece was a lot a money. But we were a team. We'd do this together or not at all.

Deena looked to me. "What do *you* say?"

There was so very much to say. I'd done a lot a ruminatin over the last three months. "Do you know all my customers—except the Bradmeyers—was nice enough to keep me on cleanin their houses? That's a gift from God." I rubbed my lip. "Tell you what, though—I ain't snoopin no more. Done learned my lesson on that."

Tully smiled.

"But I'm so tired a workin, and this opportunity would allow me to quit. I'd love to stay home and read my literature. Volunteer more at church. Plus I agree with Tully. Half the story's out there anyway but all switched round, with guesses in between. I want to set it straight."

Deena's eyebrows shot up. "So we have three yeses?"

"Yes, ma'am, we do." I raised my lemonade. "Here's to our book!"

"That's amazing!" Tully raised her glass to clink against Deena's, then mine.

"And the future of Amaryllis." Deena raised her glass higher.

We clinked again.

I took a victorious drink. Set down my glass. "You know the other reason we need to write this book? Cause Amaryllis deserves a second chance. Trent wrote bout the town when it was still in the grip a despair. Our book'll show how we got through it, with God's help."

"Yeah." Deena firmed her lips. "That's right."

I plunked my hands on the arms a the chair. "So. We gon write it like the editor wants? Each a us doin our own part, plus Trent's article in pieces?"

Tully nodded. "I think so. You think *The Jackson Bugle* will let us use the feature?"

I gave her a sly look. "I already checked."

Deena chuckled. "So you want to call the editor tomorrow mornin and tell her our decision, Cherrie Mae?"

"You bet I will. First thing."

As the baby slept, we talked bout our futures. How with the book money Tully could go to college. Deena could take a vacation once in awhile. And I wouldn't have to clean other people's toilets. I could work full-time on my part a the book. After that was done, I could sit and read all day if I wanted. *All day.* I couldn't stop smilin, just imaginin it. "Plus I can visit my son and daughter more often, see my grandbabies."

I smiled even more at that.

Our conversation turned to Amaryllis, our businesses and churches. Then to the *police.*

"Did you see Ted Arnoldson's house is up for sale?" Deena shook her head. "I hear he's movin away. Where, I don't know. Although he can't move far."

"So sad." I still mourned over Ted, as I did Trent and Mayor B. Ted had already pled guilty to his crimes, but with a clean previous record, he got off with a hefty fine and probation.

Deena *tsked.* "I still stay Chief Cotter's ego got in the way of solvin the murders earlier."

"But he did give us credit for helping him," Tully said.

"Only cause he had to. Reporters were findin out everything anyway. Otherwise he'd have claimed to crack the case all on his own."

I had to admit she was probly right. "Well, what matters is, Amaryllis is finally healin, thanks be to God."

"Yes." Deena nodded.

I stared at my closed curtains, thinkin bout it all.

Deena nudged Tully. "Look at her. What do you bet she's thinkin up a quote about now."

Tully smiled. "Bet you're right."

Now how did they know that?

They focused on me, eyebrows raised.

I nodded slowly. They wanted a quote—they'd get one. "'Neither man nor angel can discern hypocrisy, the only evil that walks invisible, except to God alone.' John Milton."

Tully tilted her head, thinkin that one over, then nodded. "Amen to that." She raised her glass.

Deena held hers up. "All too true."

I reached for my lemonade. We clinked our agreement one final time.

Cherrie Mae Devine's Quotes

Chapter 1

"My mind rebels at stagnation."
Sherlock Holmes, *The Sign of the Four,* by Arthur Conan Doyle

Chapter 7

"Behold where Ares, breathing forth the breath of strife and carnage, paces—paces on." Chorus, *Electra*, by Sophocles

"Man's conscience is the oracle of God."
The Island, by Lord Byron

Chapter 9

"Crime is common; logic is rare."
Sherlock Holmes, *The Adventure of the Copper Beeches*, by Arthur Conan Doyle

Chapter 13

"The games one plays are not the games one chooses always."
Essex, *Elizabeth the Queen*, by Maxwell Anderson

Chapter 17

"Justice, while she winks at crimes, stumbles on innocence sometimes."
Hudibras, by Samuel Butler

Chapter 19

"Circumstances may accumulate so strongly even against an innocent man, that directed, sharpened, and pointed, they may slay him."

The Mystery of Edwin Drood, by Charles Dickens

Chapter 20

"The truth is rarely pure and never simple."

Algernon, *The Importance of Being Earnest*, by Oscar Wilde

Chapter 23

"A slovenly dress denotes a disorderly mind."

Don Quixote, *Don Quixote*, by Miguel de Cervantes

"The best laid schemes of mice and men go often askew."

To a Mouse, on Turning Her Up in Her Nest with the Plough, by Robert Burns

"Fear of danger is ten thousand times more terrifying than danger itself."

Robinson Crusoe, by Daniel Defoe

Chapter 26

"What anxious moments pass between the birth of plots and their last fatal periods."

Sempronius, *Cato*, by Joseph Addison

Chapter 28

"In this world you've just got to hope for the best and prepare for the worst and take whatever God sends."

Charlotta the Fourth, *Anne of Avonlea*, by Lucy Maud Montgomery

Chapter 29

"Misery acquaints a man with strange bed-fellows."
Trinculos, *The Tempest*, by William Shakespeare

Chapter 32

"It is the nature of truth to struggle to the light."
Man and Wife, by Wilkie Collins

Chapter 33

"Silence is of different kinds, and breathes different meanings."
Villette, by Charlotte Bronte

Chapter 35

"It is no use, lying to one's self."
Dr. Rank, *A Doll's House*, by Henrik Ibsen

Chapter 37

"Let the winged Fancy roam, Pleasure never is at home."
Fancy, by John Keats

Chapter 39

"Time comes stealing on by night and day."
Dromio of Syracuse, *Comedy of Errors*, by Shakespeare

Chapter 42

"To fair request, silent performance maketh best return."
Virgil, *The Divine Comedy*, by Dante Alighieri

Epilogue

"Neither man nor angel can discern hypocrisy, the only evil that walks invisible except to God alone."
Paradise Lost, by John Milton

Discussion Questions

1. In the prologue an unnamed character is talking to Chief Cotter. As the story progressed, who did you guess this character was?

2. How did you respond to the excerpts from Trent Williams's Pulitzer prize-winning article, "Gone to Ground"? What reasons do you think the author had for including them in this format?

3. What did you think of the dialect of the three main characters? Did it help characterize them for you? Did you find it at all distracting?

4. As the story progressed, who did you think was the killer? Did your opinion change?

5. Did you relate more to one of the three main characters than the others? Which one?

6. Could the story have been told as well in third person?

7. All the characters in this book, including the three main characters, struggled with some form of hypocrisy. How did Cherrie Mae, Deena, and Tully each struggle with this issue?

8. If each of these three characters had told the full truth from the beginning, would things have gone easier for them?

9. Has hypocrisy ever crept into your life—or into the life of someone you know—in a way that surprised you?

10. If you were in Cherrie Mae's situation, how would you have handled it?

11. If you were in Deena's shoes, what would you have done?

12. How about Tully? What would you have done in her situation?

13. What classical quote from Cherrie Mae did you like best?

14. What was the biggest surprise for you in this story?

15. What did you learn from this story?

Acknowledgments

MY THANKS TO THESE WONDERFUL PEOPLE WHO GENEROUSLY gave their time to help me research this story:

Elsa James of Cielo Salon in Redwood City, California, provided background information regarding Deena's work in her hair salon.

Dan Blackledge, raised in Jasper County and a member of the Men's Garden Clubs of America since the mid-eighties, told me about Jasper County history, as well as imparted valuable information about planting and tending amaryllis flowers in Mississippi.

Keith Wilkerson, who has studied the history of Jasper County and created a Web site for that information, graciously answered questions about when my town of Amaryllis could have been founded, and what the county was like at that time. Keith's Web site is at: http://webpages.charter.net/hondapotamus/jasper.htm.

Jeff Herrin, investigator with Mississippi's 13th Circuit Ct. District, answered questions regarding law enforcement issues for the state and for Jasper County.

Peggy and Earl Schneider of Wisteria Bed and Breakfast in Laurel, Mississippi, provided a beautiful and historic place for me to stay as I researched nearby Jasper County. I enjoyed the ambiance and the conversation.

Rhonda Dyess, receptionist at Bay Springs City Hall, was warm, kind, and so very helpful. I'll be ever grateful to Rhonda for introducing me to the real Cherrie Mae and to Josephine Brown.

I also must thank the real Cherrie Mae (last name—Gammage), who granted me an interview. I hadn't expected to use her name in this story, but it was so perfect for my character, and she said she'd be "honored" if I did. The Cherrie Mae in this story is purely fictional and is in no way meant to represent the real person. Rhonda Dyess says Cherrie Mae Gammage has a hundred crowns waiting for her in heaven because of the daily Christian help she extends to her community, black and white alike. I think Rhonda is right.

As it turned out, both Rhonda's and Cherri Mae's voices were used in the book trailer for *Gone to Ground*. Cherri Mae Gammage, of course, plays Cherri Mae Devine. And Rhonda is the voice of Deena. (The book trailer can be viewed on my Web site.)

Thanks also to Bay Springs resident Mama Jo—Josephine Brown—for granting me an interview. Mama Jo cooks for many people in Bay Springs, including the high school football team (now there are some big appetites!). Through Mama Jo I learned (among other things) about turnip greens and pot liquor.

Bobby Cole Jr., jailer of Jasper County, was kind enough to take me on a tour of the jail and answer my myriad questions.

All of the above people know their stuff. Any factual errors in this book are my own.

My thanks also to the people of Bay Springs. I've tried to represent your town accurately. If I fudged a few small details, please know it was only to help my story.

Finally, I must give recognition to the real winner of the 2010 Pulitzer Prize in the Feature Writing Category: "Fatal Distraction" by Gene Weingarten. His gripping article can be read at the URL found in this book for Trent Williams' fictional "Gone to Ground."

Sometimes

the truth hides where **no one** expects to find it.

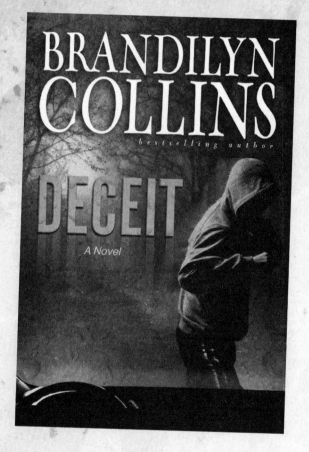

Joanne Weeks knows Baxter Jackson killed Linda—his second wife and Joanne's best friend—six years ago. But Baxter, a church elder and beloved member of the town, walks the streets a free man. The police tell Joanne to leave well enough alone, but she is determined to bring him down. Using her skills as a professional skip tracer, she sets out to locate the only person who may be able to put Baxter behind bars. Melissa Harkoff was a traumatized sixteen-year-old foster child in the Jackson household when Linda disappeared. At the time Melissa claimed to know nothing of Linda's whereabouts—but was she lying?

In relentless style, Deceit careens between Joanne's pursuit of the truth—which puts her own life in danger—and the events of six years' past, when Melissa came to live with the Jacksons. What really happened in that household? Beneath the veneer of perfection lies a story of shakeable faith, choices, and the lure of deceit.

Read the first chapter at: http://brandilyncollins.com/books/excerpts/deceit-ex.html

When your worst fear comes true.

BRANDILYN COLLINS
bestselling author

EXPOSURE

Someone is watching Kaycee Raye. But who will believe her? Everyone knows she's a little crazy. Kaycee's popular syndicated newspaper column pokes fun at her own paranoia and multiple fears. The police in her small town are well aware she makes money writing of her experiences. Worse yet, she has no proof of the threats. Pictures of a dead man mysteriously appear in her home—then vanish before police arrive. Multisensory images flood Kaycee's mind. Where is all this coming from?

Maybe she is going over the edge.

High action and psychological suspense collide in this story of terror, twists, and desperate faith. The startling questions surrounding Kaycee pile high. Her descent to answers may prove more than she can survive.

Read the first chapter at: http://brandilyncollins.com/books/excerpts/exposure-ex.html